I0664427

A WORLD GONE DARK II: SURVIVAL

A RAVAGED SKIES NOVEL

A WORLD GONE DARK II: SURVIVAL

A RAVAGED SKIES NOVEL

by Scott M. Baker

Also by Scott M. Baker

A Schattenseite Book

A World Gone Dark II: Survival
by Scott M. Baker.
Copyright © 2026. All Rights Reserved.
Print Edition
ISBN-13: 979-8-9884973-8-7

No portion of this publication may be reproduced, stored in any electronic system, or transmitted in form or by any means, electronic, mechanical, photocopy, recording or otherwise, without written permission from the authors.

This is a work of fiction. Any resemblance to any actual person, living or dead, or events is entirely coincidental.

Cover Art © Christian Bentulan

To Shannon
A teacher, a colleague, and a good friend.
You were taken from us much too soon.

DAY SIX

CHAPTER ONE

17 July

KIRSTIE COSTNER AND her friend Regan stood behind the stone wall bordering the entrance to the Atkinson Resort and Country Club. They were part of the midnight watch, their job being to warn the community of anyone approaching from the west along Providence Hill Road. The chances of raiders stumbling into the compound were slim, and even if such an event occurred, their task was not to engage the enemy but warn the compound of the approaching danger. Sure, Kirstie's nerves were on edge over a potential battle, but she could ignore that.

The silence caused her the most anxiety.

Silence was not the correct word. Plenty of noise echoed through the night. The chirping of crickets. The croaking of frogs from a nearby creek. The screech of an owl, intermittently mixed with the rhythmic pecking of a woodpecker. The scurrying of wildlife racing through the trees. The occasional howl from a coyote. Normally, the sounds of nature would comfort Kirstie, but not tonight. The striking stillness emanating from the society that once had been weighed heavily on her. A week ago, she would get frustrated if a car drove by their house, its radio blaring. Now she missed the man-made background noises: cars driving along the street, TVs or radios playing too loud, lawn mowers or hedge trimmers being used to groom backyards. The lack of such sounds only verified what she had already realized but until now refused to admit.

Society as she knew it had come to an end.

Kirstie could not believe it had only been five days since she and her friends—Regan, Mikayla, and Abbey—were stranded at Canobie Lake Park after a massive solar flare struck the planet, neutralizing all electronic devices around the world. They had been stranded at the amusement park, stuck forty miles away from their homes in Dunbarton. Luckily for the girls, Mikayla's grandmother lived in Atkinson, one town over from Salem, and only a few hours' walk. Mikayla's grandmother took in the girls, allowing them a safe haven until the emergency ended.

Only this would never end. In a matter of minutes, over a century of technology was rendered useless, plunging the world into a lifestyle that had not existed since the late 1800s. Access to media sources that informed them of world events no longer existed, limiting their knowledge to what transpired locally. Stores and online shopping had become a thing of the past; from now on, you would have to make do with whatever you had at home, scrounge for what few supplies remained, or steal from others. Growing and canning food replaced refrigeration, as did coal- or wood-fueled stoves. Candles substituted for electric lights and fireplaces for traditional heating. Transportation was limited to bicycles and horses. Overnight, the world's ability to subsist day-to-day had changed, plunging society into a battle for survival. The little neighborhood community where she now lived had to rely on the same means used by the first settlers.

The big difference was that their ancestors were accustomed to living this way and knew how to survive. For this tiny community in Atkinson, it proved to be a new way of life, and they were far behind their ancestors on the learning curve.

Despite all the adversities they faced, their group fared much better than those around them. Andrew, a former Marine with survival training and knowledge of how to respond in a crisis, became their *de facto* leader. Kathy, a science teacher at the local school, knew how to prepare the group to fend for themselves. Within the past few days, the two of them had united the neighborhood, gathered the necessary supplies, and begun preparations for a long-term existence.

They were the lucky ones. According to Andrew, most of the world, especially the larger cities, would not make it through the first week. The food supplies would run out in days. Once that happened, death would ravage the world like the Four Horsemen of the Apocalypse. Billions were already dead from lack of water, and those who made it this far brutally fought each other for what limited supplies remained. Most of them would be dead by winter, and even fewer would make it to spring. Andrew assured the compound that the supplies his team of Scavengers had procured would give them a fifty-fifty chance of surviving. Their community would fare much better than those around them, although that would not be a hard standard to meet.

The downside was that self-sufficiency significantly increased their chances of being targeted by raiders; the harsh reality was that average, usually good-natured people would do anything to keep their loved ones alive.

Kirstie could attest to that. This apocalypse had already turned her into a killer.

Kirstie always avoided conflict and never experienced a physical confrontation… until recently. In the past five days, she had taken four lives: two when Ralph, Joel, and their wives had tried to steal the community's supplies for themselves, plus the two assholes whom they ran across in the cafeteria of the local high school. Sure, each incident had been in self-defense. Yet that did little to negate the fact that she had killed them. Even more disturbing, she knew the number would increase the longer they became immersed in this nightmare. Such actions were necessary, but every life taken would eat away at her soul for the rest of her life.

These emotions paled in comparison to the concern Kirstie had for her mother, Danielle. Danielle had been working in

Boston when the solar flare hit. With all cell phones dead, Kirstie had no way of knowing what happened to her mother or where she was. As a single mom, her mother did a good job raising Kirstie, teaching her to be responsible, respectful of others, and to avoid getting into trouble. However, surviving the apocalypse was an entirely different game played on nightmare mode. Kirstie assumed her mother had tried to make it home. If the roads were as dangerous as the shit their community had encountered, she doubted her mother would have survived this long. On the slim chance her mother did find her way home, what would she do once she discovered Kirstie was not there? Wait in the hopes Kirstie would return, or go out and search for her? Neither scenario would have a good outcome. Under the circumstances, Kirstie could deal with her mother's death, though she would never get over it. However, Kirstie seriously doubted she could deal with not knowing her fate.

Kirstie felt the same about Uncle Shawn. He had taken in Kirstie and her mother after their asshole of a father left the family to shack up with that bitch in Georgia. They had grown close over the last two years, and she viewed Shawn as a father figure. He worked as the shift supervisor at the Seabrook Nuclear Power Plant. Kirstie could only imagine what he must be going through to keep the reactor from melting down. He faced an even worse situation than her mother.

Face it, Kirstie told herself. *Chances are you'll never see them again or know their fate. You'll have to suck it—*

The trees behind Kirstie rustled, snapping the teenager out of her reverie. She spun around and raised the shotgun, ready to shoot whoever attempted to sneak up on them, but nothing was behind her. Her eyes scanned the tree line, waiting for the intruder to lunge. The bushes three feet to her right rustled. Kirstie swung in that direction, aimed the shotgun, and slid her finger over the trigger.

A deer burst through the bushes and stopped, glancing

around.

Kirstie breathed a huge sigh of relief and lowered the shot-gun.

"Shit."

On hearing her swear, the deer bolted to its left, darted across the road, and disappeared into the front yard of an abandoned house.

Regan looked up from where she sat with her back against the wall. "Are you okay?" she whispered.

"Just jittery."

"That's understandable." Regan stood and patted her friend's shoulder. "Why don't you relax and let me take over the watch for a while?"

"I'll be fine." She turned around and resumed staring down Providence Hill Road. "What time is it?"

Regan glanced at her Timex, using the lights from the aurora to read the dial. "It's almost six."

"Thank God. Our shift is almost over."

As if on cue, a voice quietly called from the road behind them. "Kirstie, Regan. Are you here?"

"We're up here," Regan replied. "Behind the stone fence."

A minute later, Jordan and Theodora emerged from the shadows. Theodora smiled and waved.

"How did your shift go?" asked Jordan.

"Kirstie almost shot a deer," Regan chuckled.

Jordan scrunched his eyes. "Why?"

"It startled me. I thought it was those assholes we ran into at the school coming to raid the compound."

"Even if they do plan on raiding us, that won't happen for a while yet," said Jordan. "They'll have to find us first, and that'll take several days, maybe more. By then, we'll have our defenses up and should be able to fight them off."

"I hope you're right."

"He never is." Theodora smiled and gently jabbed Jordan in the stomach, then joined the girls at the wall. "You picked an excellent location. Provides a good line of sight and offers protection."

"It's also a good place to rest so you can take turns while on watch," added Regan.

"I like that," said Jordan.

"You're not sleeping the whole time," joked Theodora. She turned to Kirstie. "Anything you need to pass on?"

Kirstie shook her head. "It's been quiet all night."

Regan smirked. "Except for the deer."

Kirstie flashed her friend a frustrated look, then turned her attention to Theodora. "It's all yours."

"Thanks."

Jordan and Theodora took their places at the wall. As the girls walked away, Jordan whispered.

"Kirstie, Andrew wants to see you after breakfast."

"Did he say what he wanted?"

"He didn't."

"Thanks. Good luck."

They walked a few hundred feet when Kirstie asked, "I wonder what's up?"

"It can wait until morning," Regan said. "Right now, I want to crawl into bed and sleep. I'm exhausted."

CHAPTER TWO

THE LIGHT FROM the rising sun shone through the large-pane windows on the front of the Southern New Hampshire University Arena, arousing Danielle from a restless sleep as she leaned against the glass. Before the apocalypse, she would have been irritated by the inconvenience. Not now. Danielle was glad the light had awakened her out of her slumber. She wanted to… no, she *needed* to stay awake to protect Liz and Kyle from the nightmare they had been forced into.

She glanced over at the kids. Liz slept against the pane alongside Danielle, with Kyle in a fetal position beside his sister, his head resting on Liz's leg. They had fallen into a deep sleep a few hours after arriving. Danielle had not disturbed them. The kids needed to rest after what they had been through. Liz and Kyle had been abandoned by their babysitter, stranding the children for three days at home alone, waiting for their parents, who never returned. God knows what their fate would have been if Liz had not spotted Danielle walking through the neighborhood and, sensing Danielle as a decent person, followed her. Luckily for the kids, Liz had been a good judge of character. Danielle let the kids join her, unable to leave them to what would be a certain, if not violent, death. They had made it as far as Goffstown without incident and would be home by now if they had not stumbled upon a group of local police and National Guard troops who transported them to the safety of the arena.

Danielle sneered at the word safety. Granted, the Guardsmen who brought them here probably assumed they were doing the proper thing, unaware of what went on inside. As the old adage goes, you know what happens when you assume anything. Instead of a haven from the apocalypse, the area contained close to thirty-five thousand people crammed inside a facility built to hold no more than eleven thousand. Without electricity, there was no air conditioning, a situation made even more vile by tens of thousands of people who had not bathed in days, stuffed into an enclosed space without ventilation. Fourteen fifty-five-gallon drums placed around the arena floor provided the only illumination, the heat from the flames only adding to the sweltering environment. The stench was so intense it nauseated her.

While Danielle could deal with the abysmally uncomfortable environment, she was terrified by the dangers lurking in the arena's dark confines. During the night, she had heard several fights break out, one woman screaming for help, and a gunshot. As far as Danielle could tell, no one attempted to intervene on behalf of the victims. Not that she could blame them. Everyone in the foyer was too terrified to go deeper into the facility, hanging around the relative safety of the entrance. Even the National Guard troops refused to enter, which told Danielle everything she needed to know about the dangers in the arena. And it would only get worse. With so many people crowded into a building incapable of properly accommodating all of them, the situation would head south rapidly.

She needed to figure a way out of the hellhole before the arena erupted into chaos.

Danielle hoped she would be up to the task.

If someone had told her a week ago the things she would do to survive, she would have called them crazy. Yet over the past five days, she had traded sex for water, brutally killed someone who tried to rape her, and broken into someone's home and stolen from the absent owners. The situation had grown far worse since that first day, only now she was responsible for protecting Liz and Kyle. Danielle did not want to consider what she would have to do in the future to survive.

"Fuck you. That's mine."

"Not anymore."

The argument originated from the nearby bleachers, followed by the sound of a struggle. The commotion grew louder as people tried to get away from the fight. It ended a few seconds later when a woman screamed.

"You asshole. You nearly killed my husband."

"Fuck off, bitch."

Kyle stirred and raised his head. He rubbed his eyes, wiping the sleep from them. Liz stared into the arena, her eyes wide with fear.

"What happened?" Kyle asked.

"Nothing to be concerned about. Go back to sleep."

"I'm not tired. But I have to go to the bathroom."

"Can you hold it?"

Kyle shook his head. "I have to do number two."

Danielle had no idea what to do.

The elderly lady beside Danielle nudged her. "The restrooms are behind the bleachers."

Danielle hesitated.

Kyle tugged on her sleeve. "Please? I don't want to shit myself."

Liz gently slapped him on the back of the head. "Watch your language."

"But I have to go *bad*."

"Go ahead," said the elderly woman. "I'll keep your spot for you."

Danielle finally gave in, realizing Kyle fouling himself would only make the situation worse.

"Let's go." Danielle stood, her legs aching from sitting so long. She turned to the elderly woman. "Thank you."

"Don't mention it."

Danielle and the kids made their way across the arena

floor. She kept Liz and Kyle on either side of her, holding them close, being careful not to trip over anyone. Everyone they passed stared at them vacantly. One young woman with three kids of her own nodded, understanding what Danielle was going through.

When they passed the bleachers and entered the corridor leading to the restrooms, a horrible stench engulfed them, a grotesque combination of feces and urine. One hundred feet to their right, a small metal trash can with a fire burning inside lit up a sign on the wall indicating the entrance to the restrooms. Surprisingly, no one occupied the corridor, most likely because of the smell. Danielle rushed the kids to the restroom.

As they approached the doorway to the women's restroom, the stench became overwhelming. Liz broke away from Danielle and ran into the corner where she vomited.

"Are you okay?" asked Danielle.

"The smell is disgusting," she gagged.

Kyle yanked on Danielle's sleeve. "I can't hold it much longer."

"Okay." Reaching over, she took Liz's hand and led them into the restroom.

Danielle almost puked at the sight before her. Another small trash can contained a fire illuminating the area. She had not considered that without electricity, the pumps draining the toilets would be inoperable. Each stall overflowed with feces, covering the floor three feet past the doors. Piles of excrement lined the floor along the wall across from the stalls. Even more disgusting, each sink had been used as a toilet until the basins overflowed, oozing across the counter and dripping onto the tiles.

"Gross!" Liz blurted.

Kyle frantically shifted his weight from one leg to the other. "Miss Danielle, I gotta go."

Danielle looked around until she found a corner that had not yet been used. "Go there."

"No!"

Danielle crouched, making sure her knees did not touch the soiled floor. "You have to. If you go in your pants, you'll wind up getting sick."

Kyle grimaced. Moving into the corner, he started to unbuckle his pants.

"Don't let them hit the floor," Danielle warned.

Kyle began to cry, but to his credit, he slid his pants around his knees, crouched down, and did his business. Danielle grabbed Liz, and both women turned toward the door, giving him as much privacy and decency as possible.

After a few seconds, Kyle said, "I need some toilet paper."

Danielle turned around. She doubted any remained in the stalls. Even if there were, no way would she traipse through the human detritus looking for it. She moved over to the paper towel dispensers. Both had been torn open and emptied.

"Miss Danielle," Kyle sobbed.

"Just a minute."

Danielle reached up and yanked on the left sleeve of her shirt until the seam tore. Sticking her fingers inside, she ripped off the sleeve and handed it to Kyle.

"Use this."

Kyle stared at the sleeve for a few seconds, then used it to wipe himself. Because of the difficulty using it, he wound up getting feces on his palms. Still in a crouch, he held out his hands, the soiled sleeve dangling from the right one.

"What do I do now?"

Danielle approached. "Drop that thing on the floor and stand up."

Kyle obeyed. Danielle clasped the sides of his pants so they did not drop onto the shit-laden floor, pulled them up, and secured them.

"There you go."

Kyle glanced from one hand to the other. "What about my hands?"

She thought for a minute. "Wipe them on the wall."

Kyle turned to the wall, crying. He wiped away as much of the feces as possible, though residue still stuck to them.

Danielle spotted a hand sanitizer on the wall, the lid torn off. An empty bag of sanitizer sat in the dispenser. She yanked it out and waved Kyle over.

"Put out your hands."

When he did, she squeezed as much of it as she could onto his palms. It was not much, but better than nothing. Kyle wiped his hands, sniffing back tears. When finished, he hugged Danielle.

"Thank you."

"You're welcome." She leaned over and kissed the top of his head. "Come on. Let's get back to our spot."

CHAPTER THREE

SHAWN, BRAD, ANDY, and Kevin made their way north through Seabrook along Route 1. It was the first time they had left the nuclear power station since the solar flare struck. They had no choice. With the complete loss of power, the reactor's cooling system stopped functioning, and the core overheated, threatening a meltdown that would spread radiation across New Hampshire, southern Maine, and northern Massachusetts. His team and Wally's firefighting unit spent five days battling against the odds. Shawn and his crew entered the containment vessel to manually vent built-up air pressure in the reactor chamber to prevent a Chernobyl-like explosion. Wally's team pushed a pumper engine across the compound, jury-rigged the pump with car batteries, and transferred water from the nearby tributaries into the reactor, finally cooling down the core to avoid a meltdown and a worst-case scenario. Sure, in ten to twenty years, many of the locals would develop cancer, though he doubted most of those affected would survive that long.

Preventing a full-scale nuclear event came at a high price. A minor breach in the suppression chamber sent deadly doses of radiation around the reactor. Wally's team refused to abandon their efforts, continuing to pump water into the reactor until a meltdown was avoided, and in the process exposing themselves to the irradiated air vented from the reactor chamber. Each of them died at their posts from excessive radiation poisoning.

Not even Shawn's team was spared. Because of their efforts

inside the chamber, Brad, Andy, Kevin, and Libby received small doses and had a chance of living through the side effects. Shawn received a dosage of 141 milliSieverts, the effects of which had not fully hit him yet due to his age. He had already begun urinating blood, indicating radiation already ate away at his intestinal tract. Death would be inevitable. The only member of his team who underwent a more prolonged exposure to radiation was Wilson, who slipped into a coma and passed away peacefully.

Libby had left them at the main gate to the plant, heading south toward his home in Kensington. The others went north. As the four walked through Seabrook, Shawn wondered if their efforts were worth the sacrifice. Having spent days isolated inside the reactor building, none of them had a clue of the nightmare that had gripped the town.

Scores of stalled vehicles lined both lanes of Route 1, each having been looted of anything valuable for survival. Every store along the route had suffered the same level of vandalism. Larger ones like Market Basket had been ransacked, the parking lots littered with abandoned supplies. Even the smaller stores suffered, though not to the same extent. Every restaurant had endured a similar fate. Farther down the road, they passed a Burger King which had been plundered, food wrappers and cups scattered around the area, the decaying bodies of three people murdered over fast food lying amongst the carnage.

"What the fuck went on out here?" asked Brad, a look of horror on his face.

"No one was prepared for this," Shawn replied. "When the infrastructure collapsed, so did societal norms. People are willing to kill each other to take whatever is left."

"Where are the police?" asked Andy.

"Wherever they were when the power went out. We're on our own."

"Jesus," mumbled Brad.

Andy's eyes widened as the realization struck him. "What

are our families going through?"

The words struck Shawn like a thunderbolt. If such violence took place here in Seabrook, it must be just as bad, or worse, throughout the area. Danielle and Kirstie were caught in the middle. He loved his sister and admired her resilience after her husband walked out on her. Yet he questioned whether Danielle had the stamina to survive under these conditions. The two of them were raised in an upper-middle-class family. While Shawn went to a regular high school, their parents sent Danielle to a private school. She had always lived a pampered life and developed no street knowledge. He doubted his sister could survive if trapped in Boston. Based on what happened here in Seabrook, God only knew what she would face if she attempted to walk home.

Shawn was even more concerned about Kirstie. His niece was only sixteen and would be extremely vulnerable. At least she was with her friends, though a group of teenage girls would be a target. Hopefully, they found strength in numbers. He wished he could call Kirstie, find out her location and if she was safe, and make his way to help her. Unfortunately, those days were gone forever. His best hope of ever seeing Kirstie or Danielle again would be to make his way home and pray they would be there.

If he stayed healthy enough to make it home.

As they approached the interchange with Route 101, they stopped and stared at the carnage ahead of them.

Andy summed it up best when he muttered, "Jesus fucking Christ."

The southbound interchange between Route 101 and Route 1 South was clogged with burnt debris. A propane truck had been pulling out of the Tidewater Campground when it stalled. An eighteen-wheeler T-boned the tanker, initiating an explosion. Both trucks, seven cars, the outer buildings of the campground, and nearly ten acres of trees had been engulfed in flames. More than a dozen charred bodies littered the area, the corpses embedded in the streets that had melted in the fire. Thankfully, the thunderstorm that came through three days ago had extinguished the inferno. Shawn wondered how many fires that could not be put out turned into conflagrations that ravaged entire communities.

"This is fucking insane," said Andy.

"And it's only going to get worse." Shawn pointed to the northbound interchange leading to Route 101. "Let's head that way."

CHAPTER FOUR

N ATE STRATMAN LEANED against the edge of a pool table, watching Carbone try to locate the survivalist compound on the plastic-coated map mounted on the wall. The map displayed the one city and thirty-six towns in Rockingham County. Even though the territory covered was limited, it took Carbone forever to find the street.

No one would label Carbone as smart. He was a third-rate hoodlum, not clever enough to pull off a big job that would net him a large cache of money, but stupid enough to get caught. Stratman let Carbone join them because, what he lacked in common sense, he made up for in loyalty. He had been arrested four or five times previously on misdemeanor charges, never spending more than a few days in jail before being released. Three days before the solar flare struck, Carbone had been arrested for selling Fentanyl in the Domino Pizza parking lot in Plaistow and thrown into jail, which was where Stratman met him. Carbone would have spent a few years in federal prison if the apocalypse had not occurred. The town police had too much on their hands to worry about feeding the inmates, so they released them, warning them to stay out of trouble.

That was as effective as telling a puppy not to eat the sandwich left on the coffee table.

The other two released prisoners had teamed up with Stratman, knowing their only chances of survival were in numbers. Bryan Hart had been incarcerated for running a STOP sign and T-boning another driver, then beating the shit out of the driver. The fact that Hart carried a suspended license and five previous arrests for assault added to his difficulties. Stratman took on Hart as his second in command. The second prisoner, Jack Anderson, had been arrested for shoplifting, this being his fifth offense. He became third in command.

Stratman had suggested they make camp at the VFW Hall in Kingston. He knew the place well, spending a lot of time there following the fucked-up retreat from Afghanistan. Stratman had been one of those left behind, making his way home along with a bunch of civilians he had taken under his wing, only to be dishonorably discharged after chewing out his CO for stranding him. The hall turned out to be the perfect haven, having enough food and water to keep them alive for a few days.

Stratman soon discovered that a group of eleven bikers had taken over the cigar bar down the road. They agreed to team up with Stratman's crew and spent the next three days raiding abandoned homes and businesses for supplies. During that time, the team was joined by six college students from Colorado who had been touring New Hampshire when the shit hit the fan. The two males agreed to scavenge the area with the bikers, while the four women were willing to do anything to be fed and taken care of. The group also included Tyler, his wife Elena, and their two teenage daughters. Tyler served as a state trooper and, as such, could provide a cache of much-needed weapons; Elena was a doctor. Stratman agreed to let them stay, primarily because of Elena, knowing that eventually his people would need her medical expertise, and warning the bikers that the mother and daughters were off-limits so long as the husband joined the raiding parties.

As much as Stratman hated to admit it, thanks to Carbone, his people would be saved from starvation. Stratman never told the others, but their situation had become desperate over the last two days. Most of the scavenged food had been consumed, and they had only enough water for three days if rationed. He had sent a six-man team to Timberlane Middle School to scrounge for supplies. They found enough water to keep them going for another few weeks but had been surprised by another group that killed five of their people and confiscated the supplies for themselves. Carbone had been smart enough to track the group to their compound before reporting back. Now Stratman had the opportunity to not only beef up his supplies but also enact revenge for fucking with his people.

"Here," said Carbone, his finger resting on the map. He glanced over his shoulder. "They're located in Atkinson."

Stratman pushed himself off the pool table and stepped over to the map. Hart, who had been sitting down with his feet resting on a card table, joined them.

"How many people are there?" asked Stratman.

"I counted seven in the raiding party, plus at least three people who came out to greet them. One of them was a hot teenager. The guys over at the bar will enjoy her."

Stratman ignored the comment.

"There's probably more than that," said Hart.

"Agreed. Did they have guns?"

"Everyone in the raiding party except the hot teenager carried a shotgun and a sidearm. Those at the compound were also armed."

Hart shook his head. "This won't be easy. They seem to know what they're doing."

"We have something on our side they don't have."

"What's that?" asked Hart.

"Desperation." Stratman focused his attention back on Carbone. "Did you notice any defense positions?"

"No. The neighborhood seemed wide open."

HART LEANED CLOSER to Stratman. "We have to assume they've at least set up guard posts along the roads now that they know about us."

Stratman nodded in agreement. He contemplated the situation for a moment. This group seemed much better off than his people. Based on what little information Carbone provided, they probably had been raiding the local area for days, which meant they would have enough supplies to keep his people alive long enough to gather more. And they had houses, which would be a welcome change from sleeping on the floor or in recliners. Yet Stratman had to be careful. These people did not mess around. They had no qualms about killing most of the team at Timberlane and, more than likely, would hunt down his group to eliminate the threat. With better weapons and horses, they stood a good chance of wiping out Stratman's team or, at least, whittling down their numbers so his group posed no threat. The only chance Stratman had of surviving was to strike first.

But to do so without knowing the odds he faced would be suicide.

"What do you think?" asked Carbone. "Should we take them down?"

"Definitely." Stratman looked over at Hart. "But we can't go in blind. We need to have a better idea of what we're facing."

"Agreed."

Stratman turned to Carbone. "Take the nurse's husband and one of the bikers and scope out their compound. Find out everything you can. How many are there? What are their defenses? What type of weapons do they have? Where are they keeping their supplies? Take two days of water and food with you. Gather as much information as you can without getting caught and then update me."

"Gotcha."

"Then what do we do?" asked Hart.

"Then we take the compound for ourselves."

CHAPTER FIVE

K ATHY STEPPED BACK, admiring her project with pride. "What do you think?"

Kirstie stood in the center of the group gathered to witness the project's completion. Surrounding her were Regan, Andrew, Keith, Jordan, Meg, and Theodora. It reminded her of an advanced high school science project, except that, rather than earning a good grade, this would save their lives.

Three fifty-five-gallon plastic drums rested horizontally on a wooden frame erected against the rear wall of Kathy's house, each drum stacked above the others. The downspout from the gutter had been replaced with PVC piping that connected to the top bung hole. Piping extended from one tank to another, with the bottom bung hole on the lowest drum fit with a spigot.

Andrew stepped forward and examined it more closely. "How much clean water will it produce?"

"That depends on how much rain we get. So long as we get several storms this summer, we should be able to build up our reserves quite a bit before we run out."

"Thank God," said Meg. "We'll finally be able to take a shower. I've never felt this grungy before."

"No," Kathy replied with a firm tone. "This is solely for drinking water for the horses and us, and the crops if it comes to that."

"I guess you'll stink for a while longer," joked Jordan.

Meg frowned and extended her middle finger.

Kathy's attitude softened. "I'm working on a way to use the water still inside our toilets for sponge baths."

Meg scrunched her face. "Gross."

"You'd still smell better than you do now," Jordan joked again and again got flipped off.

Kathy chuckled. "I'd cleanse it first. Once we start collecting rainwater, we can put some aside for bathing, then recycle it to water the plants. Until then, we can bathe in the neighborhood's swimming pools."

"That water will become rank pretty quick," said Keith.

"And we'll all smell like chlorine," added Regan.

Kathy rolled her eyes in frustration. "It's not perfect, okay. But it's better than nothing."

"How long will it take?" asked Kirstie, ready to take a shower with radiator water from the cars at this point.

"It's not a priority. Hopefully soon."

Andrew changed the subject. "What about the other projects you're working on?"

"The gardens are all planted. We should know in a few days if they're successful, but I'm sure most of them will be productive. I've been training Andrew's daughters on how to can food so we can start storing them once they're harvested."

"Good." Andrew nodded. "We've got our supply situation under control, so now I can concentrate on our defenses."

"About that." Kathy hesitated. "Are there any more of the parts I asked for at Home Depot?"

"Jordan, Meg, and Regan were responsible for that." Andrew glanced over at his three fellow Scavengers.

"I think there were more." Jordan shrugged. "I can't remember."

"There were," added Meg. "At least most of them."

Kathy's eyes widened. "Enough to build one or two more?"

"I think so."

Kathy turned to Andrew. "Is there any chance of making another run to gather more supplies? It couldn't hurt to have at least one backup system."

Andrew thought about it for a moment.

"Do you think everything else in the store has been looted by now?" asked Kathy.

"It's not that. I'm afraid we might run into that gang again, and this time they'll be prepared. We only won last time because we caught them by surprise."

"I understand. But one or two extra rain-catchment systems, along with a few storage drums, will increase our chances of survival. I have a few other projects that would improve the odds in our favor."

"What do you have in mind?"

"A water purification filter, traps to catch the local animals and prevent them from eating our crops, and, if they have the supplies, a possible wind turbine, greenhouse, and medicinal herb garden."

"We could swing by the Carsons' place and see if they could lend us some horses," suggested Jordan. "That way, we could increase our numbers."

"And be able to carry more stuff home so we don't have to make the trip more than once," suggested Kirstie.

Andrew raised his hands in front of him. "Okay, you've convinced me. We'll go tomorrow."

Kathy smiled. "Thank you."

"You make a detailed list of everything we need."

"It'd be easier if I went with—"

Andrew cut her off. "We almost lost you last time you went with us. I'm not taking that chance again."

This time, it was Kathy's turn to give in. "Okay. I'll have the list ready in the morning."

Andrew turned to Kirstie and Regan. "Are you willing to go with us?"

Kirstie nodded. "Of course."

"That's because you're a badass," Regan said softly.

Andrew grinned. "Jordan, you and I will head down to the Carsons' to ask if they'll let us use any of their horses. Depending on how many they lend us, if they do, we'll need to find more volunteers to go on the supply run."

"I know a few who might be willing to join us."

"Can they handle themselves?"

"If not, they'll learn quickly."

Andrew agreed. "It's settled. We'll leave at sunrise tomorrow."

Kirstie raised her hand. "Regan and I have guard duty until four in the morning."

"I'll switch you two out with Mikayla and Abbey. I need you both on your game tomorrow. Are there any questions?"

No one had any.

"Good. Let's get back to work."

CHAPTER SIX

D ANIELLE HAD ALLOWED herself to doze for a few minutes. She felt as if she could take a moment to recharge because, now that the sun had risen and its rays shone through the glass facade, the arena did not seem as scary as before. She doubted anyone would try something shady during the day with so many witnesses around. With most of the people in her section of the foyer awake, even if someone did come after her or the kids, others would step in to help.

At least, she hoped so.

Her dreams ran a gamut of emotions, though as they played out, she doubted she would remember them once awake. They began with reminiscences of her time with Kirstie and Shawn. The weekend the three of them spent at York Beach two summers ago. The ski trips to Pike's Peak, not far from Concord. And the time they went hiking in the White Mountains and got lost, relying on a troop of Boy Scouts to direct them back to the proper trail. For some bizarre reason, she even recalled some of the good times with her ex before he cheated on her.

After that, the dreams took a dark turn. Danielle recalled the encounter with the rape gang near the Massachusetts border, only this time with her and Kirstie as the victims. She envisioned making her way alone through the streets of Concord, her mind playing out nightmarish scenarios, including being arrested and executed for looting a grocery store for a few bottles of water. And the National Guard dragging Liz and Kyle away from her because she was not related to them. Two Guardsmen held her by each arm while two others dragged away the kids. Kyle struggled to break free as he cried uncontrollably. Tears ran down Liz's cheeks as she reached out for Danielle, screaming her name.

Only it was not a scream. And it was not a dream. She felt a tiny hand gently tapping her shoulder.

"Miss Danielle? Miss Danielle, wake up."

She awoke suddenly, startling Liz, who knelt beside her. Danielle looked around, confused as she slipped out of her slumber.

"How long have I been asleep?"

Liz shrugged.

"About three hours," said the elderly lady beside her.

"You were snoring loudly," added Liz. "Like my dad."

Danielle balled her fists and rubbed the sleep out of her eyes. "What's up?"

"Something's going on. Everyone is forming a line."

Still groggy, Danielle glanced around. People from both the foyer and the stands had gathered in a single file at the entrance.

"Why?"

"The National Guard is handing out rations," responded the elderly lady. "We need to get in line if we want something to eat."

The elderly woman tried to stand, finding it difficult due to her age. Danielle got to her feet and helped the woman up. The four of them merged into the line that was forming, with several hundred people in front of them. Those from the other areas in the arena fell in line behind them. Danielle stared through the plate-glass windows, for the first time noticing the commotion outside.

Two military-style deuce-and-a-half trucks, each pulled by a team of six horses, approached the main doors. National Guardsmen pulled aside the barbed wire strands that formed the winding path to the arena, pushing them back in place after the transports passed. Twenty Guardsmen surrounded them, offering protection, their automatic weapons held in the low-ready position.

Liz took Danielle's hand. "Why do we have to get in line?"

"It's how they pass out the rations, dear," replied the elderly woman who stood behind Danielle. "It's time-consuming but more efficient."

Danielle slowly turned to face the woman, taking her in for the first time. She stood five feet three inches in height with the barest hint of a slouch. Her snow-white hair was disheveled and clearly had not been washed in days. Danielle guessed the woman was in her mid- to late seventies based on the spots and wrinkles on her face, particularly around the eyes. Yet she had a vibrancy that belied her age. She smiled at Danielle and held out her hand.

"I'm Evelyn, by the way."

"I'm Danielle." She shook Evelyn's hand, then motioned toward the children. "This is Liz and Kyle."

Evelyn waved at them. "It's a pleasure to meet you."

"Have you been here long?" asked Danielle.

"Since the second day. My husband died three years ago, and I live alone. My apartment is not far from here. When I heard the city was setting up a shelter at the arena, I figured my best bet would be to stay here until this blew over. I was wrong."

"Is it that bad?"

An expression of despair washed over Evelyn's face. "Much worse than I imagined. There are no medical facilities here. The National Guard ran out of boxed food supplies on day four. With no way of bringing more in, they resorted to raiding every grocery and convenience store within a fifteen-mile radius, which did little good since most of them had already been looted. Lately, they've been sharing their MREs with us. To make matters worse, four days ago, a gang stole whatever food and water they could find from the stalls and vending machines, broke into one of the suites, and set up a base there."

"Price gouging?" asked Danielle.

"Bartering for sex." Evelyn shook her head. "It's not too dangerous on the main floor, but the higher up you go in the bleachers, especially nearer the suite, it's a nightmare." She leaned closer to Danielle and whispered. "Dozens of women have been raped."

"How do you know?"

"You can hear them screaming when it happens."

"And no one tries to stop them?"

"A few did at first, but the gang members killed them. They're armed and not afraid to use their weapons."

"Why haven't the Guardsmen or police stopped them?"

Evelyn chuckled derisively. "They're too afraid to come in here. The gang runs the bleachers while the rest of us cower down here. And there's no love lost between the authorities and the rest of us. None of us are allowed to leave because of martial law. The soldiers and the police know if they came inside, they'd be overwhelmed. So, they stay outside and feed us like we're animals in the zoo."

Danielle could not believe what she heard. Damn, she had trusted the Guardsmen who had picked them up yesterday when she said they were being taken to a safe location for their protection. Instead, she and the kids had been thrust into an even more dangerous situation with no way of escape.

Once the two horse-drawn military trucks were positioned by the main entrance and the twenty Guardsmen formed a semi-circle in front of the vehicles, an officer removed the outer chains locking down the arena and opened the door. The burst of fresh air felt good, despite the heat and humidity. The line started to move, with those at the front stepping outside to receive supplies, then being ushered back into the arena through another set of doors. It took forty minutes for Danielle to reach the beginning of the line.

In front of them stood a tall, burly man and his daughter.

Danielle assumed she was in her mid-teens, maybe fourteen or fifteen. The lieutenant in charge handed them two cans of baked beans and two cans of soda.

"What the hell is this?" The man looked at the cans and back to the lieutenant. "Where are the MREs?"

"We ran out of them a few days ago. Without transportation, we have no way of bringing them to Manchester. And even if we did, the other cities have used theirs by now."

"But I see boxes of food in the truck," the man said defiantly.

"What few we have left are reserved for families."

"Fuck them!" The burly man glanced over his shoulder at Danielle and the kids, then back to the lieutenant. "These assholes don't have a chance of surviving. Why waste the food on the weak when you could be feeding the rest of us?"

From further back in line, others voiced their approval. Someone yelled, "Give the food to those who stand a chance."

The ruckus died down when four Guardsmen approached, their weapons now in the high-ready position.

Even though the asshole was twice the size of the lieutenant, the officer stood his ground without flinching. "Either take what I'm offering or move along. We have other people to feed."

"Fuck you!"

The daughter placed a hand on her father's arm and softly urged him to calm down. "It's okay. These are good enough."

"No, they're not." He shoved his daughter aside. "Give me two of those MREs and bottles of water—"

One of the Guardsmen rushed forward and slammed the stock of his M4 carbine into the man's face. Blood poured from his broken nose, and several shattered teeth fell out of his mouth. Two other Guardsmen moved behind the man while a fourth aimed his weapon at his head. A Guardsman kicked the man in the back of his left leg, causing him to fall to his knees. The other removed zip ties from his pocket, crossed the man's hands behind his back, and bound the wrists together, yanking tight. They lifted him to his feet, still groggy from the blow. Each Guardsman took an arm and escorted him off the arena compound.

His daughter ran to follow him, but a Guardsman stood in front of her, the M4 raised across his chest and his stern expression warning her not to try. She faced the lieutenant, her voice croaking with tears.

"Please don't take him away."

"Sorry, ma'am. He had a chance to stand down."

"He was only trying to protect me."

"Doesn't matter," the lieutenant replied with no emotion. "We have to maintain order at all costs."

"Can I go with him?"

"You don't want to do that." The lieutenant offered her a can of beans and a soda. "Please, take this and go back inside."

The teenager took the cans and clutched them to her chest, sobbing. A Guardsman escorted her back into the arena.

The lieutenant focused his attention on the line. "Next."

Danielle stepped forward, gently pushing the kids ahead of her.

"Are you three together?"

Danielle nodded.

The lieutenant reached into the back of the deuce-and-a-half and removed two bottles of water and a box.

"Sorry, ma'am. We're severely short on water."

"That's okay." Danielle gave one to Kyle and Liz, then took the package. "What's inside?"

"My men are gathering as many supplies as possible and boxing them." He paused and, for the first time, a hint of frustration on his face. "We're doing our best."

"We appreciate it. Thanks."

Danielle led the kids back into the arena, waiting at the door for Evelyn to get her package. They returned to their spot by the pane glass and sat down. Kyle unscrewed the top of his water bottle and began chugging it.

"Don't drink it all." Danielle took it from him, screwed the cap back on, and placed it beside her. "Save some for later."

"But I'm thirsty."

"I know. But we don't know when we'll get another one."

Kyle crossed his arms across his chest, leaned against the glass, and huffed.

Liz had already opened her bottle but only took a few sips. She offered it to Danielle. "Have some."

"No thanks, hon. That's yours."

"You need to take care of yourself, Miss Danielle. We need you." She offered the bottle again.

As much as Danielle hated to admit it, Liz was right. She took the bottle and sipped it, making sure she only took enough to quench her thirst, then placed the bottle beside Kyle's.

"What do we have to eat?" asked Kyle, still brooding.

"Let's see."

Danielle opened the lid and looked inside, her enthusiasm rapidly fading. The contents consisted of an apple and a banana, two slices of white bread, a ketchup-sized pack of peanut butter, and a package of six cheese crackers. Even more disappointing, there were several spots of mold on the bread, most of the banana's skin was brown, and the apple had a few soft spots.

Kyle glanced into the box and scrunched his face. "Gross."

Danielle did not know how to respond.

"At least we have something to eat," offered Liz, though without enthusiasm.

Danielle looked over at Evelyn. "What did you get?"

The elderly lady shook her head. "A snack bag of pretzels, a Hershey bar, a moldy orange, and an onion."

Liz's eyes widened. "An onion?"

"You want it?" Evelyn joked.

"No!"

Evelyn removed the candy bar and handed it to Liz. "This

is for you and Kyle."

Her eyes lit up. "Are you sure?"

Evelyn nodded and smiled. "Of course."

Danielle stopped Liz from taking it and leaned closer to Evelyn, her voice low. "I appreciate it, but you need to keep your strength up."

"I'm not going to survive this. And neither will the kids if they don't get more to eat. It's okay." A resignation of her fate shone in Evelyn's eyes. "They need it more than me."

"Thank you." Danielle turned to Liz. "Go ahead."

Liz grabbed the candy bar and unwrapped it. Kyle suddenly cheered up.

"Half of that is mine."

"Don't worry." Liz broke the bar into two pieces and gave one to her brother. Both kids wolfed down their portions like a pair of great white sharks devouring a sea lion.

"Enjoy it while you can." Evelyn leaned closer and lowered her voice. "Sooner or later, the military will run out of supplies to feed us. When that happens, there will be thousands of people like that asshole in front of us. You need to prepare if you want to keep the kids safe."

Evelyn leaned against the window and stared into space as she opened the bag of pretzels and munched on them.

A cold fear formed inside Danielle. What Evelyn said hit home. She had been so concerned about keeping Liz and Kyle safe, she had not considered the future. If the military had already run out of MREs, how long would it be before the local supplies were used up? Probably a day, two at the most. Then this already miserable situation would become a nightmare, one that threatened her and the kids. As their protector, she had to figure out some way to keep them safe, though she had no idea how.

Danielle handed Kyle the package of cheese crackers, telling him to share with his sister. As they wolfed them down, she pulled off the moldy portions of bread before breaking it in half and giving one slice to Liz and Kyle. As they argued over whose slice was larger, Danielle peeled the banana and ate it, struggling to keep down the rotten portions.

The banana did not upset her stomach as much as her fears for the future.

CHAPTER SEVEN

THE FOUR MEN walked along Route 101 in silence, stunned by the devastation they encountered. Abandoned ransacked vehicles, several burned out. Mail trucks and tractor trailers emptied of parcels, the contents ravaged for anything that might be of value, the rest scattered across the highway. An occasional corpse, the stench detectable from yards away, the bodies now covered in churning seas of maggots. All of this was enhanced by the silence that descended over the area, broken only by the noise of wildlife in the distance. Normally, Shawn would have found the quiet comforting, something to relax him as he sat on his back deck enjoying a can of beer. Under the circumstances, it seemed eerie and menacing.

"I feel like I'm in a dream," said Kevin, a slight quiver in his voice.

"More like a fucking nightmare," corrected Brad. "It reminds me of that movie *The Road*, only I never thought it would actually happen."

Kevin shook his head, still unable to grasp the situation. "I can't believe this all went down around us, and we were unaware of it."

"We were a bit preoccupied," Brad replied.

"We put our lives on the line to save this?"

"Enough!" snapped Shawn, then calmed his tone. "There are still thousands of people around here hunkered down in their homes fighting for their lives, including our families. Wilson and Wally's team sacrificed themselves to keep them alive and give them a chance to survive."

"Sorry." Kevin lowered his head. "You're right."

"What we have to do now is put ourselves first and get back to our families." Shawn tried to encourage his team even though he knew his chances of seeing Danielle and Kirstie were slim.

The group continued in silence until they reached the interchange with I-95 a few hundred yards ahead.

"Jesus fucking Christ," Andy whispered.

The interstate made Route 101 look like a playground. The same carnage they had encountered since leaving the power plant littered the highway, only it was five times more intense because of weekend travel to the coast. Abandoned and burnt vehicles. Dozens of collisions, several of them multi-vehicle. Scattered debris. Scores of corpses left to rot. It reminded Shawn of a war zone, as if someone had laid an air strike down on the highway. The southbound lanes were a little less congested, though still in as bad a shape. The carnage stretched north and south as far as the eye could see. The only sound came from a mile to the north, where men laughed, and a woman screamed in terror.

"Maybe we should help her," suggested Andy.

"No," replied Kevin. "We don't know how many of them there are and if they're armed. It's only the four of us, and we're feeling the effects of radiation poisoning."

"But the woman—"

"There's nothing we can do for her," interrupted Shawn. "This is the new world we face. Get used to it."

An uneasy silence descended over the group as each of them worried that their loved ones might have suffered a similar fate, or worse. Shawn tamped down the images of Danielle or Kirstie enduring the same nightmarish experience.

Shawn turned to Brad. "Are you going to risk taking 95 home?"

Brad shook his head. "It's too dangerous. I'll backtrack to Route 1 and make my way home from there. There's a lot more places to hide if I run into trouble."

"You're welcome to stay with us," offered Kevin.

"Thanks, but I have to get home to my family." Everyone noticed that Brad's attention focused on the direction of the laughing as he spoke.

"Good luck." Shawn offered his hand.

"Thanks." Brad shook it. "Someday we'll look back on this and laugh."

An awkward thing to say, but they all forced a chuckle, realizing they would never see each other again.

Brad turned and headed back in the direction they had taken. Shawn watched as his good friend left them, waiting until he disappeared behind a tractor-trailer before turning to the others.

"Let's go."

CHAPTER EIGHT

K IRSTIE SAT ON an old rocking chair on the front porch, sipping on half a bottle of spring water while watching the aurora borealis dance through the sky, less vibrant than a few days ago, dulled but still visible in the morning light. The colors were spectacular, translucent shades of red, green, and yellow running together, like celestial waves splashing ashore. It reminded her of that time in tenth grade when her mother took her to the planetarium at the Museum of Science to see the show on the Northern Lights. Though this time, rather than the classical music blaring through the speakers, the accompanying sounds belonged to nature. It would have been exotic if they were camping.

Instead, this was their life from now on.

A part of her wondered whether mankind had brought this upon itself. A rapidly increasing population placed a strain on the planet's natural resources. She never bought into the climate change advocates who kept warning for the past thirty years that the world had only five years left to exist while flying to global climate conferences in private jets. Sure, we could do more to preserve the environment, but that would never happen. People today, especially her generation, were addicted to their cellphones, making them oblivious to the world around them, allowing big business and politicians who looked out only for themselves to run everything. While her mother always made sure they had family time together, most of her friends' parents rarely spent quality time with their kids. Too much of the world had become self-focused, ignoring everything around them that truly mattered.

It suddenly dawned on Kirstie that if she had attended Friday movie night rather than going with her friends to Canobie Lake Park, she would be with her mother right now. She had selfishly focused on friends rather than family, rushing out of the house without telling Danielle how much she loved her. When Kirstie saw her mother again, she would tell her every day how much she cared for and appreciated everything Danielle did for her.

If she ever saw her mother again.

Kirstie pushed those thoughts from her mind. Danielle was tougher than she gave herself credit for. She had dealt with her father's affair, a divorce, moving into Uncle Shawn's house, and struggling to make ends meet, all the while putting up with a teenage daughter. Kirstie forced herself to believe her mother would make it through this nightmare and that, hopefully, they would get back together someday. Right now, Kirstie's priority focused on keeping herself and the new community she had become a part of safe and alive.

Kirstie's thoughts went back to a humanities teacher she had in high school, who the kids lovingly called Grandpa because he was the oldest educator there. He once said Earth is a living organism and humans are a virus infecting it. When the virus becomes out of control, the Earth will activate its immune system and cleanse the planet through wars, natural disasters, or pandemics. Maybe the solar flare was nature's way of healing itself.

The question that gnawed at Kirstie was whether she would be one of the lucky ones to survive or one of the last strains of the virus to die off.

The hinges of the storm door creaked. Regan, Mikayla, and Abbey exited, each holding half a bottle of spring water in their hands. Abbey held the screen door and gently pushed it closed so as not to make too much noise. They sat on the porch around Kirstie.

"What are you doing out here?" asked Mikayla.

"Trying to get my mind off certain things by enjoying the aurora." Kirstie glanced up. "Aren't they beautiful?"

All four girls stared at nature's light show.

Mikayla broke the silence. "How long will they last?"

Kirstie shrugged. "Not much longer. It is less intense than in the first few days after the solar flare."

"You know what I'm looking forward to?" Everyone turned to Regan. "Once the aurora is gone, we'll be able to see the stars. With no background lights to pollute the sky, the entire Milky Way is going to sparkle before our eyes."

"Have you seen it before?" asked Abbey.

"Only in photographs. I'm sure it'll be magnificent."

A blissful few minutes of silence followed as they slowly sipped their water and enjoyed the show.

Mikayla broke the mood. "What were you thinking about?"

Kirstie had been too involved in stargazing to hear the question. "Huh?"

"You said you were trying to get your mind off certain things. What was on your mind?"

Kirstie shrugged again, not wanting to discuss it.

"Did the two guys you ran into in the school cafeteria try to rape you?" asked Mikayla.

Kirstie failed to hide the surprise on her face. "What makes you think that?"

"We've made friends with Haellie. This afternoon, she finally told us what those guys she ran into in the science lab tried to do to her and Kathy, and how she stopped them."

Regan shook her head. "The two we encountered in the cafeteria tried to kill us. Kirstie shot the first one when he pulled his weapon on us. The second guy took me hostage, but she forced him to back down."

"What then?" asked Abbey.

"I shot him."

Abbey sat with her eyes wide open. Mikayla summoned the

courage to ask, "Don't take this the wrong way, but how could you bring yourself to take someone's life?"

"Someone was going to die in the cafeteria. It wasn't going to be me. I'm sure that was the same reason Haellie acted as she did. She witnessed what those assholes did to her family. She refused to be a victim, just like Regan and me. And you two are going to have to start thinking the same way."

Mikayla leaned against the wall. "I don't know if I can."

"You're going to have to if you want to survive." Abbey started to speak, but Kirstie cut her off. "You heard what Andrew said. Billions of people are already dead, and billions more will die in the next week. Only the strong are going to survive, and those people we ran into at the school have the advantage over us because they don't care. They're going to rape, murder, and loot, and the only ones who can stop them are people like us. Sooner or later, they're going to attack the compound. We're not going to make it unless we're tougher and smarter than they are."

"That'll never happen," said Mikayla.

"If I told you a week ago the people in this neighborhood would murder Dignam to steal his guns, would you have believed me? If I told you Joel and Ralph would try to steal all the supplies for themselves and would have killed us if we refused, would you have believed that?"

Mikayla lowered her head and stared at the ground. "No."

"Yet it happened. And as the situation gets worse, people are going to become more desperate. The next few weeks are going to be a nightmare."

CHAPTER NINE

D ANIELLE WATCHED THE light outside slowly fade as the sun set, the increasing darkness bringing with it a feeling of apprehension. Liz and Kyle lay to her left, both asleep. They had been here less than twenty-four hours, but that short time had been the scariest encounter since the solar event. At least on the road, she had alternatives and could avoid confrontations. However, in the arena, she had no way to escape. Even worse, they were surrounded by thousands of people on the brink. If things went south... no, *when* things went south... Danielle doubted if she would be able to protect the kids, let alone herself.

A gentle hand touched her upper arm. Danielle turned to see Evelyn sitting near her.

"I see you're upset, dear."

"Aren't you? This place is a nightmare."

Evelyn chuckled, which caught Danielle off guard. "I'm seventy-two. I'm surprised I lasted this long."

"Aren't you concerned about surviving this?"

Evelyn leaned close so Liz and Kyle would not hear. "Very few of us are going to survive this."

"Help has to be on its way."

"Dear, nothing is on the way. There's no means to ship in supplies. And even if there was, no one else will give them up because their resources are limited. Most of us are going to die in here."

Evelyn's honesty dumbfounded Danielle. It was a scenario she had not considered, though she should have. It slowly dawned on her that this was not a relocation center to keep the survivors safe until help arrived, but a prison to keep them contained until their numbers were culled. Under the circumstances, that would be a matter—

"Don't do it!"

The cry from deep inside the arena distracted Danielle. She stood to see what transpired.

Several people on the ground floor stared upward, their eyes focused on a single location. Danielle scanned the upper levels, finding it difficult to see due to the minimal light provided by the fire barrels along the ground floor. Then she spotted what caused the commotion and gasped.

A woman with two children younger than Liz and Kyle had climbed over the guardrail on the uppermost bleachers, the three sitting on the edge, their legs dangling over the side. The two kids held the woman around her waist, terrified. A small group on the arena floor attempted to talk the woman out of it. A middle-aged man stood a few feet behind the mother, calmly reasoning with her. The woman shook her head and pushed herself over the edge. She and one child plummeted from the height, hitting the floor with a loud splat that could be heard throughout the arena. The smaller child to the woman's right had been saved by the middle-aged man who raced forward and grabbed her arm. She dangled over the side, screaming for help until a younger man rushed over and helped pull her to safety. The traumatized child hugged the middle-aged man tightly and sobbed.

"What happened?" asked Liz.

"Someone tripped and fell."

"Are they okay?"

"They're fine," Danielle lied, desperately trying to spare the child from the horror that surrounded them.

What bothered Danielle most was that, except for the handful of people who tried to stop the woman from committing suicide with her kids, no one else in the arena seemed fazed by the incident.

Liz rolled over and closed her eyes.

Danielle waited until the girl was asleep and then gently nudged Evelyn. "Is there any other way out of here than through the main doors?"

"There are dozens of emergency exits, but they're all chained shut."

"What if there's a fire?"

"Then a major burden is removed from the National Guard's shoulders. And even if you managed to get through, I'm sure there are soldiers outside who would prevent you from leaving."

The emotionless way Evelyn spoke sent a chill down Danielle's spine.

"I'm sorry, dear. I don't mean to upset you, but you need to face the reality that this is where you're going to die."

Danielle did not know how to respond. How do you respond to a death sentence?

Danielle lay down behind Kyle and wrapped her arm around him, pretending to sleep, though she couldn't even if she wanted to. She had not come this far to rot away in this hellhole run by the people who were supposed to protect her. Nor would she let Liz and Kyle die under such circumstances. The kids had their whole lives ahead of them, even if it promised to be a fucking nightmare. Danielle knew the reality that they might die here, but not without a fight. And she would put up one hell of a struggle to keep them alive.

The only question was how could she get out of here?

CHAPTER TEN

THE JOURNEY WEST along Route 101 took much longer than anticipated because all three men, especially Shawn, were suffering from the early stages of radiation poisoning. They stopped for breaks more frequently than expected, with each rest lasting longer than the last, requiring more time to gather the energy to continue. Once the sun rose, the heat and oppressive humidity made walking difficult, slowing them down even more. Frustration set in at their slow progress.

As the sun began its descent on the western horizon, the glare directly in their eyes, making it hard to see, and anxiety grew inside Shawn. He had hoped to cover most of the thirty miles between Seabrook and I-93.

They had barely walked fifteen miles.

Andy perked up as they approached an overhead road sign that read:

EXIT 6
DUPONT RD
BEEDED RD
1 MILE

"That's my exit. I live only a few miles from here."

Andy quickened his pace, anxious to get home as soon as possible. Despite not feeling up to the task, Shawn and Kevin pushed themselves to keep up.

Andy's enthusiasm quickly drained when they reached the exit ramp. A Super Walmart stood adjacent to the highway. The blackened walls around the doors and the front façade indicated the store had either caught on fire or been torched. Interspersed among the stalled cars in the parking lot, the ground was littered with everything imaginable, from electronics, household goods, clothes, and even toys. When the store ignited, those inside must have panicked, grabbing whatever they could and rushing outside, only to realize these items were now useless and left them behind.

Seven people strolled around the parking lot, rummaging through the mess for anything of value. Three of them were men with scraggily beards and hair and worn clothes, probably homeless. They acted like it was Christmas, joyfully pulling clothes from the piles and stuffing them into shopping carts. Two of them fought over a winter coat, the taller of them knocking the other down, then folded the coat and placed it in his cart. The defeated guy crawled to his feet and searched for another coat.

Shawn suddenly realized that the homeless, the people who carried what little possessions they had with them and lived most of their lives without electricity, were more prepared for this disaster than most Americans.

At the far end of the parking lot, a family sorted through the debris, a man and a woman with two girls not even ten years old. The mother kept a close eye on the homeless men, worried about her daughters' safety. Glancing over to the highway, she spotted Shawn and the others watching her. She yelled to her husband, grabbed the girls by their arms, and ran toward the nearby woods. Once seeing them by the exit ramp, the husband dropped what he had gathered and raced off to be with his family.

"Fuck," muttered Andy.

Shawn knew Andy must be terrified about what his family was going through. He had the same fears.

"I guess this is where we part ways."

Andy shook his head. "It's too risky to get off here. The next exit down leads to Epping. There's fewer buildings around and less chance of running into trouble."

Kevin nudged Shawn. "You and I need to find a place to hold up for the night."

"I got you covered," said Andy. "There's a fuel depot off the next exit. You guys should be safe there."

"How far is it?" huffed Shawn.

"A mile or two. Follow me."

Andy led the way, with Shawn and Kevin close behind.

An hour later, they reached Exit 7, walked down the exit ramp, and turned right onto a side road. Shawn was relieved to see Andy had been telling the truth. The entrance to North Atlantic Fuels stood a few yards away, the compound and road surrounded by trees. They should be safe here for the night.

As they entered the area, Andy paused and turned to Shawn and Kevin.

"You two wait here. I want to check out the place and make sure no one is hiding."

Shawn nodded in agreement and leaned against the fender of a fuel truck, checking out the location. The depot extended back several hundred feet, with dozens of fuel trucks spread across the area. The place had not been looted by anyone, at least as far as he could tell. Some of the trucks appeared as though people had salvaged diesel fuel from the exterior tanks, though God only knew why. Anything that ran on diesel fuel had been disabled during the solar flare.

Several minutes later, Andy came back and flashed Shawn and Kevin a thumbs-up. "I don't think anyone has been here since the shit went down."

"Good." Shawn pushed himself off the fender, lost balance, and fell back against the truck. He tried again, this time successfully standing. "We need a break."

"The office is this way."

Shawn staggered after Andy. Kevin stayed close in case his friend needed assistance.

The office was the second building from the street. Andy

approached and tried to peer through the windows, but the blinds had been drawn. He knocked on the door.

"Is anyone there?"

No response. He knocked a second time.

"We're only looking for a place to stay for the night. We won't cause any trouble."

Five seconds passed. Andy glanced over at Shawn and gestured toward the window on the door.

"Do it."

Andy used his right elbow to shatter the glass pane closest to the knob, reached in, unlocked the door, and pushed it open. When no one lunged at him from out of the shadows, Andy stepped inside and motioned for Shawn and Kevin to join him.

Once inside, Shawn immediately made his way to the worn leather couch and flopped onto it, moaning as his body finally had a chance to relax. Kevin went over to the desk, pulled out the chair, sat down, and placed his feet on the desktop. Andy went to check the back rooms.

Shawn studied the office, which looked typical for a trucking business. Wood-paneled walls. Three metal filing cabinets with rust in the corners. Furniture that dated back to the 1980s. A banker's lamp with a large crack in the glass shade. A thin layer of dust covering everything. And a pin-up calendar on the wall showing a busty brunette in a red bikini and matching high heels standing on a crate and leaning over the open hood of a pick-up truck, just like every mechanic around the globe. The days in July had been crossed out, the last one being 15 July.

Shawn suddenly realized he had no clue what day it was and how long this shit show had been going on.

Andy exited the backroom holding seven bottles of spring water.

"No one has been here since the solar flare. I found these in the fridge. All the food has gone bad, and these are warm, but it's better than nothing."

He handed three each to Shawn and Andy, keeping the last

for himself. Each of them emptied a bottle in less than thirty seconds.

Moving over to the window, Andy raised the blind and looked out onto the compound. "We should be okay here tonight."

"What do you mean, *we?*" asked Shawn.

"I planned on staying with you."

"Bullshit." Shawn swung his legs onto the floor and sat upright. "You're too close to home. Head out now while it's still light."

"I don't feel right leaving you alone in your condition."

"Hello," said Kevin sarcastically while waving his hands. "I'm right here."

Andy shook his head. "You know what I mean."

"There's nothing you can do for me. I have Kevin if I need help. Your priority is your family. Go to them."

Andy hesitated. "Are you sure?"

"They're more important right now."

"Thanks, boss."

"I stopped being your boss when we left the reactor. I'm your friend telling you to find your family. They need you."

Andy half-smiled and headed for the door, pausing before he left. "Good luck. Both of you."

"And to you," said Shawn.

Kevin nodded.

After Andy departed, Shawn looked over at Kevin. "Lower the blind and place something in front of the door to warn us if someone tries to break in."

"Do you think that's a possibility?"

"Better to be safe than sorry."

Kevin pushed himself off the chair and secured the office.

Shawn lay back down on the couch, tried to get as comfortable as possible, and closed his eyes. He told himself that if he could get several hours of sleep, he would feel better in the morning and be rested enough to continue their trip.

Deep down, though, Shawn knew he was lying to himself.

DAY SEVEN

CHAPTER ELEVEN

K IRSTIE AND REGAN arrived in Andrew's backyard ten minutes before the run to Plaistow. Jordan and Meg were already there, saddling the horses. Instead of five, there were seven, which made her feel a bit more at ease. The two extra Scavengers would give them an advantage, however slight, if they ran into trouble. They joined Jordan and Meg.

"Can we help?" Regan asked.

Jordan glanced over his shoulder and nodded. "Thanks, but we're almost done."

"I see the Carsons' lent you the extra horses."

"They were more than willing to help. Andrew said he'd set up a water catchment system for them since they've been so helpful."

Meg glanced at the girls and said, in her worst Sicilian accent, "He made them an offer they can't refuse."

Regan giggled. Kirstie did not get the joke.

Kathy walked up, holding three pieces of printer paper. She greeted the others with a smile then asked, "Where's Andrew?"

"Rounding up the newbies who are going to join us," Jordan answered.

Meg pointed to the pieces of paper. "Is that our shopping list?"

Kathy nodded.

Meg chuckled. "Andrew will freak when he sees it."

"Well, he was able to get the extra horses, so I figured he'd be able to bring back a second cart of supplies." She paused. "We'll find out in a minute. Here he comes."

They turned to greet Andrew, each of them surprised by who he had picked. Jordan summed it up best when he mumbled, "No fucking way."

Two women accompanied Andrew. Kirstie had briefly met Theodora a few days ago. A tall, attractive trans woman in her late twenties with brunette hair down to her shoulders tied in a ponytail. Everyone in the neighborhood spoke highly of Theodora. Before the world as everyone knew it came to an end, she had worked as a therapeutic counselor at a school in Manchester. Those in the community would need her services over the next few months.

Jordan's comment centered around the second woman joining the team—Lindsey. the wife of Ralph, one of the two assholes who had tried to steal the compound's supplies for themselves. Ralph, Joel, and Joel's wife, Sarah, had gotten the drop on Keith and Andrew and might have succeeded if Kirstie and Regan had not taken them out first. Granted, Lindsey tried to stop the others, and because of that, Andrew agreed to let her stay rather than throw her and the kids out in the cold. Kirstie approved of the decision but admitted she also felt uncomfortable having Lindsey on their team.

"What the fuck is she doing here?" barked Jordan as Andrew came closer.

Andrew opened his mouth to answer, but Lindsey spoke first. "I asked to come along. Andrew was kind enough to let me stay after what my husband tried. Volunteering for this run was the least I could do."

Jordan started to protest, but Meg cut him off. "What about your kids if something happens to you?"

"I assume someone here would take care of them."

Jordan crossed his arms across his chest and glared at Andrew. "I don't trust her."

Before the disagreement could devolve into an argument, Theodora stepped beside Lindsey. "This was my idea. If we're going to allow Lindsey to be part of our group, she needs to regain our trust. I ran this by Andrew, and he agreed. Lindsey wants to go with us to prove she's reliable."

Kirstie stepped forward and offered Lindsey her hand. "Welcome to the Scavengers."

Lindsey shook her hand apprehensively. "Thank you."

Regan and Meg welcomed Lindsey to the group. Only Jordan held out.

Theodora flashed him that same disapproving look Danielle gave Kirstie when she was being difficult.

"Jordan?"

Jordan gave in. "You can join us." It did not go unnoticed he did not offer Lindsey his hand.

"Well, with that out of the way...." Andrew stepped up to Kathy. "Do you have our list?"

"Right here." Kathy handed him the three pages.

Andrew thumbed through it. "Are you serious?"

Meg nudged Kirstie and grinned.

"I know it's a lot, but everything on that list will increase our chances of making it through the winter. This is the last run you'll have to make."

Jordan leaned over and studied the list. "I hope these haven't been looted already."

"If you take me with you, I could easily find substitutes for anything missing."

Andrew angrily glared at Kathy. Kathy responded with a grin.

"You can't blame me for trying."

Andrew smiled, folded the pages, and slid them into his rear pocket, then turned to the others. "Grab your weapons, and we'll head out."

The group made its way over to the picnic table where their weapons were laid out—seven shotguns, sidearms, knives or machetes, plus seven semi-automatic weapons.

Kirstie picked up the only one she recognized, a Colt AR-15. "What are these for?"

"Extra protection in case we need it. We lucked out when dealing with those assholes at the middle school. If we encounter them again, I want to be prepared."

"I've never used one of these before," said Regan.

"Neither have I," added Meg.

"I realize that." Andrew moved behind the table and picked up a Heckler & Koch MR-27 with a scope. "They're not difficult to use. Believe me, the extra firepower they provide will shift the balance in our favor."

Andrew spent the next fifteen minutes giving his team a brief overview of how to use the weapons, emphasizing keeping the weapons set on semi-automatic mode to conserve ammo and the necessity of keeping the safety switch in the ON position so no one would accidentally shoot themselves. Once the tutorial concluded, each member of the group took their weapon of choice and mounted up.

The Scavengers mounted their horses. Andrew took the lead, followed by Jordan and Meg. Kirstie's horse towed the supply cart, with Regan riding shotgun. Theodora and Lindsey brought up the rear. The Scavengers made their way to Providence Hill Road and headed for Plaistow.

CHAPTER TWELVE

D ANIELLE CROSSED THE ground floor of the arena, thankful to see the paneled glass windows, and even more grateful when she spotted the first rays of sunlight washing across the plaza in front of the building. The past two hours had been unnerving.

She had decided early in the morning to scout out the interior of the arena, doing so when most people inside would be asleep. After her conversation with Evelyn last night, Danielle needed to know the building's layout for when she attempted her escape. Even though she avoided the bleachers where the gangs were located, it was still terrifying to walk through the side corridors by herself with the only light coming from the flames in the irregularly placed fifty-five-gallon drums. Every step of the trip, she expected to be raped or killed, scared more of the latter since that would leave Liz and Kyle alone. It was a risk she had been willing to take to find a way out of this tenth circle of Hell. Thankfully, most of those residing in the corridors slept, and the few who were awake ignored her.

Evelyn was right. Every emergency exit had been chained shut to prevent people from escaping. Two sets of chains had been wrapped three times around the handles securing the double doors, the chains held in place by double padlocks, making the chances of getting out that much harder. On the plus side, most of the fire extinguishers still rested in their mounts, which gave her a possible means of breaking the locks. Every time Danielle found an exit with an extinguisher nearby, she took the nearest entrance back into the arena, plotting out the exit's location to the main entrance, remembering land-marks to make getting back easier.t She also tried to picture where the exit was in relation to outside locations, not wanting to escape into a group of National Guardsmen, which would probably lead to her being arrested and leaving the kids on their own. However, not knowing the layout outside the building, the best she could do was make an educated guess. Hopefully, when she made the move, luck would be on her side.

After surveying the arena, identifying escape routes, and memorizing their locations, she made her way back to the kids.

Evelyn smiled when she saw Danielle approach and waved. Danielle sat down beside the kids.

"Thank you for watching Liz and Kyle for me."

"My pleasure. They stayed asleep the whole time and didn't know you were gone."

"Good."

"Did you find what you were looking for?"

Danielle nodded. "You were right. Every exit is chained up. But there are plenty of fire extinguishers in the corridors. I can use them to shatter the padlocks."

"When are you making your break?" Evelyn smiled at the prison reference.

"Later tonight, when everyone is asleep."

"Do you think that's a good idea?"

"I can't stay here. I need to get the kids to a safer place."

"Well, if you think it's worth the risk."

"I do."

Thankfully, Evelyn did not pursue the issue.

Danielle lay down beside Liz and Kyle, snuggled close to the latter, and wrapped an arm around both.

DANIELLE HAD NO idea when she had fallen asleep or how long

she had been napping, waking up only when a soft hand shook her shoulder.

"Miss Danielle. Wake up." Liz's voice had a frightened tone to it.

Danielle sat up quickly, momentarily not remembering where she was. It quickly came back to her. A crowd of nearly one hundred gathered around the main entrance of the arena, shouting and banging on the glass. Outside, the National Guardsmen nervously shifted their gazes to one another, unsure how to respond.

"What's going on?" asked Danielle.

"I don't know." Liz focused on Danielle. "But I'm scared."

"Me, too." Kyle clasped Danielle's hand, squeezing tightly.

"The morning food delivery never showed up," explained Evelyn. "People have been grumbling for over an hour. Ten minutes ago, a couple of people went up to the doors to ask what's going on. It quickly became a mob."

"Will we be okay?" asked Liz.

"Of course, hon." Danielle hugged her. "I'll take care of you."

As they watched, more National Guardsmen filtered into the plaza out front. They seemed as nervous as the crowd inside was angry. Several protestors taunted the Guardsmen; a few pounded on the glass or flipped the middle finger at them.

Several minutes later, a tall Guardsman passed through the line of troops with two others on either side. His demeanor suggested that of an officer. Without hesitation, he stepped up to the main entrance. The crowd inside became increasingly vocal, shouting questions and insults, none of which could be heard amid the noise. Others from inside the arena surged forward, not to join in the protest but to see what would happen.

The officer stopped five feet from the glass. "What's the problem?"

Dozens of voices yelled out.

"Where's our food?"

"What the fuck is going on?"

"You're trying to starve us to death." The last shout incited even more fury among the crowd.

The Guardsman to the officer's left raised his M4. The crowd panicked until the officer placed his hand on the barrel and pointed it toward the ground. He turned his attention back to those inside the arena. He shouted something, his words inaudible above the protests. The officer stepped closer, raising his hands and motioning for the crowd to quiet down. After a few seconds, an uneasy silence descended over the protestors.

"I want to answer your questions, but it's hard for me to do that from out here. Please, stand back so I can come in."

The shouting resumed.

"Screw that."

"Fuck you."

"Where's our food?"

"We want out of here."

The protests ended when a tall, muscular African-American yelled, "Everyone, shut up! Let him inside so we can hear what he has to say."

Quiet mumblings went through the crowd, but no one objected.

The tall, muscular man ushered everyone away from the door, creating a space fifteen feet square, then turned and nodded. The two Guardsmen accompanying the officer shouldered their weapons, raced forward, and removed the chains and padlocks securing the entrance. Without hesitating, the officer pulled open the glass door and entered. The two Guardsmen started to follow, but the officer stopped them.

"I'll be fine. Wait out here."

"But, sir—"

"Do as I tell you."

The Guardsmen stood down, positioning themselves near the entrance.

"I'm Colonel Laney of the New Hampshire National Guard. Despite what you think, we're here to help you and keep you safe."

"Bullshit!" yelled a man near the back of the protestors. "You're keeping us prisoners!"

The tall, muscular man spun around. "Shut up and let the colonel speak!"

The crowd simmered down.

"I know you're all angry because you missed the morning food delivery," continued Laney. "The reason is that we've been scouring the city for days and can't find enough supplies. I've sent out—"

The crowd shouted questions at the colonel, who raised his hands for them to be quiet before continuing.

"As I'm trying to tell you, I've sent out squads to the neighboring towns in search of supplies, but so far, they've come back with nothing. We've expanded the search to include—"

"You mean there's no more food?" screamed a young woman.

"We don't have enough to feed everyone. Once we've gathered—"

"You do have food!"

Laney hesitated. "As I said, not enough to feed everyone."

"Give us what you have. We'll divide it amongst ourselves."

"I can't do that. It would cause   "

"Fuck them! The military is hoarding it for themselves!"

The protests grew even angrier.

Panic overwhelmed Danielle.

Evelyn tapped her on the shoulder. "Get the kids out of here now."

"What?"

"This situation is going to head south quickly. Escape while you have a chance."

Danielle hesitated a second before realizing Evelyn was correct. None of the scenarios she ran through her mind ended peacefully. She stood.

"Let's go."

Liz and Kyle stared at her, overwhelmed by everything.

"Where are we going?" asked Kyle.

"Just do as I tell you." Danielle yanked the kids to their feet.

Kyle cried. Liz said, "You're hurting me."

She ignored them and turned to Evelyn. "Come with us."

"Thanks, dear, but I'd only slow you down. Get out while you can. And God bless you."

Danielle knew arguing with Evelyn would be useless. Grabbing the kids by the hands, she made her way into the arena, circled around the mob, and headed for the emergency exit she had selected as their escape route. She made it halfway across the building when a commotion broke out behind her.

Glancing over her shoulder, she watched the crowd attack Colonel Laney, dragging him to the floor. The two Guardsmen standing outside rushed inside to save the officer. Before they could raise their weapons, the crowd swarmed them, beating the soldiers to the ground and stealing their weapons. The line of close to thirty Guardsmen that had formed in the plaza raised their weapons and rushed into battle.

Knowing she had only seconds left, Danielle turned and entered the closest passage leading to the exterior corridor. She had chosen an emergency exit by one of the feces-fouled bathrooms, knowing the stench kept people away, which meant she would have to deal with fewer people.

Automatic weapons fired echoed through the corridor, followed a second later by screams and cries of pain. Those mobbed around the door scattered, trying to avoid the gunfire. In a few seconds, they would stampede into the corridors looking for safety. Danielle had not experienced anything this terrifying since this whole nightmare began. She increased her pace, dragging the kids behind her.

"I'm scared!" Kyle cried.

"Shut up and keep running!"

Danielle reached the exit later and shoved the kids against the wall. They stared at her, fear filling their eyes. She could not be certain if the situation or her behavior terrified them. Screw it. Saving their lives was more important than protecting their feelings.

"Stay here and don't move."

Grabbing the fire extinguisher from its mount, she slammed the bottom against the first of the two padlocks, hammering it three times before the shackle broke. She was about to work on the second one when Liz cried out.

Danielle spun around to see a young man with a scraggly beard and matted hair holding Liz against him, his hand wrapped around her neck.

"I'll release her if you let me go with—"

He never got the chance to finish his sentence. Danielle raced forward, raised the extinguisher, and slammed the bottom with all her might into his face. Bones cracked, and fractured teeth fell from his mouth. Blood dripped over Liz, who screamed. The asshole kept his hold on the girl. Danielle struck him a second time. He released Liz and collapsed onto the floor. Grabbing Liz, Danielle pushed her against the wall and stepped over to the young man.

He raised his hands above his face. "Please, don't—"

Anger, fear, and adrenaline had taken over. She slammed the bottom of the extinguisher into his face, repeating the assault until his skull caved in.

She went back to the exit, savagely attacking the second padlock. The shackle broke on the second attempt. Danielle quickly removed the chains, pulling them free as the sounds of multiple weapons firing echoed through the corridor, soon drowned out by the panic that erupted amongst those trapped inside. They had seconds to escape.

Danielle pushed open the door, the fresh air a relief from the clamminess inside. She turned to the kids.

"Come on!"

Neither Liz nor Kyle moved, hugging the wall, their lips quivering.

"What's wrong?"

"Y-you're scaring us," croaked Liz.

Danielle did not have time for this bullshit. Grabbing each kid by the arm, she dragged them over to the exit and shoved them through the doors.

"Freeze!"

A National Guardsman barely eighteen years old stood ten feet away, his weapon aimed at Danielle. He looked more terrified than the kids. His hands shook. Luckily, his finger was not on the trigger.

Danielle tried to calm her voice. "Please, we're just trying to escape from what's going on."

The Guardsman said nothing, keeping the weapon aimed at Danielle, not sure what to do.

More weapons fire erupted from inside the arena, accompanied by cries of pain and panicked yells. The Guardsman lowered the barrel toward the ground and motioned behind him with his head.

"Get out of here while you can," he said, pointing to the right.

"Thank you." Danielle grabbed the kids by their arms and ran, getting as far away from the battleground as possible.

CHAPTER THIRTEEN

S HAWN SLOWLY SLIPPED out of a deep sleep, only vaguely aware of the world around him. Deep sleep was not accurate. That implied a long, restful slumber. Instead, he had experienced several hours where exhaustion shut down his body, forcing him to rest. It did little good. He felt worse today than last night due to the effects of radiation poisoning. As for being more energetic, if he were a battery, Shawn doubted he would be above fifty percent charged.

Shifting from his right side to his back, Shawn felt something leather beneath him. He listened, expecting to hear the sounds of nature, but everything remained quiet. Were they back in the control room at the reactor? No, that couldn't be. There they were isolated in the dark. Shawn sensed sunlight on his face.

He suddenly remembered that last night Andy had led him and Kevin to the office of a fuel depot station and broke into the main office so the two would have a safe place to rest. They must still....

Shawn's stomach churned painfully. Vomit raced up his throat. He sat upright, his foot bumping into a small plastic wastebasket. Grabbing it by the rim, Shawn shut his eyes, leaned over, and puked three times into the container. Even after emptying his stomach, he dry-heaved for another thirty seconds. Once his insides calmed down, Shawn opened his eyes. The vomit mixed with blood indicating radiation poisoning had worsened.

"Are you okay?"

Shawn glanced up. Kevin crouched in front of him.

Shawn gave him a thumbs-up and waited until he caught his breath.

"You don't seem okay. In fact, you look horrible."

"Thanks." Shawn attempted to say it sarcastically, but the words fell flat.

"I meant because of the radiation poisoning."

"I know." Shawn leaned back into the couch. "What time is it?"

"A little after nine in the morning."

"Why did you let me sleep so long. We have to get moving."

Shawn tried to stand. His legs gave out, and he fell back onto the cushions.

"That's why. You can hardly move. Relax for a few minutes."

As much as Shawn hated to admit it, Kevin was right. He took a deep breath, which almost made him vomit again, except nothing remained to heave.

"Thanks for staying with me."

"My pleas... you know what I mean."

"You're new to the team. I don't even know where you live."

"I have a studio apartment in Hampton."

"Hampton? That's across the tributary from Seabrook. Why didn't you go home? What about your loved ones?"

"My parents and siblings live south of Chicago. My fiancée was going to join me when she finished college in December." A look of sadness washed over Kevin's face. "I guess that's not going to happen now."

"I'm sorry."

"It is what it is. Maybe someday I'll get back to them. If they survive this."

"They will." Both men knew Shawn was lying.

Kevin leaned over and tapped Shawn on the arm. "At least

we prevented a meltdown and saved thousands of lives."

But at what cost to ourselves, thought Shawn. "How are you feeling? You also absorbed a high dose of radiation."

"A little tired, but that's from going non-stop for the past six days. The rest last night did me good."

"Did you sleep well?"

"Like a rock." Kevin motioned toward the chair behind the desk. "That was way more comfortable than sleeping on the floor."

"Good." Shawn realized how dry his throat had become. "Where's that water Andy left for us?"

"Right here." Kevin went over to the desk, came back with a bottle, and unscrewed the cap.

Shawn gulped down three mouthfuls, instantly regretting it. His stomach churned again. He grabbed the waste basket in time to vomit, again mixed with blood.

"Try sipping it," advised Kevin.

Taking a mouthful of water, Shawn swirled it around his mouth to rinse out the taste of puke, then spit it into the waste basket. He followed that with a few sips. This time, it stayed down.

"Thanks." He waited a minute before taking another sip. "Once we make it home, you're welcome to stay with us."

"I can't do that."

"Why?"

"I'll be a burden. You don't have enough room for me."

"It's a two-family house. We have plenty of room."

"What about food and water?"

"We barely have enough for ourselves."

"That's my point."

"You can help me scavenge for supplies and protect the girls. I won't be in shape to do that for a while." Kevin started to protest, but Shawn cut him off. "No arguments. I'm your boss."

"You stopped being my boss when we abandoned the

plant," joked Kevin, paraphrasing Andy.

"Then you're my friend, and friends stick together in times like these."

"Okay. Deal."

Shawn spent the next few minutes sipping more water. His stomach had settled down, and his dry throat felt better. Gathering what little strength he had left, Shawn pushed himself off the couch and paused until the dizziness stopped.

"Let's head out. I want to cover as much ground as possible before nightfall."

CHAPTER FOURTEEN

THE RIDE INTO Plaistow was stressful yet uneventful. Andrew had initially considered taking an alternate route into town to avoid a possible ambush but ruled it out. Staying on the main roads would have led them through the commercial district, which could have exposed them to looters, while taking back roads would have added miles to the trip. Instead, Andrew followed the same path to Home Depot that the group had used earlier. Things became extremely uncomfortable when they passed the house where Haellie's mother and siblings had been murdered.

The only difference between now and their previous trip a few days ago was the increase in the number of animals. With fewer people around and no vehicles to worry about, wildlife had become bolder, especially deer. They had come across at least eight of them grazing in people's front yards or roaming through the streets, and each seemed less intimidated by humans than a week before. Half an hour ago, they ran into a rafter of close to forty turkeys waddling down the center of the road, prompting the horses to avoid the gang of gobblers by circling around them through someone's yard. At this rate, it would not be long before animals became the dominant species.

As the Scavengers approached the Dunkins on the corner of East Road and Plaistow Road, Andrew raised a hand for the others to stop, then he and Jordan moved on ahead. As Jordan stood guard, Andrew used the binoculars they had commandeered from the local library to carefully scan the area north and south of their position for signs of trouble. Once certain the coast was clear, Andrew waved for the others to join them. The group turned right and proceeded to Home Depot.

As they entered the parking lot, Kirstie noticed not much had changed. The sliding glass doors at Home Depot remained open, and nothing seemed disturbed from last time. At the other end of the strip mall, discarded food and looted items still littered the parking lot in front of Walmart. Only now, five wild dogs and a cat, probably family pets left alone when their owners never returned home, wandered through the debris, devouring anything still edible. On seeing the Scavengers approaching, the dogs barked and raced across the parking lot while the cat scurried back inside the store.

Andrew stopped in front of the Home Depot entrance and turned his horse to face the others.

"Jordan and I are going inside to make sure the coast is clear. If you hear gunfire, head back to the compound."

"What about you?" asked Meg.

"We'll lead them away and circle back around later. Wait here."

As the two maneuvered their horses through the sliding doors, Kirstie mumbled, "I hope they'll be safe."

"I'm sure they will be," Regan reassured her friend. "It's not like there's food and water in there."

"I know. I'm just nervous after what happened at Timberlane."

"With luck, we won't run into him again. If he's smart, he'll stay away from us." Regan chuckled. "Especially if he knows what a bad ass you are."

Kirstie wanted to protest but thought better. Doing so would only egg on her friend's teasing.

A few minutes passed before Jordan emerged from inside the store and waved for the others to come in. Kirstie and Regan waited until the rest of the group entered, then backed their horses up to the doors, Jordan helping them maneuver the trailer into the lobby. After everyone had dismounted and tied up their horses, Andrew issued them their assignments.

"Kirstie and Regan, bring in one of the trailers from outside and rig it so the horses can pull it. Theodora, you go with them. You're the lookout. If you see anyone approaching, fall back inside and warn us." He turned to Jordan and handed him the third page from Kathy's list. "Meg and I will start rounding up the items from these two. You and Lindsey gather the rest of the supplies."

Jordan lowered the list he was reading and glared at Andrew. "Really?"

"What's wrong?"

"You're teaming me up with her?"

Meg huffed in frustration. "I'll team up with Lindsey."

"No. Jordan will." Andrew flashed Jordan a look that warned him not to start any trouble.

"Fine." Jordan rolled his eyes and headed into the store to look for the things on the list, not even glancing at Lindsey. "Come on."

As THEODORA STOOD watch by the door, Kirstie and Regan searched the store for the items they needed to hook up the trailer to the horses' saddles. On the way out, the girls rounded up the Carsons' horses and led them into the parking lot. Theodora followed, taking up a position behind a pick-up between the girls and the access roads into the strip mall. After ten minutes of spotting nothing more than a chipmunk, she stepped over to Kirstie and Regan, still scanning the area.

"Do you need help?"

"We've done this several times. Meg taught us." Kirstie paused to look at Theodora. "Aren't you worried someone might find us?"

Theodora grinned. "They're the ones who'd have to worry. My dad used to take me to the gun range a lot when I was a kid. He was always trying to toughen me up."

"No offense," began Regan, "but you don't seem like the shooting range type."

"My ex-boyfriend thought the same thing, so he took me shooting one night. Claimed he wanted me to learn how to protect myself, but in truth he wanted to show off and impress me. He set up the target twenty feet away, handed me a 9mm Makarov, and told me to shoot without aiming. I put seven rounds into the chest and one in the groin, then turned to him and said that's a warning in case he gets out of line."

Kirstie smiled. "I bet the relationship didn't last long after that."

"He broke up with me the next day. Believe me, no loss on my part."

All three women laughed.

After completing the rigging, Kirstie announced their success by slapping the side of the trailer. "We're done."

Theodore slung the semi-automatic rifle over her shoulder. "What now?"

"Help us back the trailer into Home Depot."

ANDREW AND MEG walked up and down the aisles, Andrew pushing the shopping cart while Meg used a flashlight to search the shelves for the items on Kathy's list. It felt like trying to find multiple needles in numerous haystacks.

"Is that one of them?" Andrew pointed to the fourth shelf from the floor.

Meg moved the flashlight around until she spotted two items on the same shelf—rigid foam insulation and clear silicone caulking. She scooped the items off the shelf and placed them in the cart.

"What's Kathy planning on doing with these?"

Andrew shrugged. "I only get what she asks us to. She did a great job with the water catchment system, so I don't question her on any projects she has in mind. Without her, I don't know how long we'd survive."

The two continued cruising along the aisle, slowly filling up the cart. They had made a U-turn and were halfway down the next aisle when Andrew said, "Wait. What's that?"

"Where?"

"Second shelf to the left."

Meg shined the light around but did not find it.

"Let me." Andrew gently took the flashlight and centered the beam on dispensers containing one-sided heavy blades used for box cutters. Reaching out, he pulled it off the shelf and examined it.

"Is that something Kathy is looking for?"

"No, but I can use these to ramp up the compound's defenses."

JORDAN WALKED DOWN the center of the aisle, pushing the cart while simultaneously moving the flashlight between the list and the shelves.

"What can I do to help?" asked Lindsey.

"Stay out of my way," snapped Jordan, his tone angry enough that Lindsey slowed to put a few extra feet between the two of them.

After a few more minutes of awkward silence, Lindsey stopped in the center of the aisle. "Jordan?"

He spun around and glared at her, his tone unusually harsh. "What?"

Lindsey pointed to the blue plastic fifty-five-gallon drums stacked on the shelves to her left. "Isn't that one of the items Kathy's looking for?"

Jordan huffed angrily for missing it, but this time did not vent his frustration on Lindsey. He loaded the items into the cart and glanced over at her.

"Thanks for catching that."

"You're welcome. What's next?"

Jordan studied the list. "Lumber."

"If you want, I'll bring this cart up front and bring back a dolly to load the lumber."

"Okay."

Lindsey wheeled the cart to the front of the store where Kirstie and Regan loaded the gathered supplies onto the trailers. She found one of the carts for carrying large-scale items and headed toward the lumber section, homing in on the beam from Jordan's flashlight. As Lindsey rounded the corner, she said, "I've got the—"

A gasp ended her sentence. Jordan had begun pulling 2x4s out of the pile, placing them on the floor. He struggled with one board, yanking to pull it free. He failed to notice the shaking had shifted the lumber on the shelf above him, which were about to topple over.

Rushing down the aisle, Lindsey grabbed Jordan's arm and yanked him back.

"What the fuck are you—?"

The thunderous sound of collapsing wood cut Jordan off. He stared at the spot he had stood a second before, now covered with a couple of hundred pounds of wood, realizing the close call he had avoided.

"What's going on?" Andrew yelled from the other side of the store.

"Nothing to worry about." Jordan shouted. "Some lumber collapsed."

"Are you okay?"

"I am." Jordan turned around and smiled. "Thanks to Lindsey."

"Be careful."

"I will." Jordan patted Lindsey on the shoulder. "Let's load up what we need."

TWO HOURS LATER, the group had scavenged everything from Kathy's list and loaded them onto the two trailers. Andrew and Meg conducted a final sweep of the store to make certain they had not missed something that might be of use on the compound but found nothing. The Scavengers had done a good job of cleaning out Home Depot of what they needed.

Andrew rejoined the group.

"We're heading home. We'll follow the same route we did getting here. Meg and I will take the lead. Kirstie and Regan will follow us with the first trailer and Theodora and Lindsey with the second. Jordan will bring up the rear. Any questions?"

There were none.

"Then let's head out."

Everyone mounted their horses and exited Home Depot, taking up their positions as they crossed the parking lot. Once they reached Plaistow Road, the group turned left, then turned left a few hundred feet later onto East Road. Kirstie took the opportunity to look into Plaistow, certain it would be months before she would ever see the town again.

The town resembled a scene from one of those apocalypse movies Shawn used to make them watch. Streets littered with garbage. Desolation. No traffic, human or vehicular, moving along the roads. No people milling about. No signs lit up declaring they were open for business. The only thing missing was collapsed buildings, but that would happen in time. Those movies always give her a sense of unease. Now she faced it as a stark reality.

"Is anything wrong?" asked Regan.

"No." Kirstie focused on the group and moved the horse forward, shoving the disturbing image into her subconscious along with dozens of other repressed memories over the last seven days. Nothing could be done about the past. However, if they put in the effort now to build up their resources and defend themselves against the raiders, then maybe... maybe... the future would be better.

CARBONE LED HIS team along the back roads of Atkinson, occasionally checking his map to make certain they were heading toward the compound. Nicolai followed. Just over six feet in height, bald, with a dark red beard and tattoos running down his arms and across his neck, Nicolai had a menacing presence. Carbone chose him because Nicolai happened to be the toughest gang member among the bikers and would be helpful if ambushed. Unfortunately, he was the least controllable of the gang, possessing a violent temper and a short fuse, which hopefully would not be an issue. Tyler, the former state trooper, of average height with unkempt blonde hair and rapidly growing facial hair, appeared less threatening, though he possessed an aura of confidence due to his experience with stake outs and seemed more level-headed, evening out the team.

"Hold up." Carbone raised his hand, warning the others to stop.

"What's up?" asked Nicolai.

Carbone did not respond, concentrating instead on the road two hundred feet ahead of him. Two horse-drawn carts and three independent riders were proceeding down it, heading west. Carbone recognized the lead rider as the asshole he had encountered at Timberlane. He could not believe their luck.

Rushing toward the trees, he shoved Nicolai and Tyler toward the woods.

"What the fuck are you doing?" snapped Nicolai.

Carbone placed a forefinger across his mouth. "Those people up ahead are from the compound Stratman wants us to scope out."

"What people?" asked Tyler.

"Shut the fuck up." Nicolai rolled his eyes. "What are we going to do?"

"Let them get ahead on us, then we'll follow but stay hidden. They should lead us to where their supplies are stored."

CHAPTER FIFTEEN

DANIELLE TOOK LIZ and Kyle by the hands and dashed across the street, rushing into the park east of the arena. The sound of weapons increased in intensity, accompanied by screams of terror or fury from those still trapped inside. Halfway across the park, she moved behind a tree and used it as cover.

"Liz, Kyle, get down."

"Shouldn't we run?" asked Liz.

"We will. I need to see what's going on." Danielle placed a hand on the girl's shoulder and gently pushed her onto the ground where she would be safe, then turned her attention back to the arena. People emerged from around the front of the arena, most of them rushing across the main road, heading for the safety of the side streets. Others circled around and tried to escape along the side of the arena to get away from the carnage. A pack of seven civilians carrying weapons moved north, firing at what Danielle assumed were National Guardsmen. Several innocent bystanders collapsed, caught in the crossfire. One of the civilians with a weapon yelled out to the others and turned to run. Machine gun fire erupted from in front of the arena, the barrage of bullets tearing apart those with stolen weapons as well as scores of innocent people caught between them.

Turmoil broke out behind the arena. The Guardsman who had let her and the kids go remained in position, allowing those who came through the emergency exit to escape into the surrounding neighborhoods. A family of five passed close by the Guardsman when the father jumped him, struggling to take the automatic rifle. He succeeded, knocking the Guardsman to the ground and rushing back to his family. The Guardsman withdrew his sidearm and warned the father to stop. The father spun around and aimed at the Guardsman, forcing the latter to empty his sidearm in defense. Several rounds struck the father, the rest missing and striking his family. The father's finger tightened around the trigger, peppering the Guardsman with five bullets, killing him instantly. The only survivors were the mother and the oldest child crying over the bodies of the two dead siblings.

This is fucking insane, thought Danielle, *and it's only going to get worse*. She needed to get the kids out of here before they were next.

Danielle helped Liz and Kyle back to their feet and ushered them toward the other end of the park.

"Let's go."

"Where are we going?" asked Kyle.

"Somewhere safe."

Liz looked up at her. "Where's that?"

Sadly, Danielle did not have an answer. All she could think about was making it out of the area before a stray round killed her or one of the kids.

Once at the end of the park, she veered toward the road on the right and headed down it, entering a residential neighborhood. She saw no one around, though the streets showed what type of nightmare had occurred in the city. Abandoned cars, most with the doors open and everything of value stolen. Garbage littering the streets and sidewalks, the wind having blown most of it into the bushes and front yards. Most of the houses had been broken into, with electronics and personal items strewn across the street. It reminded her of the post-apocalypse movies she had watched on family movie night. Only this was not fictional. It was reality.

And reality was far worse than anything Hollywood could

imagine.

They kept running until the sounds of gunfire and screams faded into the distance. By now, they had covered at least seven or eight city blocks, maybe more. Danielle had not been paying attention, focused on getting the kids to safety. Only then did Danielle realize she had difficulty breathing and her legs ached. Kyle cried from exhaustion. As they slowed, Liz looked up at Danielle.

"Can we rest? Please." The young girl drew out the last word so it sounded like a plea.

"Let me find a safe place to hide."

Liz squeezed her hand.

The problem would be finding a safe place to rest. Danielle assumed other survivors from the arena would soon be heading in this direction though, at the moment, she could not see anyone following them. At least a dozen houses had their front doors ajar, so getting in would not be a problem. The fear came from what she might find inside. Dead bodies. Terrified families who would do anything, including kill her and the kids, to defend themselves. Or worse, people who would rape and/or kill them merely for fun.

Danielle came upon a driveway that led a hundred feet to a house on the left and a two-car garage on the right. The latter would be the perfect hiding place. She doubted anyone would seek shelter there. And with luck, she might find something inside the garage that could be used as a weapon. She checked the surrounding area and, when certain no one was around, led the kids up the driveway.

"Where are we going, Miss Danielle?"

"We're going to rest in the garage."

"Yay!" answered Kyle.

Danielle stopped by the garage and made one final check of the surrounding area and the windows of the nearby houses to make sure no one noticed them, then grabbed the handle to the garage door on the right. It did not move. She had not anticipated it being locked.

"Damn it."

"You shouldn't swear," chastised Kyle.

"I'm sorry." Though she knew the odds were slim, Danielle tried the other garage door. To her surprise, it lifted off the ground. She quickly scanned the interior but spotted no one hiding in the shadows. A blue Subaru Forester sat in front of the locked garage door. Good. The kids would have a comfortable place to relax. She ushered them inside and closed the garage door behind her. Sunlight shone through the two windows in the rear wall, providing enough illumination to see.

Danielle opened the side doors to the Subaru and stood aside. "Get in."

Liz looked up at her. "Miss Danielle, you know it doesn't work."

"We're not going to drive it. I want you both to take a nap. The seats are more comfortable than the floor."

"I call the front seat!" Kyle jumped into the driver's side and played with the steering wheel, making engine noises.

Liz turned to Danielle and rolled her eyes.

"You take the back."

"Where are you going to sleep?"

"I'll find a place. First, I want to check the garage to see if I can find anything we could use."

"Okay, Miss Danielle. Be sure to get some rest."

"I promise."

Danielle leaned over and kissed Liz on the top of the forehead. The girl hugged her for several seconds before climbing into the back and lying down.

"Kyle, get some rest."

He pretended to slam on the brakes and smiled. "I'm on my way to Canobie Lake."

For the first time since being picked up by the National Guard, Danielle thought about her daughter, praying Kirstie was not going through what she and the kids had to endure.

"You can finish your drive later. Right now, rest."

"Aye, aye, ma'am." Kyle saluted then lay back against the driver's seat.

Both kids fell asleep in less than a minute.

Danielle took the opportunity to search the garage. Eight plastic containers labeled Xmas ornaments in black magic marker sat in two stacks in the right rear corner. Beside it stood a shelf with gardening supplies, an old microwave oven, five canisters of motor oil, a container of anti-freeze, and another of windshield washer fluid. Beside the shelf, a gas-powered lawn mower and a weed whacker lay propped against the wall.

On the opposite wall sat a small work bench. Danielle checked it out. Boxes of nails and screws sat stacked on the bench top against the wall. Above it, various tools hung from a two-by-four drilled into the wall. She pulled down an eighteen-inch crowbar, a foot-long screwdriver, and a hammer for herself plus two smaller screwdrivers for the kids. They may not be the best weapons, but at least it offered some protection against attackers.

Danielle went over and lay down a few inches from the garage door, leaning against the cement wall. If anyone tried to break in, which seemed unlikely, she would be close enough to ambush them.

CHAPTER SIXTEEN

H EAT AND HUMIDITY beat down on Shawn and Kevin, their predicament made all the more unbearable by being on a highway, constantly exposed to the sun and the heat radiating off the asphalt. They could have exited off Route 101 and taken the back roads to Dunbarton, which would have been a safer alternative and kept them out of the direct sunlight for much of the journey, but that would have added days to their journey, time Shawn knew he did not have.

Other than the group of people spotted back at the Super Walmart and a few stragglers along Route 101, all of whom avoided Shawn and Kevin as if they had plague, they had seen anyone. Not that it surprised Shawn. He assumed everything of value had been looted during the first few days. Every vehicle or truck they passed had been ransacked, those items not necessary for survival left scattered along the highway. Several vehicles had blood streaks on them or covering the asphalt, now dried out after baking in the sun for a week. Occasionally, they stumbled across a corpse in the middle of the road, most of them having been ravaged by wildlife and birds.

A terrible stench greeted them as they approached a FedEx van. The driver's door stood open. As they passed by, both men looked inside. The nauseating odor came from the driver who sat in the front seat, a bullet hole in his left temple. Not being exposed to sunlight, the corpse was still moist. Liquified flesh stained the seat and floor mat. Maggots covered most of his body. Shawn reached in and tapped its shoulder. The body collapsed onto the passenger seat, disturbing a swarm of flies that swarmed around Shawn's head. He closed the door before swatting away the annoying insects.

"This is insane," mumbled Kevin.

"What is?"

"That people would do this to each other." Frustration welled up inside him. "We're not some third world country. This is America. Nobody acted this bad during COVID."

Shawn chuckled, which sent a wave of nausea through his stomach. "COVID was the apocalypse played on beginner mode. We're now playing the nightmare scenario."

Kevin huffed and shook his head, his faith in humanity shattered.

Shawn understood how Kevin felt. He had always expected a societal breakdown in a situation like this, though never imagined it would be so severe. The last twenty-four hours had awakened him to the reality the world faced. If it was this bad in the suburbs, in a state as peaceful as New Hampshire, how intense was the nightmare in major metropolitan areas around the world?

That thought only increased his determination to make it home and check on Danielle and Kirstie.

Shawn took a few steps before his stomach erupted. Supporting himself on the fender of a Nissan Altima, he vomited across the hood, mostly blood and bile. Catching his breath, he steadied himself, then dry heaved.

"You need to rest." Kevin stepped over to help his friend stand up, only to be pushed away.

"I'm fine."

"We both know that's not true. Your radiation poisoning is getting worse."

"Fuck you."

"No thanks. I have higher standards."

Kevin placed Shawn's right arm over his shoulder and escorted him to the side of the Altima that provided shade. This time, Shawn did not object. Once out of the sunlight,

Kevin propped his friend against the rear tire. He reached into his backpack, removed an unopened bottle of spring water, and twisted off the cap.

"Drink some of this."

Shawn waved him off. "We need to conserve our supplies."

"You need liquid." Kevin placed the bottle in Shawn's hand and closed his friend's fingers around it. "Drink."

Shawn did not argue. He filled his mouth with water, swished it around to remove the taste of vomit, and swallowed, immediately regretting his decision. His stomach churned. Shawn swallowed hard, forcing down the vomit. A few seconds later, his stomach settled down. He took another sip of water. This time he did not feel the urge to puke.

"How do you feel?"

"Like shit."

"What are your symptoms?"

Shawn hesitated to answer, but realized Kevin deserved the truth. "This is wearing me down. I'm exhausted and sometimes feel dizzy. But that could be from the heat."

"That's not the reason. What else?"

"The last time I urinated, which was two days ago, I pissed blood. My stomach only began acting up this morning."

Kevin's expression darkened. He knew Shawn did not have much time left before becoming incapacitated.

"You need to rest before we go on. Close your eyes and take a nap. I'll keep watch."

"I want to keep moving." Shawn attempted to stand, making it only a few inches before falling back against the car.

"You're not going to make it very far if you don't rest."

Shawn knew Kevin was right. "Alright. I'll rest for a few minutes, but I doubt I'll take a nap."

"Fine. Take a few minutes to build back your energy."

Leaning back against the car, trying to get as comfortable as possible, Shawn closed his eyes.

Within minutes, he fell asleep.

CHAPTER SEVENTEEN

JORDAN RODE HIS horse alongside Andrew and Meg, speaking softly. "We have company. Three guys have been tailing us for half an hour."

Concern flashed through Meg's eyes. "Are you sure?"

Jordan nodded. "I spotted them out of the corner of my eye when we passed Meditation Lane. They've been following us since."

"Shit." Andrew thought for a moment before he turned to Meg. "Jordan and I are going to dismount at the country club and check these guys out. Take our horses and head back to the compound. I don't want anyone to know where we're located."

"Do you want me to stay behind and help?"

Andrew shook his head. "I need you to make sure the supplies get back safely. But if you hear more than one gunshot, come back with reinforcements."

When the group reached the road leading to the country club, Andrew and Jordan dismounted and ran behind the stone wall. Meg took the reins and led the convoy to the compound. Andrew placed his Heckler and Koch with a scope against the wall and lay prone, only his head extending beyond the edge of the wall, using his binoculars to scan the road. He paused only long enough to glance over at Jordan and motion toward the rifle.

"Do you know how to use one of those?"

"Of course." Jordan picked up the gun and aimed down Providence Hill Road, using the site to focus on a mailbox. "I used to hunt with my old man when I was a teenager."

Both men waited to see if the trio still followed them.

CARBONE, NICOLAI, AND Tyler moved along Providence Hill Road, rushing across front yards and making their way through the woods, staying at least ten feet from the road so no one would accidentally spot them. Every five minutes, one of them would make their way out to the pavement and check on the group before rejoining the others.

"How much farther do we have to go?" bitched Tyler.

"About a mile." Carbone spun around to confront Tyler. "And keep your voice down. Do you want to give away our position?"

Tyler flipped Carbone the bird.

"Why are we still tracking them if you know their location?" asked Nicolai.

"I want to make sure it's the same group I ran into earlier. If it's a second group, that's twice as much shit for us."

Nicolai nudged Tyler. "And twice as much pussy."

"We're almost there." Carbone pointed through the trees to the stone wall bordering the entrance to the country club. "Take a break. I'm going to check on the group."

ANDREW SPOTTED SOMEONE emerging from the trees across the street one hundred feet down Providence Hill Road. The man moved farther into the road, trying to get a clear view around the bend. He concentrated so much on following the others he never noticed Andrew by the wall.

"One of them exposed themselves," Andrew whispered.

Jordan slowly rose and aimed the hunting rifle, focusing the scope on the man's head. Anger welled up inside Jordan when he recognized the face of the asshole who ambushed him in the school gym.

"That's the motherfucker who tried to kill me a few days ago."

Andrew studied him again. Damn, Jordan was right. Andrew had seen him for only a few seconds when they ran into each other in the school corridor. The other five gang members with him that afternoon were total assholes. Two of them had tried to rape Kathy and Haellie, two more had attacked Kirstie and Regan, and this guy's partner had almost killed Jordan. No way would Andrew let these guys know the location of their compound.

"Fire a warning shot."

"My pleasure."

Jordan adjusted his aim, took a deep breath, and slowly pulled the trigger. He watched through the scope as the bullet slammed into the asshole's forehead. The bullet tore off the back of his skull, creating a cloud of blood, brains, and bone fragments.

"FUCK!" TYLER WATCHED, frozen in shock, as Carbone's head exploded.

"Get down, asshole." Nicolai grabbed Tyler by the shoulder and shoved him to the ground. Scurrying over to a tree, he checked the road to see where the gunshot came from. It took a moment for him to spot the gunman behind the stone wall, still scanning the road with his hunting rifle. Another one lay prone by the wall's edge with a pair of binoculars. He considered firing back but thought better. If they had spotted him and Tyler, they would have fired at them by now. If Tyler remained calm, they had a chance of escaping.

Nicolai said in a low voice, "Crawl deeper into the woods."

"What about Carbone?"

"Fuck him. He was a dick. I don't wanna get shot. Now move."

"We're heading back to camp, right?"

"Stop being a pussy," answered Nicolai. "We can't go back to Stratman without knowing where this group is located and how many there are. He'll shoot us both and give your wife to the bikers."

The thought of his wife being one of the gang's whores made Tyler more pliable to the risks involved.

Both men stayed low and made their way deeper into the woods, Nicolai checking over his shoulder every few seconds to see if the gunman chased after them. He waited for either him or Tyler to be taken out, but no more shots were fired.

After a hundred feet, they turned left and moved parallel to Providence Hill Road, following the others at a safe distance.

"I THOUGHT I told you to fire a warning shot?" snapped Andrew, watching the woods through his binoculars.

"It was a warning to the others."

Andrew forced himself not to laugh.

None of the other raiders engaged them. After a few seconds, Andrew heard the rustling of leaves and tree branches, the sounds growing dimmer. The other two must be trying to escape. He considered going after them but thought better of it, knowing doing so would only put him and Jordan in danger. At least they had succeeded in stopping the raiders from following them to the compound.

Five minutes passed and Andrew neither saw nor heard anything from the raiders, assuming they had retreated.

"Do you see anything?"

Jordan shook his head. "I spotted movement in the trees, but it looks like the other two are heading away from us."

"Cover me."

Andrew stood and slowly emerged from behind the wall, half expecting to be caught in return fire. When nothing happened, he cautiously made his way to the body lying in the middle of the road. Jordan's shot had been spot on, killing the raider instantly. Not that he cared. This motherfucker would have done the same thing to them if given the chance. Andrew searched the body for anything that might tell him where this group was located, finding a box of matches with the logo of the VFW emblazoned on it. He had no idea where that was located but would check it out later. Taking the dead man's weapon, he returned to Jordan.

"What did you find?"

"Just this." He handed Jordan the book of matches. "I doubt it's a coincidence that we ran into that asshole and his friends. He must have followed us back here after the encounter at Timberlane."

"Shit."

Andrew nodded in agreement. "We have to assume they know everything about us. Where we are, what we have in the way of supplies, and how many of us there are. Considering what happened at the high school, I doubt they'll want to work with us and will take what we have for themselves."

"Maybe they were going to sneak in and steal some of our food."

"They would have done that at night when most of us were asleep. My bet is that these three were a scouting party. They'll be back with more."

"How many more?"

Andrew shrugged.

"What are we going to do now?" asked Jordan.

"We need to strengthen our defenses before they come back. I figure we have a minimum of twenty-four hours before they return, maybe thirty-six if we're lucky. We need to be ready by sundown tomorrow night."

"Do you think we can do it?"

"We have to." Andrew motioned toward the compound. "Let's get back. We need to have a group meeting."

CHAPTER EIGHTEEN

DANIELLE LAY IN bed, peacefully sleeping on a soft, comfortable mattress. A warm breeze blew through the open window, ruffling the white curtains. A floor-mounted fan stood at the end of the bed set on low, providing enough flowing air to keep her cool. It had been a long time since she felt this relaxed. She could stay in bed for another hour.

"Wake up," whispered a voice beside her.

Danielle rolled over to see Kirstie, her daughter, a bright smile on her face, the teenager's brown eyes staring at her lovingly. Her presence warmed Danielle's heart. She loved Kirstie more than anything in the world and would do whatever it took to keep her safe and happy. The young girl had her whole life ahead of her. College. Marriage. Children of her own. Danielle so looked forward to someday being a grandmother.

"Wake up."

Kirstie still smiled, a pleasant gleam in her eyes, though her voice seemed scared.

A small, soft hand touched her shoulder. "Miss Danielle, please wake up."

Danielle woke up from her dream with a start. For a moment, she had no clue of her setting, only that she was not resting in her bed but on a hard, cement floor. Dim light flowed through the twin windows to her left. Rather than being safe in her bedroom, she sheltered in a garage after having escaped from the riot at the arena. The face staring at her was not Kirstie but Liz, and the look in her eyes was not adoration but fear.

"What's up?"

Liz placed a finger over her lips, warning Danielle to be quiet, then whispered, "Someone's outside."

Danielle listened. A plastic garbage container fell over followed by the sounds of someone rummaging through the trash, more than likely searching for food. She got up, took Liz and Kyle by the hands, and moved them into the corner so no one could spot them through the window.

"Stay quiet. Hopefully, he'll go away in a few minutes."

"I'm scared," Kyle said louder than Danielle wanted.

The noise outside stopped. A few seconds later, the intruder began playing with the handle on the garage door.

Danielle quickly ran through her options. No other way out of the garage existed except the two bay doors. If they stayed inside, they would be trapped and would have to fight off whoever tried to get in. Danielle had only chance to save herself and the kids—to strike first, catching the intruder by surprise and taking him down quickly.

She leaned close to the kids and spoke softly. "Kyle, you stay here. Liz, I need you to raise the garage door so I can ambush him."

"I… I don't think I can," stuttered Liz.

"You have to. I need to take him down before he gets inside. If something happens to me, run away as fast as you can."

"I won't leave you behind," Liz protested.

"Promise me you will."

Both kids nodded reluctantly.

Danielle hugged them both tightly, then stood. She picked up the three-foot-long crowbar and moved to the garage door. Liz followed and grabbed the handle, focusing on Danielle. Danielle held the crowbar like a baseball bat, took a deep breath to steady her nerves, then mouthed a single word.

"Now."

Liz stood, pulled the garage door up several feet, placed her hands beneath the rim, pushed it up, then ran back to be with Kyle. Danielle ran out and swung the crowbar with all her strength. No one was there. The weapon passed through empty space. The force of the swing knocked her off balance. Danielle toppled onto her back, landing hard enough to knock the wind out of her for a few moments. As she lay partially stunned, someone approached from her right, aiming at her head. She blocked her face with her hands, worried about what would happen to Liz and Kyle if the attacker took her out.

A sloppy wet tongue lapped across her cheek.

"Oh my God!" Kyle joyfully squealed.

"He's adorable," added Liz.

Danielle lowered her hands, watching as a Boxer gave her a face bath. When the kids knelt beside the dog, it switched its attention to them, rubbing its head across Kyle's face as Liz scratched its back.

Kyle glanced at Danielle as the dog licked his face. "Can we keep him?"

"We barely have enough supplies for ourselves."

"Please," pleaded Liz. "I'll share my food with him."

"Besides," added Kyle, "he'll make a good guard dog."

The Boxer turned his head to Danielle and barked as if agreeing with them.

Slowly getting up, Danielle considered allowing them to keep the dog. If she said no, she knew the kids would be heartbroken, and they had already gone through enough. Besides, he would not be a huge drain on their limited resources; he could eat and drink things they couldn't. Kyle made a good argument, and considering this was the second time she had swung a weapon at a potential enemy and landed on her ass, having the dog around would increase their chances of survival. He would be useful in detecting threats and defending the kids. Though Danille hated to admit it, even in the apocalypse she could not ignore a stray dog.

"We can keep him."

"Yay!" both kids cheered as they increased their level of affection on the Boxer.

Danielle smiled. "What are we going to name him?"

Kyle responded without hesitation. "Chase."

Liz rolled her eyes in frustration. "Chase is a German Shepherd."

"But they look the same."

"Fine." Liz sighed and shook her head.

"What are you talking about?" asked Danielle.

The kids stared at her as if she had stepped off a flying saucer. Kyle finally replied, "*Paw Patrol.* Chase is the police dog. The character protects people, like he'll do for us."

Danielle smiled again. "Chase it is."

The Boxer barked, approving of the name.

Kyle changed the subject. "I'm hungry and thirsty. And I have to go to the bathroom."

"Me too."

So did Danielle. She considered her options, quickly narrowing them down to one—seeing if there was anything to eat or drink in the house across from the garage.

"You stay here with Charles—"

"Chase."

Danielle suppressed a grin. "You stay here with Chase while I go see if anyone is home."

Climbing the steps to the back porch, Danielle glanced through the window to see if anyone was there but saw no one through the silk curtains. She knocked loudly on the door three times.

"Is anyone home?"

No answer.

Danielle knocked again, a little louder this time. "If anyone's home, please open up. I only want some water and food if you can spare any. And to use your bathroom. I have two kids out here."

Still no response.

She tried turning the knob only to find the door locked. Looking through the window one final time and seeing no movement inside, Danielle decided to take a chance. An old-style lattice window was on the door leading into the kitchen. She used her elbow to smash the lower right window, half expecting to be raked with gunfire from inside. When nothing happened, Danielle reached in, unlocked the door, opened it, and stepped inside the kitchen.

"I don't want any trouble. I only want to get some water for my kids. If anyone is here, please let me know and I'll leave."

Silence.

Danielle stepped onto the back porch and waved to get the kids' attention. "Come on. And bring Chase with you."

Once everyone was inside, Danielle closed and locked the door, checking the backyard to make certain no one had spotted them.

"Let's find the bathroom."

Danielle found it off to the right in a small hall leading from the kitchen to the dining room. She told Liz and Kyle not to flush because the pumps might not refill the basin, and to wash their hands together when they were done. Leaving the kids alone to do their business, she returned to the kitchen to find food. Chase fell in behind her, his stubby tail wagging.

She opened the refrigerator door and gagged as the stench of rotten food washed over her. Seven days without electricity in the heat and humidity, everything edible inside had spoiled. She held her breath while rummaging through the items, the only thing worth saving being two seven-ounce plastic bottles of orange juice. A large crock pot covered with tinfoil, its spoiled contents especially foul, sat on the center shelf to the right. She pushed it aside to reach the seven bottles of spring water against the back wall. Pulling them out, she placed them on the counter.

Next, Danielle checked the cabinets. They contained the usual items one would expect, from spices and flour to canned goods. She removed everything they could use: five cans of peas or mixed vegetables, three cans of fruit, a jar of peanut butter, a box of Frosted Flakes, a box of Ritz Crackers, an opened pack of double-stuffed Oreo cookies, and three cans of chili for Chase. Danielle then searched the cabinets above the sink, finding two large bowls, one of which she filled with the contents of the chili can and the other with water from the faucet, placing both on the floor. Chase devoured the chili in seconds and emptied the water bowl, which Danielle refilled for him.

Only a third of the box of cereal had been eaten, and the Ritz box contained two sealed packs of crackers; they would bring both with them on the road. The jar of peanut butter was almost empty, so they would finish it off for dinner. Only seven Oreos remained, so she ate one and saved the other six for Liz and Kyle. Spotting a loaf of whole wheat bread on the counter, she checked it out. Mold had consumed most of the loaf. Danielle salvaged five slices, using four of them to make peanut butter sandwiches for the kids and loading the remainder of the jar on the fifth slice for herself. Grabbing two plates and glasses from the cabinets, she placed a sandwich and three Oreos on each plate and divided one bottle of spring water between the tumblers. When Liz and Kyle came back from the bathroom, Danielle gestured toward the table.

"Dinner is served."

The kids cheered and ran to their seats. Liz started on the sandwich while Kyle wolfed down the Oreos. Chase stood between the kids, his tail wagging furiously, giving them sad puppy eyes. Both kids gave him one of their Oreos.

"You stay here with Chase. I'm going to check out the house to see if I can find anything we can use."

Danielle quickly scanned the dining and living rooms, knowing there would be nothing there. Heading upstairs, she checked out the first room on the right. Judging by the posters of scantily clad anime girls, the *Star Wars* paraphernalia on the bookshelf, and the clutter spread across the floor, she assumed it belonged to a teenage boy. A backpack with Deadpool on the front rested against the foot of the bed. She emptied the contents onto the floor before crossing to the room across the hall.

Danielle's heart sank. She had entered a nursery. A thousand thoughts raced through her mind. Were the kids at school and daycare and the parents at work when the shit hit the fan? Did the parents ever make it back to their kids? Hopefully, the family was on vacation when the apocalypse began. She pushed all those thoughts aside. They reminded her too much of Kirstie, and right now she needed to concentrate on keeping Liz and Kyle safe.

The room beside the teenager's served as a guest bedroom with a laptop on a desk by the window overlooking the garage, probably someone's workspace. Rummaging through the dresser drawers and closet, she found nothing useful.

Across the hall sat a small bathroom. Danielle took the toothbrush, toothpaste, and dental floss from off the sink and placed them in the backpack, which to her were Godsends since she had not cleaned her teeth in three days. Opening the medicine cabinet, she rummaged through the contents. The only items of any value were a box of *Star Wars*-themed band aids, an unopened bottle of NyQuil, and a half-used container of underarm deodorant, all of which she tossed in with the oral hygiene products.

The room at the end of the hall was the master bedroom. Danielle checked the bathroom first, confiscating the dental hygiene products for Liz and Kyle. The medicine cabinet and drawers beneath the sink were like hitting the jackpot. Bottles of Ibuprofen, antacid, allergy meds, stool softeners, and anti-diarrhea medication. Three rolls of bandages, gauze pads, and a bottle of rubbing alcohol. Two tubes of sunscreen lotion. An unopened bottle of Nyquil. And tampons. They were something she had not even thought about until now. Thank God, she found them because her period would start in a week.

Moving over to the closet, Danielle found two empty back-packs sitting on the floor and threw them onto the bed. She sorted through the clothes and shoes, the only items that would fit any of them being three baseball caps that would help keep the sun or rain out of their eyes and prevent their scalps from getting sunburned. Rummaging through the dressers came up with nothing of value except panties which were too small for her to wear.

Danielle next checked out the end tables on either side of the bed. The one on the right had an 8x10 photograph of the family at the beach mounted in a silver frame. The husband and wife were in their mid-thirties, both attractive. In between them stood a teenage boy, his blonde hair tussled by the wind and a huge smile on his face, his teeth covered with braces. The mother cradled a sleeping baby not more than a year old. Danielle prayed they had survived this event and were currently in a safe place, though she doubted it. Opening the drawer, she chuckled. Several sex toys and plastic bottles of lubricant filled the area.

Moving over to the end table on the left, she noticed a dead alarm clock and a multi-item charger sitting on top. Relics of the past. Opening the drawer, her eyes widened.

A pistol case with an electric lock rested in the center. The LED lights were off. Danielle lifted the lid. Inside sat a semi-automatic pistol and two magazines of ammunition. She hesitated, afraid to pick it up. All her life, she had been anti-gun, convinced they were nothing but a threat to whoever owned them and those around them. What she had experienced over the past week, though, had changed her mind. This would help protect her and the kids from the assholes out there.

Danielle removed the weapon and studied it, turning it around in her hand. Other than pulling the trigger, she had no idea how to use or maintain it. Shit, she did not even know how to replace an empty magazine with a full one. Shawn had once mentioned a safety switch that would prevent the gun from firing, but she had no clue where it was located or how to use it. Danielle considered putting it back and leaving it but, on second thought, slipped it into the backpack with the other supplies. Hopefully, she would never have to fire it, but better to have it and not need it than to need it and not have it. If she did bring it out, maybe it would scare off whoever threatened them.

Grabbing the three backpacks, Danielle headed downstairs. Liz and Kyle had finished eating and sat on the living room floor playing with Chase. Kyle had taken a small throw pillow off the sofa and teased the Boxer who would grab it in his mouth, the two engaging in a tug of war. The pillow must have split open a while ago because stuffing littered the floor. Every few minutes, Liz would grab the dog's stubby tale, getting a face bath in return until Kyle nudged the dog with the pillow, starting the tug of war all over again.

"I see you're having fun."

"Chase is adorable," said Liz.

Before Kyle could say anything, Chase let go of the pillow and lunged forward, pinning him to the floor and licking his face. Kyle laughed loudly.

Liz turned her attention to Danielle. "Did you find anything upstairs?"

"A lot of good stuff, including toothbrushes and toothpaste."

"Yay. My mouth feels gross."

"Noooo," whined Kyle. "I hate brushing my teeth."

"You're going to brush them. If you get a cavity, there's no dentist to take care of it."

Kyle moaned.

"I have a surprise for you." Danielle reached into the backpack and pulled out the three baseball caps.

Kyle squealed with joy and grabbed the one with a flying saucer on it with the words "Exeter UFO Festival" beneath. He placed it on his head. The cap slid down over his eyes. Kyle laughed again.

"Let me fix that." Danielle took the cap off his head, adjusted the Velcro strap, and placed it back. This time it fit perfectly. She offered the other two to Liz. "Which one do you want?"

Liz studied them as if her life depended on her choice. She eventually took the one with the American flag on the front. "I like this one."

That left the baseball cap with an embroidered image of the Eifel Tower and the word PARIS written underneath.

"What are we going to do now?" asked Kyle.

"We're going to spend the night here. There's a king-size bed upstairs we can share. Tomorrow morning we'll continue heading north."

"Can Chase sleep in the bed with us?" asked Liz.

Kyle became excited. "Please!"

Chase looked at Danielle, his stumpy tail wagging.

"Of course. He's part of the family now."

Both kids yelled in happiness. Chase barked his approval.

CHAPTER NINETEEN

T HE SUN HAD already begun its descent toward the eastern horizon, which aggravated Shawn. Not because of the approaching dusk. Once darkness fell, hopefully the heat and humidity would be more bearable. What pissed off Shawn was that he had not covered as much distance as he had originally hoped to.

Shawn had taken this route home five days a week since he started working at Seabrook and knew it like the back of his hand. He had mentally calculated the distance home, figuring if he walked at least fifteen miles a day, he would reach his place in Dunbarton on the fourth day. Only he had not calculated the physical effects of radiation poisoning on his health. Shawn had hoped to reach Exit 3 before nightfall since a country club sat nearby where they could safely bunk down for the night. They were only halfway between Exits 4 and 5. At this rate, they would add at least another day to the trip. Maybe two.

Assuming Shawn lived that long.

Kevin plodded along beside him, purposefully keeping his pace slow so Shawn could keep up with him.

"We shouldn't have taken that nap," protested Shawn. "Now we won't make it to the country club in time."

"You only slept for an hour." Kevin kept his voice pleasant, though frustration showed in his eyes. "Even if we continued on, we would barely be at Exit 4 by now. And without that nap, your body would have given out by now."

Shawn wanted to argue back but knew Kevin was correct.

He should not get upset with his friend because his body slowly gave out on him.

"You're right. I'm sorry for being such an ass."

The frustration disappeared from Kevin's eyes and a smile pierced his lip. "Don't worry about it. I know you want to get home to check on your family."

"You're worried about your family, too."

"I am. But they live out of state. I doubt I'll ever know what happened to them. I have to live with it."

An awkward silence developed between the two men.

After a few hundred feet of walking, Shawn's legs gave out, too exhausted to keep on moving. He stumbled against a nearby Volvo and collapsed, his knees slamming onto the asphalt. A jolt of pain shot through his legs, which upset his stomach. Before Shawn could lean over, vomit shot up his throat. He puked, most of it splashing across his legs. Some of the vomit stuck in his throat, causing him to gag. It took several seconds to cough up the vomitus and spit it out, leaving him gasping for breath.

Kevin knelt beside his friend. "Take slow breaths."

Shawn focused on suppressing his gag reflex, soon getting it under control. He took a deep breath and coughed again, causing more gagging. For a few seconds, Shawn thought this would be how he died—choking on his own puke. He took a second deep breath. This time air filled his lungs with no adverse reaction. As his breathing returned to normal, Shawn leaned back against the Volvo.

"I need to rest."

"Take your time." Kevin scanned the area for a better place to relax, one not in the sun. He spotted something a quarter of a mile up ahead and tapped his friend on the shoulder. "Look. There's an RV."

"Where?"

Kevin pointed to the recreational vehicle.

"It's probably been ransacked."

"Who cares. It has a bed where you can rest and be out of the sun."

Kevin helped his friend to his feet. Shawn staggered, unable to walk on his own. Kevin wrapped Shawn's arm around his shoulders and helped him walk.

It took almost twenty minutes to get there. The RV had been gone through, though not as bad as either of them had thought. Several suitcases and boxes lay open on the ground, the clothes having been rummaged through and tossed onto the asphalt. Someone had left the entry door open. Kevin leaned Shawn against the exterior wall and moved to the opening.

"Is anyone inside?"

When no one answered, he called out.

"My friend and I are coming in. He's sick and needs to rest for a while."

Kevin helped Shawn inside.

The interior of the RV had been rummaged through but, like outside, not bad. All the cabinets had been opened, some of the contents either thrown to the floor or placed on the counter. Nothing had been vandalized.

A strong odor of feces and urine wafted over them.

"What stinks so bad?" asked Shawn.

"Smells like someone took a shit in here." Kevin helped Shawn onto the sofa. "You stay here while I check it out."

Kevin made his way through the RV, checking the cabinets for anything of value but finding nothing. As he made his way through the small hall leading to the bedroom he peered into the bathroom and grimaced.

"I found the source of the stench. Everyone must have been using the toilet to take a leak or a shit. It's filled to the brim."

"That sucks."

"We'll get used to it."

Kevin closed the bathroom door then disappeared into the bedroom. He emerged a few seconds later and rejoined Shawn.

"Everything's good back there. The bed looks like it's been slept in a few times, but it's passable. Come on. You need to lay down."

Kevin helped Shawn to his feet and led him to the bedroom. Shawn's eyes widened when he saw the queen size mattress, never so happy to see a bed in his life. Kevin propped him against the wall then straightened out the blanket and covered the sheets with it. Shawn stumbled over and dropped onto the mattress, breathing a deep sigh of relief.

"Jesus, that feels good."

"Good. Now relax for a bit."

"What will you do?"

"I'm going to lock the door and sleep on the sofa in case anyone tries to break in."

Kevin moved over to one of the side windows not directly in the sun, pulled the curtains aside, and opened the pane to let air in.

"That will help air the place out."

When he turned around, Shawn had already dozed off.

CHAPTER TWENTY

N ICOLAI TOLD TYLER to lead the way to the compound, partly because his experience as a cop would help them avoid any more lookouts or patrols, and partly because if Tyler fucked up then he would take the bullet, not Nicolai. They cautiously made their way through the woods, careful to avoid making noise or being discovered, and found the outskirts of the compound ninety minutes later. Both men hid themselves behind a large copse of trees and reconned the area.

The house off to the left on the opposite side of Providence Hill Road appeared to be the center of the compound. Nicolai noticed the group they had been tracking stopped there. Five or six people gathered around them and unloaded a portion of the supplies. When the garage door opened, he spotted a stacked row of ten-gallon bottles of water used in dispensers, a collection of water bottles wrapped in plastic, canned food, several dozen packages of toilet paper and paper towels, and what from this distance appeared to be medical supplies. After unloading similar items from the cart, the man who Nicolai assumed to be the leader of the group entered the house, followed by a beautiful woman and her teenage daughter. He would enjoy trying them out at the bar. An older, attractive blonde led the two horse teams further down the street.

Nicolai leaned over and whispered to Tyler. "I'm going to climb this tree. Hopefully, I'll find out where they store the other supplies. Keep an eye out for patrols. If things go south, get the fuck out of here and report back to Stratman."

"Be careful."

Scanning the area first to make sure no one was nearby who could spot him, Nicolai scaled the tree, pulling on each branch first to make sure it would hold his weight. He stopped forty feet up, enough to give him a view of the compound while staying hidden among the leaves. The older, attractive blonde stopped two houses down and helped the others unpack the construction supplies and load them into the garage. At first, Nicolai had no idea what these items were intended for until he spotted the water catchment system set up in her backyard. Damn, these motherfuckers had collected more supplies than he imagined.

Once unloaded, three sweet-looking girls untied the horses from the cart and led them back the way they had originally come, turning down a side street. They brought the animals three doors down and led them into the backyard. The two teenagers removed the saddles and stored them in the garage while the other chick gave the animals food and water.

Directly across the street from him, another pair of teenage girls tended to a large garden set up inside the fenced in backyard. God damn, these people had a good set-up here. A garden, horses, supplies, real houses to live in. And tons of new, sweet pussy. He would advise Stratman to take over this compound and move their group here where they could sit out the end of the world in style.

Nicolai waited until the sun had begun to set, studying the area and mentally noting where the key targets were, before climbing back down and rejoining Tyler.

"What did you see?" whispered Tyler.

"This place is fucking awesome. They're living like fucking royalty while we're sleeping in chairs and struggling to find food. What did you discover?"

"Surprisingly, they don't have patrols, at least during the day. My bet is they've set up other checkpoints, but none I could see."

"Doesn't matter. These woods provide the perfect cover.

We'll follow this path into the compound and take these assholes by surprise. What do you think?"

"It sounds like the best plan," Tyler replied optimistically, confirming to Nicolai this would be the best option.

Both men waited until sundown then used the darkness to head back to the VFW Hall.

DAY EIGHT

CHAPTER TWENTY-ONE

A NDREW AND KATHY spent most of the night discussing the best way to defend the compound despite the odds against them, working until sunrise. Andrew called an emergency meeting after breakfast to discuss the run-in with the raiders yesterday afternoon. Word about the incident traveled fast after the Scavengers arrived back at the compound. And so did the rumors. When Theodora came up to him last night and asked for more details about the incident with the raiders at the school a few days previous, Andrew knew he needed to fully brief everyone.

Even more important, he needed to prepare them for what was ahead.

Andrew opened the French door to his kitchen and stepped out onto the patio. All eyes focused on him. The looks of fear of the unknown he noticed at the first meeting had been replaced by anxiety over the developing situation. Only now the group looked to him for guidance. Without realizing it, he had become the de facto leader. Up until this moment, Andrew did not mind. However, now he would be leading them into combat. Two years in the Marines trained him for this. The question was whether he could train his neighbors to defend the compound.

As he approached the picnic table, Jeanette mouthed, "You got this."

Andrew stopped in front of the others and took a deep breath.

"Let me get straight to the point. The gang we ran into at

the school the other day knows where we're located and is going to raid our compound."

"Are you sure?" asked Theodora.

"We are."

Jordan shifted in his seat to face Theodora. "The raider I shot yesterday was the same one who tried to kill me in the gym at Timberlane."

Several people asked questions at once, while others mumbled amongst themselves. Andrew raised his hands to quiet them down. Once settled, Victoria, a middle-aged woman with her brunette hair tied up in a bun, stood up to ask a question.

"Are you sure they're dangerous?" Victoria asked hesitantly. "Maybe they were only searching for supplies like we are."

Jordan rolled his eyes. "Didn't you just hear me say that one of them tried to shoot me?" "We also ran into two of them at the school." Kirstie motioned to Regan. "They tried to kill us."

"Yes… but.…" The middle-aged woman struggled to find the right words. "Maybe they thought you were a threat."

"They're the threat." The stern voice came from the front of the group. Haellie stood and turned to face Victoria, her tone seething with anger and hatred. "They butchered my family for fun. Two of them forced my mother to her knees and made her watch as they executed my siblings one at a time, taunting her with each killing before shooting her through the head. At the school, two of them tried to rape me and Kathy. I burned my hand with acid trying to stop them."

Kathy stood and placed her hands on Haellie's shoulders, attempting to comfort her, but Haellie shrugged them off.

"I lost everyone dear to me because of these people. I'd be dead by now if Andrew and the others hadn't taken me in. No way am I going to sit back and let those assholes walk in here, butcher us, and take what you've been working so long to set up. Unless you want to wind up dead, grow a pair and listen to Andrew."

Victoria focused her gaze onto the grass. Haellie glared at her for a moment before sitting down.

Andrew noticed the group's indecision suddenly shifted to resolve. Everyone focused their attention on him. Time to take advantage of the opportunity.

"Haellie is right. These people are brutal and dangerous. We can't reason with them. We can't negotiate with them. I had hoped they wouldn't find us, but obviously they have. Which leaves us with two options—surrender or fight for what we've built."

"How many are there?" asked Fallon, who lived on the outskirts of the compound. It was the first time she had asked a question at any of the meetings. "And where are they located?"

"As for the first question, I don't know. There could be five or fifty. As for their location, the raider we took out yesterday had a book of matches on him from the VFW Hall in Kingston."

"Shit," said Victoria. "My husband and I used to go there. That's not far from here."

"Exactly. I'm estimating, worst case scenario, they could launch a raid against us as early as tonight."

Mumbling broke out amongst the group again, this time with undertones of fear. Andrew calmed them down.

"If we know where they are," said Keith, "why don't we attack them first? We have the element of surprise."

"We lost that element when we took out one of the raiders. Even if we could take them by surprise, we have no idea how many we're facing and what their defenses are. Our best option is to fortify the compound and prepare to defend ourselves."

"Do we have enough weapons to do that?" asked an older man in the back of the group.

Andrew motioned to the house across the street. "We do thanks to Dignam."

"No." A woman Andrew knew by the name Martha Lee leaned over and pulled close her young daughter. "I don't want any guns around my children."

Andrew started to reason with the woman, but Meg stood and turned to the woman. "And what are you going to do if one of the raiders breaks into your house and comes after you and your daughter while the rest of us defend the compound? Beg him not to harm you?"

Martha Lee straightened in defiance. "I have my principles."

"Your principles became useless the moment the solar flare hit. There are no longer any police to protect you. That's up to you now. Do you really want to put your daughters in that situation?"

"I can protect her without guns, thank you."

Meg shrugged in frustration and sat down.

Kirstie used the momentary silence to change topics. "How do we prepare to defend the compound when we have no idea how many raiders there are?"

"As we used to say in the Marines, 'hope for the best but plan for the worst.'"

Andrew removed a folded paper tablecloth from his back pocket and spread it across the picnic table. The group gathered around, looking over each other's shoulders. Andrew spent the next thirty minutes going over his layout for defensive positions and traps, the best locations to place them, and how to build them. No one spoke throughout the briefing. When finished, he tapped the table with his right hand.

"Any questions?"

Andrew knew there was a slew of them, but no one dared ask.

"I have one," said Jordan. "How do you plan on putting this together in twenty-four hours?"

"I don't, but we'll accomplish as much as we can before the raiders strike and hopefully it'll be enough. We'll start with the defenses and traps I circled in red, then move on to the blue ones and hopefully the green ones. Until we get everything set up, I'm suspending all other projects. We'll continue tending to the horses and the gardens, but the children can do that. Being behind fences will protect them if the shit hits the fan early. Haellie will oversee them."

Haellie's head shot up, her expression a combination of surprise and anger. "I can handle being on the front lines."

"You can't with that bandaged hand. I'm not using that as an excuse. With those wounds, you're more of a liability in combat. When we've taken down the raiders—"

"If," someone mumbled.

"*When* we take down the raiders, and when your hand heals, I'll post you to the scavenging parties."

Haellie nodded reluctantly, hating the decision but realizing Andrew made the correct one.

Andrew withdrew four folded sheets of paper and spread them out across the tablecloth. "These three are directions on how to set up the defenses and traps, plus where we'll post guards. This last one is the schedule for work shifts and guard duty."

Kathy examined the sheet of paper. "You have us working our asses off."

"Better than getting them shot off," Jordan responded.

Andrew glanced around at the group. "All the stuff you'll need is sorted out in Kathy's garage. Let's get to work."

CHAPTER TWENTY-TWO

DANIELLE LET LIZ and Kyle sleep in late so they could get some rest.

At least, that's what she would tell them. It had been so long since she had spent the night in bed that, once Danielle had dozed off, she slipped into a deep sleep. She would not have woken up when she did if it had not been for Chase standing beside her, nudging her head with his snout every ten seconds. Opening her eyes, she smiled at the Boxer, who responded with a wagging tail and a face bath.

Danielle pushed herself up on the pillow. "Good morning, boy."

Chase barked, waking up the kids who groggily sat up and opened their eyes. The dog waded into them, getting plenty of hugs and pets in return.

After a few minutes of doting on Chase, Liz glanced over. "Good morning, Miss Danielle. How did you sleep?"

"Excellent. And you?"

"Great." Liz kissed Chase on the forward.

"It was the first time I've had good dreams in over a week," added Kyle. He turned to the window. "The sun seems awfully high. What time is it?"

Danielle looked to the nightstand beside her bed. A battery-powered alarm clock read 8:19.

"That's later than we usually start," said Liz.

"It's okay. We needed the sleep." Danielle threw off the covers and swung her legs out of bed. "Who wants breakfast?"

Both kids raised their hands and excitedly yelled, "Me."

Chase barked twice.

Everyone put on their shoes and headed downstairs. Chase rushed by them, nearly knocking the three humans over to be the first in line to eat. Once in the kitchen, Danielle removed two cans of kidney beans from her backpack, opened them, and divided the contents among four bowls. She placed one each in front of the kids and a third on the floor, taking the bowl with the least amount of beans for herself.

Liz stared at the plate, her face expressing her unhappiness. "Cold beans? Seriously?"

"That's all we have, hon." Danielle motioned with her head toward Chase, who had already devoured his portion and pushed the bowl around the kitchen floor trying to lick it clean. "The dog likes it."

"That doesn't count," said Kyle. "He eats his own poop."

Danielle laughed.

She finished her breakfast while the kids ran forks through theirs, eating with a slow reluctance. As they did, she went over to the backpack and removed two bottles of water, then took three glasses from the cabinet, pouring one and a half bottles into the glasses and adding the remainder of the last bottle to Chase's bowl.

With the meal over, Danielle told the kids to go upstairs and use the bathroom, reminding them not to flush. She used the downstairs bathroom. While they were gone, she divided the supplies evenly among the three backpacks, slid the sidearm between the small of her back and her pants, covering it with her t-shirt, and placed the two extra magazines in the front pocket of her backpack. By the time Liz and Kyle rejoined her, they were ready to move out.

Danielle helped the kids with their backpacks. "Are we all set?"

"What about Chase?" asked Liz. "Don't we need a leash for him?"

"We don't have one."

Liz became anxious. "What if he runs away?"

Kyle rolled his eyes and huffed. "Where's he going to go? We're the only family he has."

Danielle nodded in agreement and led the kids to the kitchen, pausing by the back door to the driveway. "You three stay here. I'm going to check and make sure no one is in the streets. I'll be back in a minute."

"Okay," said Liz.

Kyle saluted.

Making her way down the driveway and using the front porch as cover, Danielle scanned the road they had been on earlier. Nothing moved in either direction. She moved out into the center of the road to expand her view. Still nothing. Satisfied they were not in danger, she headed back down the driveway and waved for the kids to join her.

Chase ran over to the garage, peed on the wall, then completed his business.

"Should I lock it?" asked Liz.

"No. Someone else may want to use it later."

Once in the street, they headed west.

Only now did Danielle realize how much last night's stay in a quiet house and a comfortable bed had reset her mood. Trying to survive in this post-apocalyptic climate, especially while protecting two young children, had drained her. Physically, mentally, and emotionally. While there was no way Danielle felt like her old self—and she doubted she would ever feel that way again—the break had reenergized her. They would have to do this more often.

Danielle smiled. *Look at you,* she thought. *Becoming a post-apocalypse badass. You should change your name to Mad Maxine.*

They walked less than a mile when Danielle stopped and muttered a single word.

"Fuck."

Rather than call her out for swearing like he usually did, Kyle sensed her anxiety and followed her gaze to the sign on the side of the road.

"What's wrong, Miss Danielle?"

She did not respond, her attention focused on the road sign that bore the symbol for I-93 and, beneath it, an arrow pointing in the direction they were heading.

CHAPTER TWENTY-THREE

S HAWN SLOWLY EMERGED from a deep slumber, his eyes still closed, and yawned loudly. For a moment, he had no clue where he was. Then he stretched, feeling a mattress underneath him. God, it felt good to finally be in a bed. It had been…. Shit, how long had this nightmare been going on?

He opened his eyes. Between the limited light in the room and his blurred vision, the only detail he could make out was the shadow of a figure standing at the foot of the bed.

Shawn yawned a second time. "Good morning, sis."

"Do I look like your sister?" chuckled Kevin.

"No. You're much prettier."

"I'll tell her you said that when we see her."

Shawn pushed himself up and leaned against the wall. The shades were closed, but sunlight shone bright outside.

"What time is it?"

"A little after nine."

"In the morning?"

Kevin wrinkled his eyes. "Yeah."

Shawn closed his eyes and sighed.

"Here. Drink this." Kevin handed him a bottle of spring water. "It'll make you feel better."

"I don't want to use up our last one."

"It's not. I checked out the RV while you were asleep. There was a second storage unit at the rear no one had noticed. I broke it open and found two cases of bottled water and a box of canned goods, mostly chili and vegetables. I had an awesome breakfast."

"Thanks." Shawn took the bottle.

"Be warned. The cases were sitting in an enclosed area in direct sunlight, so it's still hot."

"As long as it's wet."

Shawn twisted off the cap and swigged a mouthful. Kevin was right. It had the temperature of a cup of tea that had been sitting around for ten minutes. Not that he cared. His dry palette absorbed the wetness. He swirled the water around for a few seconds before swallowing. The water caused his throat to reflex a bit. This time Shawn was ready and forced back the cough. His stomach churned and a wave of nausea washed through him, but he did not vomit.

"Feels good, doesn't it?"

Shawn nodded.

"Drink slowly. You don't want to make yourself sick. Excuse me."

Kevin rushed out and into the bathroom. Shawn heard the toilet lid being raised followed by his friend puking. Kevin heaved four times, the sound of the vomitus hitting the porcelain bowl even from this distance. He gagged and spit a few times, then urinated. Kevin returned several seconds later, wiping his right arm across his mouth.

"Radiation sickness?" asked Shawn.

"Stupidity. I overindulged and ate two cans of chili for breakfast. I'm now paying for it."

"Great. Now this place will smell even worse."

Kevin smiled. "You don't have to worry about that. I opened the exterior valve to the septic tank this morning. Everything now empties onto the highway."

"That's gross and illegal."

"Like there's a cop around to fine me." Kevin chuckled, then became serious. "How are feeling?"

"I thought sleep would help. I feel rested but am still dizzy and nausea."

"That's a combination of the radiation poisoning and dehydration. I drank three bottles of water this morning and still peed orange."

Shawn raised the bottle. "Let me finish this and we'll head out."

"We're staying here today."

"No," argued Shawn. "I need to get home and check on the girls."

"Neither of us will make it there unless we rest up and hydrate. We'll hit the road tomorrow if you're up to it."

"I can't abandon—"

"Enough." Kevin cut him off, his voice stern. "We both know the chances are slim either of them will be home when we get there."

What little positivity he had dissolved. Both men knew Kevin was right, only this was the first time either of them had spoken it.

Kevin must have seen the fallen expression on Shawn's face and tried reassuring him.

"Danielle and Kirstie are smart and resilient. I'm sure they both found a safe place to ride this out. Once we get home, if they're not there, we can go looking for them. But that's not going to happen if we don't take care of ourselves. Besides, I don't want you dying out there."

The last sentence bothered Shawn. Not because of what Kevin said but because of the reality of the situation. Up until now, he refused to admit the effects of the radiation poisoning were getting worse. He always knew the chances of making it home were slim given his physical condition. Only now they both admitted to it. Kevin was not forcing them to stay in the RV to rest. He wanted his friend to die in comfort. While a part of Shawn was furious that Kevin made that decision on his own, the other part thanked God he had Kevin watching out for him.

"Okay. I give in. We'll spend the day here and see how I feel tomorrow."

Kevin's expression indicated he knew Shawn had accepted his fate.

"Thanks. Now take it easy and drink. Let me know if you want anything to eat."

CHAPTER TWENTY-FOUR

KIRSTIE PAUSED FROM digging, pushed her shovel into the dirt, and wiped her brow with her sweaty arm. At Regan's suggestion, she had tied a bandana around her forehead, though in the heat and humidity, that proved of minimal use. In less than ten minutes, the bandana was drenched and sweat ran down her face and back. Her tank top and shorts were soaked, making the manual labor even more unbearable.

"This sucks."

"Quit your bitching," replied Regan, half in jest.

Haellie paused from loading the dirt into a wheelbarrow, sticking the blade into the mound and using the handle for support. "She's not complaining about the heat. We'd be sweating even if we were lounging around in the backyard. It's digging all these pits and lugging the dirt away. Why aren't the men helping?"

Kirstie sighed. "Because they're doing the heavy lifting."

"I think we can take five," said Regan, leaning against the side of the pit.

Andrew had assigned the girls to dig these pits, or raider traps as he called them, throughout the compound, mostly near the homes where the supplies and horses were stored. Kirstie, Regan, and Haellie made up the first of the four groups. Mikalya and Abbey comprised the second, Andrew's daughters Sarah and Stephanie made up the third, and Victoria and Martha Lee the fourth. Each trap was ten feet long, three feet wide, and three feet deep. So far, the groups had dug eight traps: three each around Andrew's and Kathy's houses to protect the garages with the supplies; one by the gate to Justin's house to defend the horses; and one by Mikayla's grandmother's house to shield the garden. Next, they would dig these defensive positions at other houses in the compound, starting with those homes with children.

"Are you sure these will do any good?" asked Haellie. "Won't the raiders see them?"

Regan shook her head. "Andrew is convinced they'll attack at night."

"They'll see them with their flashlights."

"I doubt they'll use flashlights," replied Regan. "That would give away their positions."

"And with no lights in the neighborhood, it'll be too dark to notice them," added Kirstie. "The idea is not to stop them but slow them down and hopefully incapacitate a few of them."

"Especially with what Andrew has planned," added Regan. She pushed herself off the side of the pit. "Time to get back to work. We have several more hours of daylight and plenty of traps to prepare."

"THIS PLACE SMELLS like shit." Justin only half meant the complaint. He had grown up in the countryside near a farm and loved the smell. It reminded him of those days as a kid when life was good, and he did not have to fight raiders to survive. However, having it in his backyard went a bit overboard.

Justin agreed to use his house as a stable for the horses they had saved from that abandoned farm because he had a two-car garage and a large, enclosed backyard. He had pushed his car into the driveway and dragged the plastic containers filled with Christmas decorations into the kitchen, emptying two of them to use as troughs. A quick run back to the farm where they had found the horses provided over thirty bales of hay to keep them fed. As an animal lover, he enjoyed taking care of the horses, finding it relaxing.

What he did not enjoy were the piles of manure they created.

Twice a day, Justin shoveled it into a wheelbarrow that, when full, he would bring over to Lori's house, where the farmers could use it as fertilizer to help the crops grow better. Even bringing the pile over after each cleaning did little to diminish the stench, which had made its way into the house, adding another level of discomfort to the heat and humidity.

One of the female horses, an American quarter horse, walked up to Justin and rubbed her head against him. He wrapped one arm around her neck and petted her with the other.

"You're a good girl, Jezebel." Justin gave her that name because she flirted with everyone who came into the stable.

Jezebel neighed, rubbed her head against him one more time, then wandered off to the trough for a drink.

Justin passed through the garage and entered the kitchen, making sure the Mossberg shotgun lay propped up against the wall. After the encounter with the raiders the other day, Andrew assigned one of Dignam's weapons to every member of the compound over the age of sixteen. Because of the vital function their house played in ensuring the compound's survival, his house, Kathy's house, and Mikayla's grandmother had been given three extra weapons, either semi-automatic rifles or shotguns, to keep by the main entrances to those houses plus the garage, added security if the raiders attacked.

He corrected himself. *When* the raiders attacked.

Justin checked the time. His watch along the perimeter began in twelve minutes.

RYAN STARED AT the stone wall with the words Timberlane Country Club on it, then turned to Keith, who headed for the golf course.

"Why can't we use this location. It worked well enough last time."

"Because the raiders know we're using it. They'll try to take out whoever is here. It's too dangerous."

He fell in behind Keith. "It doesn't make any sense. Chances are they won't even come this way next time."

"You're probably right, but this spot is too valuable not to defend."

Keith did not explain to Ryan that the country club was a key choke point. He and Andrew had studied a map of the neighborhood for over an hour to determine the best locations for the guard posts. The raiders would be coming from Kingston. If they approached from the east, the most likely route, the roads they could use merged onto Providence Hill Road before the country club, which meant they would have to pass by this spot. If they attacked from the south, their best option was to enter the country club from Hunker Farm Road, which paralleled Providence Hill Road. This meant the lookout had the possibility of seeing them come from two different directions. Despite having been utilized before, this location still provided the best opportunity to spot their approach.

If the raiders circled the country club or approached via Route 111, the only way to reach the compound would be from the west end of Providence Hill Road, so Andrew set up the second lookout a quarter of a mile away from the center of the compound in that direction. Any approach from the north would eventually lead to the only other route into the compound: Old Coach Road, so a third lookout post had been established a quarter of a mile from the compound along this route.

With luck, one of the three positions would spot the raiders in time to warn the others.

"Where are we going?" asked Ryan.

Keith pointed along the small stone wall that separated Providence Hill Road from the golf course, indicating the woods up ahead. "That's the perfect position to set up our post. If they come down the road or through the country club, they won't spot us until it's too late. And if we engage in a firefight, we can use the wall as protection or, if necessary, retreat into the woods."

KATHY WALKED UP behind Andrew, who stood on a ladder installing a defensive position around the fence surrounding her backyard.

"The final preparations are finished. Our supplies should be safe."

"Great. Thanks for doing that."

"Like we had a choice." She walked over and watched Andrew work.

On each vertical board of her fence, he placed a one-sided razor blade extending half an inch above the top, anchoring them in place with Philip's head screws. So far, he had completed one wall and was three-quarters of the way through the second.

"What are you doing?"

Andrew finished screwing in the second nail and climbed down the ladder, turning his attention to Kathy. "We don't have any barbed wire, so this is the next best thing. If anyone tries to scale the fence, they'll slice their hands up. I completed the fence around the garden this morning. When I'm done here, I'll do the same to Justin's fence to protect the horses."

"Do you think it'll work?"

"It has to." Andrew glanced over at her, the concern in his eyes sending a cold chill down her spine. "We only have one chance to stop these assholes. If we fail, everyone here is going to wind up dead."

Or worse, thought Kathy.

CHAPTER TWENTY-FIVE

DANIELLE STARED AT the sign pointing to I-93, trying to remain calm as the nightmare images of what she had endured traveling north along the interstate raced through her mind. The tryst with the college boys for water. Having to walk miles along an open highway in the heat and humidity with no shade. The encounter where she watched a family of three being raped and murdered, and how she had to take a human life to prevent herself from being next. Danielle doubted she could make it through that experience again without breaking down.

And there was no way she would put Liz and Kyle through that.

A small hand squeezed her. "Miss Danielle, is everything all right?"

Danielle forced a smile. "Everything's fine. I'm nervous about crossing the highway. It can be dangerous."

"I know. We had to be careful when we crossed Route 293 after you found us."

Why hadn't Danielle thought of that earlier? After she had finally gotten off I-93 and taken the kids under her wing, they had crossed the Merrimack River at night and snuck across Route 293. After that, it was all safe back roads. They had made good time after that and would have been home by now if they had not run into that National Guard unit that brought them to the arena. She reasoned that it would be much safer to use this path than to attempt to navigate the interstate again. The only problem was that she had only visited Manchester once or twice since moving to New Hampshire and had no clue where Route 293 was located.

"Do either of you know where Route 293 is?"

"That way." Liz pointed in the direction they had come from.

Fuck.

Danielle made a quick calculation. If they headed back along this road, it would take them near the arena. God knows what kind of shitshow waited there. And if they were unfortunate enough to run into the National Guard again, the chances were good that she and the kids would be rounded up and carted off to another hellhole. She would rather starve to death out here than be stuck in one of those places again. She decided to turn left at the next street, travel north for several blocks, then back track to the river.

At the next street corner, Danielle stopped the kids and told them to wait close to the bushes while she checked and made sure the coast was clear. Residences stretched for the next mile. More than a dozen stalled cars filled the street. Many of the houses and apartments had been ransacked. After studying their surroundings for several minutes, she saw no signs of danger. Sure, there might be someone living in one of the residences who could pose a threat, but it was a chance she had to take.

Danielle reached behind her to make certain the firearm was still there, then waved for Liz and Kyle to join her.

They had walked several blocks when Liz pointed to the street ahead. "We want to turn left here."

"Why?"

"This is Bridge Street. It'll take us to one of the bridges across the river."

"You know your way around the city."

Liz smiled. "I pay attention to the roads when my mother drives so I'll know where I'm going when I'm old enough to get my driver's license."

Turning left onto Bridge Street, they made their way through another residential neighborhood. There were a few businesses on the road, including two restaurants and a gas station/convenience store that had been looted. Danielle did not bother checking them out since she doubted anything of value had been left behind.

After traveling a few more blocks, Danielle noticed several buildings ahead of them had been burnt out. She slowed her pace, scanning the street ahead and the surrounding area. So far, the kids had not noticed, and Chase seemed content to plod along between them, so Danielle risked continuing ahead.

She soon wished she had not.

A twin-engine passenger airliner had crashed, probably on its approach to or from Manchester International Airport. The plane had struck the roofs of the houses on one side of the street and belly landed in the park, the cabin of the airliner digging its way across the ground before smashing into a school on the opposite side. The front façade of the school had collapsed, as had several classrooms inside. The fuel tanks must have exploded because the school interior, the grass and trees in the park, and several nearby homes had been gutted by flames. The tail section jutted out from the school and the starboard wing lay across Bridge Street, the space in between littered with parts torn from the plane as well as bodies and luggage charred by the fire. Danielle remembered the airliner that had struck the Prudential Center on the first day of the power outage, a nightmare she had desperately tried to forget. Her heart sank thinking about the inferno that had killed so many students and passengers.

Liz dropped to her knees and vomited. Chase went over and comforted her.

Not being old enough to realize the intensity of the devastation before them, Kyle said, "Wow. I've never seen a plane crash before."

The comment snapped Danielle back to reality. "Come on.

Let's go around this."

She helped Liz back to her feet and led them down the road to their right, traveling several blocks before turning onto Union Street and heading toward the river.

CHAPTER TWENTY-SIX

S HAWN WOKE SLOWLY. Opening his eyes, Shawn remembered that he and Kevin had bunked out in an RV to get away from the blistering sun and to rest in a more comfortable setting. Glancing through the open window to his left, he noticed the sun did not beat down from above, which meant he had either slept all day and the sun was rising, or through the night and the sun was setting. Climbing out of bed, he stumbled over to the window to check the highway. The shadow from a nearby Subaru stretched toward the east, so it must be sunset.

Surprisingly, Shawn felt better than he did when they first arrived at the RV. The constant churning in his stomach had settled down and his dizziness had passed. His energy level was at its highest since leaving Seabrook. Shawn convinced himself the worst was behind him.

He slowly grew aware of the pressure inside his bladder, which had woken him. He made his way to the bathroom, waving at Kevin, who rested on the couch. The urge to urinate became intense. He barely had time to unzip his pants when the stream began. Shawn glanced into the bowl. Blood mixed with his urine, though not as much as last time. Rather than being dark orange, this time his pee was light yellow. The water Kevin found had rehydrated him, which helped him feel better. When finished, Shawn zipped his pants and flushed the toilet out of habit, chastising himself for forgetting Kevin had opened the septic tank.

Damn, he had not felt this good in days.

Exiting the bathroom, Shawn joined his friend at the front of the RV.

"You're looking better," said Kevin.

"I'm feeling better. Once the sun is down, we should head out and make up for lost time."

Kevin's expression changed to one of concern. "I don't think that's a good idea."

"Why? I'm rested enough we can make it to Dunbarton."

"I disagree."

"We can't stay here forever."

"We won't, but…." Kevin hesitated, not wanting to speak his mind.

Shawn called him out. "But what?"

"You know as well as I do that it's not unusual to recover slightly before the full effects of radiation poisoning hit. That's going to happen to you."

"It won't."

"Yes. It will." Kevin's defiance caught Shawn off guard. "I know you want to get home and check on your sister and niece. But when you have a relapse—"

"If I have one."

"*When* you have a relapse, if we're on the road, there's a good chance we won't find a place as comfortable as this for you to…." Kevin paused, awkwardly looking for the correct word before completing the sentence. "Rest."

Shawn's anger rose. "You think I'm going to die here?"

"We both know it."

"Stop being such a pessimist," Shawn snapped.

"I'm a realist." Kevin took a deep breath, hoping to break the tension. "I know your primary concern is your family. If I had family nearby, they would be mine. But they're not. My goal is to take care of you. Wilson was lucky enough to pass away peacefully on a gurney. I don't want you to suffer the same fate as Wally's team."

Shawn turned his back and stormed off, pausing after a few

feet. As angry as Kevin had made him, Shawn knew his friend was right. He had done everything possible to keep his crew safe while dealing with the reactor meltdown, though he had failed in Wilson's case. Right now, Shawn struggled with the conflict between common sense and his sense of duty to his family. It took several minutes for him to come up with a workable compromise. At least workable in his mind.

Shawn stepped back to Kevin. "I'll make a deal with you. We'll spend the night here and rest. If I feel good in the morning, we'll continue to Dunbarton. Deal?"

Kevin paused for a moment to consider the options. Finally, he stood, approached Shawn, held out his hand, and, without enthusiasm, replied, "Deal."

Both men shook hands.

Kevin quickly took back control. "Grab a couple of bottles of water and go lie down. You need to stay hydrated."

"Yes, sir," Shawn replied sarcastically.

"Do you want anything to eat?"

"I'm not hungry."

"You need to eat."

"Are there any cans of mixed vegetables left?"

"Plenty. But I need a can opener, and the only one here is electric. I still have cans of chili."

Shawn frowned.

"At least it's protein."

"You win. But if I clog the toilet, you can clean it up."

CHAPTER TWENTY-SEVEN

STRATMAN STOOD IN front of the wall of the VFW Hall, studying the county map Hart had tacked to it and the layout of the intended target Nicolai had sketched on a whiteboard from the closet. Nicolai, Tyler, Hart, and Anderson formed a loose line behind him, waiting for him to ask questions. Dozens raced through Stratman's mind. Based on Nicolai's information, the compound appeared larger and more populated than they had first believed. It also had more supplies than they had initially estimated. If his crew could pull off this raid, they could sit out the winter in comfortable homes and live off the hoarded supplies until spring, at which point his people could begin planting crops and scrounging for supplies for next winter.

However, if his crew failed, his people would be back to square one, with no supplies and proper accommodations for the winter, and fewer men in his crew.

Stratman sat on the fence regarding his decision.

"How many people did you see on the compound?"

"Thirteen," responded Nicolai. "Half of them women or teenagers."

"And all of them armed," added Tyler.

"No big deal." Anderson shrugged. "We have twelve men in our crew, and all but two of them know how to fight and use weapons."

Stratman glanced over his shoulder at Anderson. "Anyone carrying a firearm poses a threat. Remember, they took down five of our people at the junior high school."

Stratman went back to studying the chart. "Which houses have what we're looking for?"

Nicolai stepped up to the whiteboard and placed an X over the house on the corner of Old Coach Road and Providence Hill Road. "That's where they're growing the garden." He drew an X on the house across the road two doors down. "That's where I saw the construction supplies." Another X on the house to the left of the latter. "They stored their food and water here." And the final X over the house three doors down on Geary Lane. "And the horses are being kept here." Nicolai then drew a circle around the four homes. "Everything we need is in the center."

Hart studied the whiteboard. "Where's their command center?"

Nicolai pointed to the house containing the food supplies. "Best as I can tell, it's right here. It belongs to the guy in charge."

"A woman and two young girls live there," added Tyler. "They won't pose much of a threat."

Anderson stepped forward and tapped his finger against the whiteboard where Nicolai had drawn the copse of trees. "If we took the route Nicolai and Tyler did through the woods, it would put us a few hundred feet from all four targets."

Hart shook his head. "Too risky. If someone spotted us before we reached the end of the woods, they could pin us down long enough for the entire compound to attack."

"What do you suggest?" asked Stratman.

"We divide into three groups." Hart drew an arrow through the woods into the compound along the path Anderson had suggested, then added two more arrows, one northwest of the compound and the other to the east. He pointed to the middle arrow. "This will be our main attack. The other two groups will flank the compound from either side."

"That weakens each of our groups," said Anderson.

"On the contrary. It triples our chance of success." Hart

placed the marker in the whiteboard's tray. "If one of our groups is spotted, the defenders will concentrate their resources on them, allowing the other groups to circle around, seize the houses, and catch the enemy in a pincer movement."

"Makes sense," said Tyler.

"I think it's a great idea," added Nicolai. He looked over at Stratman. "What do you think?"

Stratman did not respond, moving close to the map and whiteboard. What Hart proposed made sense. Stratman studied the map. If he was defending the compound, he would place checkpoints on the closest road junctures leading to the center—the country club, the western end of Providence Hill Road, and along Old Coach Road. If his people broke up in the woods after they passed the first checkpoint, that increased their chances of seizing the homes before a proper defense could be mounted. Even if his people managed to seize only two homes, Stratman could threaten to destroy them if the defenders did not surrender. The plan was not foolproof. No plan ever is. But it gave his crew the best opportunity for success.

After a few minutes, Hart asked, "What's your decision?"

Stratman turned around to face the others, focusing on Hart. "We'll do it your way."

Hart nodded. "Thank you."

The other three men high-fived each other.

"Work out a plan of attack. I'll lead the group toward the homes at the center of the compound. Hart, you lead the flank attack from the northwest, and Nicolai, the one from the east."

"What about me?" asked Anderson.

"I want you to stay here and keep an eye on the women and children. If we don't come back, you do what you think is best."

Anderson nodded his approval.

"Tell the rest of the guys to party up tonight and get some rest. We leave tomorrow afternoon."

CHAPTER TWENTY-EIGHT

DANIELLE LED LIZ and Kyle down Union Street for eight blocks before turning left onto Harrison Street, heading west toward the river. She chatted with the kids and urged them to play fetch with Chase using an old tennis ball they found in the gutter, anything to keep them distracted from the nightmare they had recently witnessed. All the while, she maintained a close vigil on the surrounding neighborhoods.

When they reached Elm Street, Danielle reached out, stopped the kids, and ushered them toward the wall of the closest building.

"Is everything okay, Miss Danielle?" Liz asked.

"Yes. I want to check out the area before we continue. Stay here and don't make any noise."

Kyle saluted.

Elm Street was a main thoroughfare that ran through the center of Manchester on the east side of the Merrimack River. It included hundreds of apartment buildings, homes, small businesses, and restaurants. By now, Danielle had grown accustomed to finding stalled vehicles and litter wherever she traveled, but downtown Manchester looked like a war zone. Every building had been ransacked, especially homes and restaurants. Shattered glass covered the sidewalks, mixed in with non-essential items looted from the stores. A high-rise apartment building sat several blocks to their left, with one balcony near the top sporting a sheet tied to the railing bearing the word HELP. A house four doors down on the right had four corpses, now in an advanced state of decay, scattered across the front lawn; an older man in a wheelchair sat on the front porch, a shotgun on the deck beside him, his body riddled with bullets, an indication of how violent things had become in the city. Other than a stray cat crossing the street, Danielle spotted no movement.

"Let's go."

The three of them sprinted down Elm Street for a few yards before turning onto Langdon Street. Chase wagged his tail and followed, thinking they were playing a game.

After walking for a few minutes, Liz crinkled her nose. "What's that smell?"

"Yuck," added Kyle. "It stinks."

Danielle detected it a few seconds later—the stench of decayed flesh. She had smelled it before when encountering the dead, only this odor was more intense than usual. By the time they reached Canal Street, which paralleled the river, it overwhelmed her senses.

Liz grew excited. "I know this street. Mom used to take it all the time when leaving the city." She pointed to the right. "If we keep going that way, it'll eventually take us to a bridge that crosses the river and the highway."

"Are you sure?"

Liz stared at Danielle, a hurt expression on her face. "Yes, I'm sure."

"I'll follow you."

Liz took the lead and headed down Canal Street, a small defiance in her steps. Danielle could not help but grin.

When they entered the on-ramp leading to the bridge, the stench became overpowering. Danielle's eyes began to tear up.

Kyle closed his eyes and shook his head. "Gross!"

"I think I'm going to puke," said Liz.

"Pull your t-shirts over your nose and breathe through your mouth."

The kids did as they were told.

As they crossed the bridge, Danielle suddenly realized what

caused the stench, nearly vomiting at the sight.

Beneath them, thousands of rotting corpses filled the Merrimack River. A small dam blocked the western half of the river, with most of the bodies piled up behind it. Even from this distance, she could hear the buzzing of thousands of flies and wasps feeding off the carcasses. Maggots swarmed over those bodies exposed above the waterline.

Off to the dam's right sat Amoskeag Falls. Hundreds of corpses had wedged themselves between the rocks, creating mini dams that trapped those bodies not caught up against the main structure. Three bodies flowed south down the river, the first in line bloated. It struck the human dam and ruptured, semi-liquified intestines and organs flowing over the top and cascading into the river below. The second corpse became entangled in the obstruction, only partially passing over the edge, its upper torso dangling. The third careened into the bodies, rolling over them and plummeting into the river, slowly drifting toward the coast.

As Danielle stared at the nightmare, aghast, the flow of water tore a rotted arm off a corpse that tumbled down the falls until it joined the bloated remains and the third body.

Kyle ran over to the guardrail and peered down at the carnage. "Why are there so many bodies?"

"People upriver are probably tossing the dead in it so they don't become contaminated."

"Gross!" repeated Kyle. "I'm not drinking any river water now."

Liz tugged on Danielle's sleeve. "I'm scared. Can we go?"

"Of course." Danielle hurried the children onto the bridge and rushed them to the other side.

Once across the river, they passed a motel, took the overpass over Route 293, and entered another residential neighborhood. For some reason, this area looked familiar. Liz confirmed it a few seconds later.

"This is the road we took before the National Guard

brought us into the city."

"You're right," added Kyle. "We've come full circle."

Danielle checked out the street sign at the next corner. They were traveling along Goffstown Road. If she stayed on this route, it would eventually take them into Goffstown, which bordered Dunbarton. With luck, they will reach her house sometime tomorrow.

"Good news, kids. We're almost home."

"Yay!" Kyle skipped the next few steps. "I'm exhausted."

Liz was more reserved. "Hopefully, we won't run into any National Guardsmen who'll take us back to the arena."

Danielle leaned over and hugged Liz around the shoulders. "Don't worry, hon. I won't let that happen this time."

DAY NINE

CHAPTER TWENTY-NINE

KIRSTIE AND ABBEY silently walked along Old Coach Road heading north. Abbey had unslung her Mossberg and held the shotgun by the stock in her right hand, ready to fire it on a second's notice. Kirstie led Fred by the leash. Fred, a three-year-old Beagle/Bassett mix, belonged to Theodora. Unlike most dogs, Fred did not get excited by the wildlife that roamed the area, especially night critters like raccoons. He only barked at other people, which made him ideal as a guard dog. The downside, being a hound, Fred paused to sniff anything he came upon, then marked his territory by peeing on it. They were on their fifteenth stop-and-sniff and had only been on the job for ten minutes.

Fred bolted to the other side of the road, dragging Kirstie with him. He stopped to sniff a mailbox post for several seconds, turned around, and peed on it.

Abbey sighed. "At this rate, we'll be lucky to complete our first round in an hour."

"Be glad we have Fred and not Smokey." Smokey was Keith's Pitbull. "He's barely controllable on his walks. The dog knocked Jordan off balance on the last shift."

"Are you serious?"

Kirstie nodded.

"At least Smokey would tear apart the raiders."

"He's so dumb and lovable, if the raiders gave him a treat, he'd lead them to Andrew's house."

They reached the intersection of Old Coach Road and Hawthorne Drive, the latter of which circled the neighborhood and connected with Old Coach Road next to the center of the compound. Fred changed direction, raced over to the clearing between the trees where most of the neighborhood dogs did their business, and began sniffing around and staking his claim.

"How much urine does he have in him?" asked Abbey.

Kirstie ignored the complaint, happy to spend these six hours with Fred. She had always wanted a dog, but Danielle would not let her have one. Considering they now lived in the time of the apocalypse, this would be the closest experience to owning a pet she could hope for.

Kirstie gently pulled on the leash. Fred trotted down Hawthorne Drive.

Andrew set up three teams of roaming guards to warn the others of the raiders if they bypassed the lookout posts on their way to the compound. He divided them into two shifts—the first from sundown until midnight and the second until sunrise. Their task was not to engage the raiders but to fall back and warn the others who would defend the compound. This was the first shift for the two teenagers.

Two-thirds of the way along the road, a twig snapped in the woods off to the left. Abbey dropped to one knee and raised the Mossberg, ready to fire if necessary. Kirstie removed the semi-automatic pistol from her holster as she studied where the noise came from. Fred stared into the woods.

Another snapping of a twig sounded several seconds later, followed by a deer emerging from the tree line. It paused and looked around, sensing their presence. Fred tilted his head to one side and stared at the deer, never having seen one before.

Abbey lowered the shotgun and whispered, "Jesus, that scared the shit out of me."

On hearing the human, the deer spun around and noisily bolted back into the woods. Fred stood still, gawking at the wildlife as if he had seen an alien from another planet. Kirstie gently pulled on the leash.

"Come on, boy. Let's keep going."

REGAN AND MIKAYLA strolled west down the center of Providence Hill Road, the latter holding the leash for Roxie, a tan and white Boxer who belonged to Jordan. Roxie's stubby tail wagged furiously, the dog viewing her guard duties as nothing more than an extra walk that she loved so much.

As they approached the guard post, Roxie became excited and barked, smelling her master a hundred feet ahead of her. The bark was met by a shotgun being pumped, loading a round into the chamber.

"Whoa," said Regan. "It's only us. Don't shoot."

"Is that Roxie?" asked Jordan from the dark.

On hearing his voice, Roxie strained on the leash to see him. Mikayla let go, and the dog ran down the road. She hurried over to Jordan, rubbing against him and giving him a face bath. The teenagers approached the guard post.

"Sorry," said Meg as she placed the shotgun by her feet. "You startled me."

"My fault," offered Regan. "I didn't realize you were this close to the compound."

Jordan ignored the conversation, scratching Roxie behind the ears while she licked him. The dog paused, sniffed his pants pocket, then sat down and begged.

"Smart girl." Jordan removed a Milk Bone from his pocket and gave it to Roxie, who lay down and began eating.

"Any signs of the raiders?" asked Mikayla.

"Thank God, no," Meg answered.

"It'll happen sooner or later." Regan studied the woods around her, realizing they made too much noise. "We should get going."

When Roxie finished her treat, she stood, wagging her tail. Jordan scratched behind her ears and kissed her nose. "You go with the girls."

Roxie ran back to Mikayla, who picked up the leash. The teenagers headed back toward the compound.

"WILL YOU CALM down?" huffed Lindsey, yanking on the leash to keep Smokey from bolting.

"You want me to take him for a while?" asked Haellie.

"I doubt he'll be any better behaved for you."

Haellie slung her Daniel Defense MK18 semi-automatic rifle over her shoulder, took the leash from Lindsey, and crouched in front of the Pitbull, speaking in a firm but friendly tone. "Calm down."

Smokey stopped pulling.

"Sit."

The dog obeyed.

"What are you?" asked Lindsey. "A dog whisperer?"

Haellie chuckled. "When I was little, my family had a rambunctious Husky, and being the oldest kid in the family, I had to take him for walks. I learned quickly how to control our dog, otherwise he would have taken me for a drag through the neighborhood."

No longer having to deal with Smokey, Lindsey stretched and shifted her upper body from side to side, then glanced down Providence Hill Road. In the light of the waning aurora, she spotted the golf course several hundred feet ahead of them.

"Who's on duty now?"

"I'm not sure. I haven't met everyone here yet. All I know is their position is set up so the guards can watch the road and the entire golf course." Haellie stood. "Do you want me to take him for a while?"

"You don't mind?"

"Not at all." Haellie leaned over and looked Smokey in the eye. "Who's a good boy?"

The Pitbull danced around, his tongue hanging out of his mouth.

Haellie led the way back to the compound.

CHAPTER THIRTY

DANIELLE CAUTIOUSLY MADE her way along Main Street through Goffstown. Liz and Kyle followed, holding hands and staying close to Danielle, scared and silent after she told them this part of their trip could be the most dangerous. Sensing their anxiety, Chase stayed beside Kyle to protect him if anything bad happened.

They had reached the Cumberland Farms service station south of Goffstown an hour before sundown. Danielle decided to take a break and continue later that night, partly because the kids were exhausted, but mostly because she wanted to make the passage through town in the dark. Goffstown was the largest town in the area and, as such, had the greatest chance of housing a raider hangout or being patrolled by the National Guard, and no way would she allow the kids to be taken back to a detention center. Instead, they held up in the ransacked service station, the kids getting a good sleep while she and Chase kept watch. A little after midnight, they set out for the last leg of their journey, Danielle calculating they would be at her house within the next eight to ten hours.

So long as nothing happened to them while in Goffstown.

They passed dozens of vehicles stranded during the solar flare. Unlike the I-93, where every vehicle had been stripped of anything valuable for survival, with the doors left open and junk strewn across the road, most of those they came across had their doors and trunks closed, as if the owners had left them and would come back later with a tow truck.

Crossing the stone bridge over the Piscataquog River, the

group entered the downtown area. Danielle ushered the kids to the side of a building, gesturing for them to stay in place. She then moved to the corner and studied the town.

Danielle had expected everything to be ransacked, which it had been, but not in such an orderly manner. No broken glass lay scattered along the streets and sidewalks. Thank God, there were no corpses. The front doors to the local restaurants and Ace Hardware remained open, suggesting they had been cleaned out of food and the necessary supplies. It seemed as if Goffstown had avoided looting and rioting. It gave her hope the situation out here may not be as desperate and violent as everywhere else.

Rejoining the kids, she crouched in front of them and whispered. "It doesn't seem to be as bad as everywhere else, but it's better to be safe than sorry. Don't talk and stay close to me."

"I'm scared," Liz said in a soft voice.

"I know you are." Danielle hugged her. "We all are, but things will be okay as long as you listen to me. Understood?"

Liz nodded. Kyle saluted. Chase wagged his tail.

Danielle brandished her semi-automatic pistol, then the group stepped onto the sidewalk and headed north. Danielle walked slowly, pausing inside every doorway to study the road and buildings ahead of her. Thankfully, the aurora remained, though lessened in intensity, providing enough light to scope out their path. Once certain no one was around, she waved, and they moved to the next doorway.

At the opposite end of town, St. Matthew's Episcopal Church sat off to the left. Luggage and backpacks lay neatly stacked by the stairs, none of them having been rifled through, which struck Danielle as odd. Across the street, at the corner of Main and High Streets, stood Sully's Superette with nearly twenty vehicles in the parking lot. As with everywhere else in town, the grocery store had been cleaned out of food and water, but no litter lay scattered across the asphalt. It seemed as if everyone in Goffstown vanished overnight.

Liz grabbed Danielle's shirt to get her attention. Danielle leaned over. "What is it?"

"Shouldn't we check out those suitcases for cloths?" Liz whispered. "I'm covered in blood."

"We need to get home as quickly as possible. I have cloths there."

"Any that fit me and Kyle?"

Shit, thought Danielle. *She had not considered that.*

"You two stand watch. Let me know if you see anything, and I mean anything."

Liz nodded. Kyle saluted.

Danielle scanned the stack of luggage, eventually finding a suitcase with the Hello Kitty logo on it wedged underneath two larger suitcases. Reasoning it would be the best option for finding kids' clothes, she removed the top two pieces of luggage, being careful not to knock anything over and attract attention. She placed the Hello Kitty suitcase on top of the others and began to unzip it.

"May I help you?" The question came from the front doors of the church.

Liz gasped and pushed Kyle behind her. Danielle spun around, moved in front of the children, removed the semi-automatic pistol, and aimed it. Chase moved beside Danielle and growled menacingly.

A young man, no older than his mid-thirties, stood at the top of the stairs. He had collar length hair that had not been washed in a week. The young man extended his arms to the sides, palms facing Danielle to show he was unarmed. He descended the stairs.

"I'm sorry to have startled you."

Danielle raised the semi-automatic into firing position. "Don't take another step closer."

He stopped. A smile spread across his handsome face. "Trust me, if I meant to harm you, I wouldn't have announced my presence. I'm Reverend Sanders. This is my parish. I only want to help if I can."

Danielle kept the weapon trained on his chest, her trust having long since been eroded away.

Liz stepped beside Danielle. "Sorry, mister. We didn't mean to upset you. Miss Danielle was looking for clothes for me and my brother. We've been wearing these things for over a week."

"Help yourselves. The people who owned the luggage are no longer here."

Liz glanced up at Danielle. "Can we?"

"Go ahead."

Liz and Kyle opened the suitcase and rummaged through the contents.

Danielle lowered the weapon several inches but kept her finger near the trigger, then placed herself between the kids and Sanders.

"What do you mean the people who owned the luggage are no longer with you?"

Sanders pointed to the stairs. "May I?"

"Just don't get too close."

"Agreed." Sanders slowly descended the steps. "After the solar flare struck, the town panicked. The mayor had everyone gather here for safety. Search parties went to Sully's and the local restaurants to gather up as many supplies as possible. The local doctor brought over the medical supplies from his office. Several of the local residents brought their firearms. We were going to ride out the disaster until help came."

"Did it?"

Sanders nodded. "Four days ago, a National Guard unit came by and took everyone to a relocation center where they would be safe and well fed. They also took our supplies. I volunteered to stay here and gather up any survivors who came this way."

"Do you mean the SNHU Arena?"

"Yes, that's the place. You know about it?'

"We were there."

Sanders' face brightened. "How was it?"

"It sucked," answered Kyle without looking up.

Liz gently slapped him off the back of the head. "Language."

The reverend's expression changed. "I don't understand."

Danielle hesitated to tell him, but reasoned sugar-coating reality died along with the rest of civilization. "The place was a nightmare. Close to thirty thousand people were stranded there. No plumbing. No electricity. Two days ago, the National Guard ran out of food and a riot broke out. We barely made it out alive."

"Dear God." Sanders closed his eyes, folded his hands, and said a silent prayer. "That explains why the National Guard never came back."

"Sorry to be the bearer of bad news."

"No one expected the end of days to be easy."

Liz moved beside Danielle clutching a pile of clothes. "We found stuff that should fit us."

"Do you mind if we take these?" Danielle asked Sanders.

"Be my guest. They'll be of use to someone. And take the suitcase with you. It'll be easier to carry."

"Thank you."

Liz placed the clothes inside the suitcase and zipped it shut. "We're ready, Miss Danielle."

"You're welcome to spend the night here," offered Sanders.

"Thank you, but we're heading to my house. It's nearby. I want to get there as soon as possible."

"I understand. The good news is we haven't had any trouble in the area. The locals who have sheltered in place have made sure no bad elements stay around for long."

"That's good to know." Danielle turned to the kids. "Are you ready?"

They both nodded.

"Thank you again. We appreciate it."

"No need to thank me. I'm carrying out God's will to help those who need it. May He keep you safe on your journey."

Sanders waved and entered the church, closing the door behind him.

"Let's go."

Danielle led the kids away from the church and turned right onto Main Street, which would take them home.

CHAPTER THIRTY-ONE

THANK GOD SHAWN had listened to Kevin. Last night the effects of the radiation poisoning hit him with a vengeance.

Shawn woke up around three in the morning, his stomach and intestines in agony. He barely made it to the toilet when the explosive diarrhea struck, covering the interior of the bowl with blood and liquified feces. Before he finished defecating, his stomach heaved. Fortunately, a small plastic trash bucket was within reach. Shawn held it to his mouth and puked, the vomit mixed with chili and blood. After cleansing his body, Shawn sat on the toilet and leaned back.

His head pounded. He had experienced a few migraines in his life, but none of them had been as bad as this. After resting for several minutes, the throbbing behind his eyes slowly subsided. Only then did Shawn realize his body was doused in sweat, his clothes soaked through and clinging to his skin. He ran his hand across his scalp to wipe it away. When he checked his palm, clumps of hair stuck between his fingers.

"Fuck."

Kevin centered himself in the doorway, checking on his friend.

"Please don't say I told you so."

"I won't. Is there anything I can do?"

Shawn shook his head. After a few minutes, he pulled off several pieces of toilet paper and used them to wipe his mouth and spit out the contents.

"Do you want me to get you some water to clean out your mouth?"

Shawn waved off Kevin.

Gathering his strength, he ripped off several more pieces of toilet paper and used them to wipe his ass. It took eight attempts to clean himself enough to try and stand. When he did, Shawn fell forward.

Kevin ran in and propped up his friend. "I got you."

Shawn's pants and underwear lay bunched around his ankles. "Could you help me pull them up?"

"Of course."

As Shawn steadied himself on the shower door and sink, Kevin bent over and lifted his friend's clothes up to his waist, then held him upright as Shawn buckled his pants. He did not have the energy to zip them.

Kevin led Shawn back to the bedroom and helped him lay down. Once Shawn had gotten as comfortable as possible, Kevin felt his forehead.

"You're running a fever."

"Of course, I am." Shawn mumbled the words, his tone resigned to his fate.

Kevin waited until his friend settled down a bit. "Can I get you anything?"

"No. I'll just throw it up. But thanks."

"No problem. Do you want me to stay with you?"

Shawn shook his head. "I'll let you know if I need you."

As Kevin turned around to leave, Shawn called out to him.

"Get me a pen and paper. I want to write a letter to the girls."

"Sure." The look of resignation on Kevin's face said it all.

He came back a few minutes later with a notebook filled with lined paper and a ballpoint pen, handing them to Shawn.

"I found these in the glove compartment. Looks like someone was keeping a journal of their trip. There's a few blank pages left."

"Thanks."

"Do you want me to write it for you?"

"I'm still able to do that. Besides, it's personal."

"I understand. I'll be out here if you need me."

As Kevin left, Shawn began writing his final letter to Danielle and Kirstie.

CHAPTER THIRTY-TWO

ANDREW STOOD ON the street in front of his house. He held an unopened bottle of water in his right hand, too lost in thought to have pried off the lid, let alone drink. His eyes scanned the compound, looking for anything he might have missed.

Everyone had spent the last twenty-four hours preparing the defenses to repel the raiders. The houses containing the supplies, garden, and horses had been secured and traps set up to stop or slow down any attempts to seize them. Guard posts had been set up along the main roads leading to the compound, assuming the raiders were bold enough, or dumb enough, to come that way. In case the raiders attempted to approach through the woods, Andrew had established neighborhood patrols. Except for the children, every adult carried a weapon and had been trained in how to use them, if you considered an hour of instruction training. Most important, they held the defensive position, which gave them a major advantage. He should feel confident about winning the upcoming battle.

However, if his time in the Marines told him anything, it was that all plans fall apart upon first contact with the enemy.

Andrew worried about how many raiders would be attacking. He had less than twenty people available to defend the compound, twelve currently on duty and the remainder ready to respond at a moment's notice. The odds were fifty-fifty his force outnumbered those of the raiders.

What caused Andrew the greatest anxiety was who made

up the raiders. Other than himself, no one in the neighborhood had served in the military. The only one with any security experience was Ryan, who had served as a guard at the BAE facility in Nashua. Families, single people, and six teenagers, including his daughter Sarah, comprised the rest of the compound. Except for those who ran into the raiders at Timberlane, none of them had ever faced a situation as dangerous as this. If people like themselves, average people trying to survive, launched the attack, the compound had a good chance of winning. However, if the raiders were former military or hardened criminals—

"Andrew."

He spun around, surprised to see Kathy standing behind him. He had not heard her approaching.

"Are you okay? I called your name three times."

"Sorry. My mind was elsewhere."

"I can relate." Kathy paused. "Are you worried?"

Normally, Andrew would have lied, maintaining a front to not worry the others. He had come to know Kathy quite well these past nine days. The two of them had worked hard to prepare the compound to survive this crisis. Without her, many of them would be dead by now. She deserved the truth.

"Anxiety is eating me up. I have no idea who we're facing or how many there are. This is a life-or-death moment. Based on those assholes we ran into at the school, we're screwed if we don't win."

"I'm worried about what will happen to the women if we lose." Kathy took a deep breath. "In that case, I plan on taking my own life. It's better than being a sex slave."

Andrew had not considered that until now. He could not let Jeanette and his daughters go through that nightmare, yet he did not know if he could bring himself to kill them. Such thoughts eroded what little confidence he had. There was only one way to prevent this horrifying scenario.

"Well, that means we have to kick the raiders' asses or die trying."

CHAPTER THIRTY-THREE

"ARE YOU READY?" asked Hart.

Stratman studied the map of the compound, re-membering as many details as possible, and did not hear him. He turned to his second in command.

"Sorry?"

"I asked if you were ready. They're waiting for you at the bar. The sun is going down."

Stratman hadn't even noticed the time. "Let me grab my gear."

"You seem distracted. Are you worried about tonight's raid?"

"Worried about taking the compound? No." Stratman slung the Remington 870 shotgun over his shoulder, checked the magazine of his 40 caliber Glock to make sure it was full, and slid it into his holster. "But I am concerned about possible losses to our group. We've already lost six bikers. That's almost half the men."

"We still have the other six. Tyler is a major asset. And those two pussy college guys are holding their own."

"You mean Sam and Mark?"

Hart nodded.

"Counting you, me, and Jim that only leaves us with thir-teen able-bodied fighters. The more men we lose taking that compound, the fewer we'll have to defend ourselves against other gangs."

"We'll be getting some fresh pussy when we take the com-pound. We could give the college girls a break and make them fighters, putting them to a different use. The bikers are getting bored with them. Who knows, maybe some of the guys at the compound will be willing to switch sides after we take over."

Stratman considered what Hart had said. He had a point. The only reason Stratman had let the college students stay was because he needed the extra hands provided by Sam and Mark. The girls earned their keep by servicing the bikers whenever they got horny, which was all the time. If anyone from the compound joined them, that would even out their losses.

First, they had to take the compound.

"We'll cross that bridge when we come to it." Stratman grabbed his backpack and headed for the door. "Let's join the others."

Both men left the VFW Hall and crossed the street to the biker bar where the rest of the group had gathered. Those going on the raid sat in the leather chairs in the smoking area. Tyler's wife and two daughters stood behind the bar with him, putting as much space as possible between the family and the others. So far, no one had violated Stratman's order that the three women were not to be touched, but that did little to alleviate their fear. The four college girls sat at the bar, each of them appearing defeated and anxiety ridden after continued sexual abuse. Anderson sat with them.

Stratman stood in front of those going on the raid and studied them. Sam and Mark were reliable and dependable but, being college students from middle-class families, they had no experience with the world the rest of them lived in. Under normal circumstances, the bikers would have eaten them alive. So far, neither of them had been in any conflicts, mostly going on supply runs.

The bikers were the exact opposite. Some of them made Stratman nervous, and he had spent time in jail. Especially Spaz, their leader. He stood six feet two inches in height, two hundred and ten pounds of muscle, with small scars across his face and hands from all the fights he had gotten in. The others called him Spaz because he had a volatile temper and became uncontrollable when someone pissed him off. Stratman almost felt sorry releasing him on the compound.

The other bikers in the group were also bad ass, but nowhere as extreme as Spaz. Sarge, the second in command, had spent five years in the army before spending several years in the brig and being dishonorable discharged for assaulting his commanding officer. He had a scar on his right shoulder where he had used acid to remove his Army tattoo. Nicolai had defiance issues, even arguing with Spaz on several occasions. Spaz kept him around because he was the best street fighter in the gang. Shank was a thin, small Latino who stood five feet five inches in height. He used a knife as his weapon of choice, making his victims suffer before finishing them off. Shank continued the practice in prison where he did five years for drug dealing, using a makeshift knife to assert his dominance, thus his nickname. Big Daddy, a man of normal height and average looks, got his nickname because of his eleven-inch cock. Unfortunately for the girls, he liked his sex rough and abusive. Pounder sat up front smoking a cigar. Six feet in height and two hundred pounds of muscle, he got his name from enjoying beating people up, one of whim he beat to death. Carlson, the newest member of the gang, had been with them for less than a year. Lean and exceptionally handsome, Carlson looked more like a businessman than a biker. No one knew his backstory. The reason Spaz let him join the gang was because he had taken two years of Taekwondo and proved exceptionally effective as a street fighter.

This was the nightmare Stratman planned to release on the compound. He felt much more confident of their chances of success.

Except for Tyler, each of the raiders had a bottle of beer or a tumbler of liquor on the tables in front of them.

"You guys have been drinking?"

"Just one drink before they set out," replied Anderson. "The alcohol will wear off before you get to the compound. I figured they could use some liquid courage."

"Not that we need it," said Spaz. "We're going to fuck up that compound."

"Remember, our goal is to take the supplies and horses for us, so don't hurt any of them."

"What about the assholes in that compound?" asked Sarge.

"Do what you want with them. They're going to fight to the death to keep what they have. Make sure they're the ones who die."

"Except for the bitches." Nicolai pointed to the bar. "We need some fresh pussy to fuck. These whores are all used up."

One of the college girls broke down in tears.

Big Daddy grabbed his crotch. "I call dibs on the new chicks."

"Enough!" yelled Stratman. The room went silent. "Our goal is to take over the compound so we have decent places to stay and enough supplies to get us through the winter. Save your raping for later. Besides, according to Nicolai and Tyler, all the women on that compound are armed, so they're going to fight back. Is that understood?"

When no one responded, Hart stepped up beside Stratman. "He asked if that was understood."

Most of the biker gang mumbled yes. Nicolai flipped Hart the finger.

"Has everyone been briefed on what they need to do?" asked Stratman.

Hart nodded. "I went over the plans with them this afternoon."

Spaz gave Stratman a nod. "Don't worry, boss. We got this. That compound will belong to us by this time tomorrow."

"Damn straight," said Shank.

Nicolai, Big Daddy, and Sarge high-fived each other.

Hart looked over at Stratman and nodded.

"All right, grab your stuff and let's head out."

As the others prepared, Stratman walked over to Anderson. "Once we've secured the compound, I'll send someone back with the horses and carts, then you can move everything to the new place."

"Roger that." Anderson offered his hand. "Good luck."

Stratman gave it a firm pump. "Thanks. You'll hear from us soon."

When everyone was ready, Stratman led the way out of the bar, giving one last look over his shoulder. Hopefully, this will be the last time he sees it. Once outside, the raiders turned left onto Mill Road and headed for the compound.

CHAPTER THIRTY-FOUR

A FEELING OF hope surged through Danielle as she turned onto Ray Road. After more than a week on the move, they were within a mile of her home.

If someone had told her when she set out on this journey it would take her nine days to make it home, and what she would go through to survive, she would not have believed them.

If someone had told Danielle she would adopt two children and a dog along the way, she would have laughed.

Danielle closed her eyes and prayed, something she had not done in years.

God, let the nightmare end here.

The last leg of their trip after leaving the church had been the easiest. Granted, they had been traveling at night, so the chances of running into trouble were slim. The only living things they encountered were stray livestock released from their farms and the occasional raccoon or possum. Only a few homes had candlelight shining through the window, families merely trying to survive.

Maybe things will get better now.

"Can we rest for a minute?" Kyle sighed. "I'm exhausted."

"Me, too," added Liz.

"Let's keep moving. We're almost home."

Kyle's eyes lit up. "Really?"

"We're the fourth house down."

"We'll finally be safe?" asked Liz.

"Yes." Danielle hoped she told the truth. "And soft beds to sleep on."

Liz clapped excitedly.

"And working toilets?" Kyle chimed in.

"Sorry. They run on electricity."

"Crap."

Liz slapped her brother gently off the back of the head. "Language."

"I said crap, not shit."

Danielle laughed.

Ten minutes later, Danielle stopped, glanced up the driveway leading to her house, and cried.

"What's wrong?" asked Kyle.

"Nothing. They're tears of joy."

The house was untouched on the top of the incline. No damage. No broken windows. No personal items scattered across the lawn.

Danielle was finally home.

"Is that our new home?" asked Liz.

"Yes."

Both kids jumped up and down with joy. Excited by their reaction, Chase wagged his tail and barked excitedly.

Liz started up the driveway. "Let's go. I'm exhausted."

Danielle grabbed her arm, common sense overriding her happiness. "We need to check it out first in case someone is squatting there."

The happiness drained from the kids.

"You stay here with Chase while I check it out."

Liz took her hand and squeezed. "Be careful."

"I will."

Danielle slowly made her way up the driveway, focusing on the windows for any signs of someone lurking inside. Crossing the walkway to the porch, she cautiously climbed the stairs. Taking a deep breath, she wrapped her hand around the knob and turned.

Locked.

Moving down the porch to the second front door, she tried

that knob.

Also locked.

Danielle leaned over and peered through one of the windows, half expecting a bullet to shatter the glass.

Nothing.

She knocked on the pane. "Is anyone there?"

Silence.

Danielle exited the porch and went to the garage door, hoping they were unlocked, but then remembered Shawn had installed automatic garage door openings, so trying to enter this way would be useless.

Making her way around the side, Danielle climbed the porch to Shawn's apartment and tried the front door, finding that one locked as well. Figured this would be the one time everyone remembered to lock up before leaving. Peering through the window, no one seemed to be inside.

Exiting the porch, Danielle motioned for the kids to stay put and circled around to the back of the house. All three rear doors were locked. Even more hopeful, no windows were broken, suggesting no one had broken in. For the first time since the crisis began, she felt a sense of hope and confidence.

Heading over to the enclosed porch attached to her apartment, Danielle used her elbow to shatter the pane nearest the knob, reached in, and unlocked the door. Stepping inside, she paused, listening for any movement inside the house, but heard nothing. Crossing the porch, she opened the door leading inside.

"If anyone is here, please don't shoot. I mean no harm."

No one responded.

Removing the semi-automatic pistol from the small of her back, Danielle held it ready to fire, stepped inside, and turned right toward the kitchen.

The kitchen appeared the same way it did that morning when Shawn went to work and Kirstie joined her friends for their trip to Canobie Lake. No one had raided the house.

Tears flowed down her cheeks as memories of those better days flooded her thoughts, those days when her family was together. She remembered making breakfast for them that morning, and Shawn and Kirstie rushing out without eating, typical for them. Back then, it aggravated her. Now she would give anything to have them back, ignoring all the effort she made for them.

Danielle pushed those thoughts away. She had a new family to take care of.

She slid the semi-automatic between her back and her pants and made her way to the front door, opened it, stepped onto the porch, and waved for the kids to join her. Liz and Kyle screamed in happiness and ran up the driveway. Chase barked and ran after the kids, passing them and being the first to reach the door. The dog sat in front of Danielle and barked. She crouched in front of him, kissing him on the nose and scratching his ears.

Liz reached the porch next. "Is everything okay inside?"

"Yes. No one has been here."

Liz clapped her hands. "Can I go in?"

"Sure."

Liz rushed in. Chase stayed close to her. Kyle rushed by seconds later, joining his sister as she went from room to room on the first floor.

"Look," called out Kyle. "Miss Danielle has a fireplace. We'll keep warm in the winter."

Danielle closed and locked the door, then joined the kids in the living room.

"This place is awesome." Liz rushed over and hugged Danielle.

"Where are the bedrooms?" asked Kyle.

"Upstairs."

"Can we check them out?"

"Sure."

The kids bound up the steps, reminding Danielle of Kirstie's dramatics when going to her room.

"This must be the daughter's room," Liz squealed. "I love it."

"I claim this room," shouted Kyle.

"No way. I'm a girl. I get it."

Danielle joined them by the doorway. "For the next few nights, I think we should all sleep together in my room where we'll be safe."

Kyle's eyes lit up. "Where's your room?"

Danielle pointed to the door at the end of the hall. The kids ran down and opened it.

"Yay," said Kyle. "She has a king size bed."

Liz, Kyle, and Chase raced into the room, followed a second later by all three of them jumping onto the mattress. Danielle entered and smiled. Liz and Kyle had already claimed all the pillows for themselves. Chase sat along the end of the bed, his tongue hanging out, his tail wagging.

Liz glanced over at Danielle. "Can we take a nap?"

"We can take a long sleep. You two scoot over to the other side. I want to sleep near the door."

The kids bounced over to the other side of the bed. Chase jumped up and pushed his way between them, wanting to sleep next to his favorite humans.

The room was hot and humid, having been closed up for over a week with no AC available. Danielle opened the windows in the bathroom, at the end of the bed, and on the other wall, allowing somewhat cool air to flow through the house.

Going back to the bathroom, she turned on the faucet, grateful that some water remained in the system. She used what little came out to wash her face, barely getting rid of the accumulated dirt and sweat. When the faucet ran dry, she gazed into the mirror. The woman who stared back was so different from the one who had left here nine days ago. Thinner from a lack of food. Circles under tired eyes. Matted hair showing signs of gray. Stress wrinkles along her brow.

What surprised Danielle was not the wear and tear but the confidence she saw. Long gone was the woman who two Fridays ago had been concerned if she looked pretty enough, the terrified woman who left Boston to make her way home. A toughened reflected in the mirror, a woman who taken a human live, who had saved two children from certain death numerous times, who had survived the nightmare of the SNHU Arena, and who had successfully made the journey from Boston back home. A strong, independent woman who had done things she never imagined she would do gazed back at her, a woman who would protect Liz and Kyle with her life if necessary. Danielle could not bring herself to use the term bad ass, but she was someone not to be fucked with. Thankfully, she had changed to deal with the collapse of society and would make it through all this.

Going back to the bedroom, everyone else had fallen asleep. Liz and Kyle lay on their sides, each wrapping an arm around Chase, who snored loudly. Danielle could not help but smile. For the first time since this shitshow began, she felt at ease.

Keeping the bedroom door open to hear if someone tried to break in, and placing the semi-automatic by the bed, Danielle crawled in and kissed Liz on the forehead. The girl smiled. Danielle lay her head on the pillow, sleep getting ready to swarm over her.

With luck, things would be better now for her and the kids.

CHAPTER THIRTY-FIVE

Dear Danielle and Kirstie,

If you're reading this, you already know I'm dead.

It also means Kevin made it this far and was able to deliver the letter. You can trust Kevin. I've worked with him for the last six months. His role was vital in preventing Seabrook from melting down. He also stayed with me while I tried to make it back to you, keeping me safe and making sure my last days were as pleasant as possible under the circumstances. (He can fill you in on any details or questions you have.) Kevin has no family members living in New Hampshire, so I said he could stay with us... you... and help out. Please take him in.

You have no idea how much it upsets me that I couldn't make it home to check on both of you. The solar flare disabled all back-up systems at Seabrook and the reactor began melting down. If we had abandoned our posts, tens of thousands of people would have been exposed to lethal doses of radiation, including both of you. We were able to prevent that but at the cost of seven people. Eight if you include me. The cost was high, but the results were worth it.

I know I always teased you about what a

burden it was taking you in, but that was just me being an asshole older brother. I loved having you there. The two of you have made these past few years the best time of my life. I used to hate coming home to an empty house. Then you moved in. You brought laughter and love into my life, and for the first time in a long time I felt like I belonged. Thank you. I only wish I could be there to hug you both before I pass on.

I have faith you'll survive this nightmare. You're a strong, smart, independent women and have what it takes to make it through this. Stay safe and strong.

I love both of you.

Shawn

Shawn spent nine hours drafting that farewell letter, partly because he wanted to get the wording perfect, mostly because the effects of the radiation poisoning took every ounce of his energy. And dignity.

Not long after his first round of bloody diarrhea that morning, Shawn suffered a second round. Kevin had cleaned the waste basket and placed it on the bed beside his friend, giving him a place to vomit. However, during his heaving, Shawn fouled himself. Even more embarrassing, Kevin came in to check on him, wincing at the stench. Rather than let Shawn wallow in his filth, Kevin immediately set to work cleaning him up, removing his soiled clothes and stained bed sheet, cleaning him with a towel from the bathroom, then replacing the old sheet with a new one from the closet, all the while comforting his friend and telling him this was normal given his medical condition. Shawn appreciated Kevin's efforts and encouragement, though it did little to lessen his feeling of humiliation. He felt like an aged invalid in a nursing home, the worst possible way to end his life.

To make matters worse, Shawn suffered the same bouts of diarrhea three more times throughout the day, and each time Kevin cleaned him and replaced the sheets. They had run out of sheets and towels on the second purge, forcing Kevin to use whatever clothes he found in the closet. Shawn never thought he would die in such an undignified manner at the age of forty-nine. When Kevin left him to rest last time, Shawn cried in disgrace.

Despite how he felt, Shawn pushed through with writing the letter, wanting to make sure he gave Danielle and Kirstie closure.

After he finished signing off, Shawn tore out the two pages and folded them.

"Kevin," he croaked.

His friend came into the bedroom, expecting to clean Shawn again, relief washing over his face when he saw that was not the case.

"What do you need?"

"Not much." Shawn handed him the folded letter. "I finished my letter to Danielle and Kirstie. Would you give it to them when you get to my house?"

"I'll do that." Kevin placed it on the nightstand. "I'll leave it here in case you want to add anything to it."

"I don't have the energy." Shawn sighed from exhaustion. "You can read it if you want."

"It's personal, only for your sister and niece."

"I told them how you helped me try and get home and asked them to let you stay and help out."

"Thank you, but you didn't have to do that."

"You need a place to stay until this blows over."

"Do you think they'll let me stay? They don't know me."

"Danielle is a good woman even though she's my little sister." Shawn chuckled, which sent him into a coughing fit. He expected to foul himself again but, thankfully, did not. There probably wasn't much left inside him. "I want to thank you."

"For what?"

"For staying with me. For taking care of me. For making my last days…." Shawn had trouble putting his thoughts into appropriate words.

"You're welcome. But there's no need to thank me. You'd do the same if our roles were reversed."

"I appreciate everything you've done, both now and back at the reactor."

Exhaustion overwhelmed Shawn. He slumped back onto the pillows.

"Take it easy and get some rest," suggested Kevin. "I'll check on you later."

"Thanks," mumbled Shawn.

He regretted not being able to say goodbye to Danielle and Kirstie in person and not knowing whether they were safe. It gave him a sense of reassurance that Kevin would do everything in his power to give the girls his letter and, if they were at the house, take care of them.

Shawn closed his eyes and dozed off in seconds.

CHAPTER THIRTY-SIX

DANIELLE WOKE UP from a deep sleep to the sound of Chase growling. She bolted upright. The dog stood at the end of the bed, staring out the open window, his ears back against his head. Outside, she heard footsteps slowly coming up the driveway.

Fuck. When will this shit be over?

Chase dove off the bed, ran over to the window, placed his front paws on the sill, and began barking. Danielle jumped up and crouched by the dog, comforting him. He continued barking. Glancing outside, in the light from the aurora she spotted a figure on her front lawn, scanning the house.

"What's wrong?" asked Liz as she sat up, rubbing sleep from her eyes.

"Be quiet," Danielle whispered. "Someone's out front."

Fear filled Liz's eyes. "Who is it?"

"I don't know." Danielle grabbed the pistol off the nightstand. Pulling Chase away from the window, she led Liz and Kyle to the walk-in closet and ushered them inside, pushing the dog in with them.

"Stay here and don't come out until I come for you."

"I'm scared," whined Liz.

"So am I. You have Chase with you. Everything will be alright."

Kyle started to protest, but Danielle closed and locked the closet door, then slowly made her way into the hall. At the top of the stairs, she peered around the corner and scanned the porch windows. No one stood outside. Maybe the intruder had given up and left.

Or maybe he had gone around back.

Danielle suddenly remembered she had busted the pane to unlock the rear door, giving the intruder access to the house.

Racing down the stairs, she circled around through the living room and down the hall, stopping a few feet from the door to the back porch. No one roamed around outside. Moving closer and using the door as cover, she peered through the window. Still no one. Carefully opening the door, she slid onto the enclosed porch, crossed over to the windows, crouched so no one could see her, and scanned the backyard.

Movement in Danielle's peripheral vision caught her attention. Spinning her head to the right, she spotted someone looking around the corner where Shawn's apartment was. Shit. The intruder was still here. If Danielle could sneak out without being seen, she had a chance of catching him by surprise.

Danielle unlocked and opened the rear door to the house. The screen would be more of a problem. The rusting hinges squealed like a pack of mice. Shawn had been promising to oil them but never got around to it. Slowly pushing open the door so as not to make any noise, she slid through the opening onto the stairs, moved down two steps, and slowly closed the door.

The sound of a shotgun shell being loaded sounded behind her, followed by a gruff voice. "Put the weapon on the ground. Slowly."

Fuck.

Danielle bent over and placed the semi-automatic pistol on the stairs then stood.

"Hands above your head and move away from the stairs."

She obeyed.

"Now turn around. Any sudden moves and I won't hesitate to shoot you."

Danielle did as told. A bright light flashed into her eyes, blinding her. She expected at any moment to be gunned down or raped.

Instead, the intruder said in a surprised tone, "Miss Costner? Is it really you?"

"Do... do I know you?"

"Sorry." The intruder lowered the shotgun and the flashlight so the beam shown on the grass. "It's Corvin. I live across the street."

As Danielle's vision returned, she recognized her neighbor. Corvin was a burly man who stood a little over six feet in height and had a slight beer belly. He smiled at her through an auburn beard. He wore his usual clothes—a baseball cap, flannel shirt, jeans, and work boots. Danielle never knew his name, always referring to him as the Redneck. They had never spoken, though they had waved to each other on numerous occasions. He seemed friendly enough, though it always aggravated her when he would fire weapons in his backyard on the weekends.

Now she thanked God Corvin was well armed.

"You guys can come out now. It's safe."

The intruder Danielle had spotted earlier rounded the house and slung the weapon over his shoulder. A third person moved up behind her and joined Corvin, still holding his shotgun but with the barrel pointed toward the ground. He had the same build as Corvin, though six inches shorter and with no beard.

"Who is she?" he asked.

"This is Debbie Costner—"

"Danielle," she corrected.

"Danielle Costner. She lives here with her daughter Kirstie and her brother Shawn."

"Have you seen or heard from them?" Danielle asked excitedly.

Corvin shook his head and offered a sympathetic, "Sorry."

The guy slung his shotgun over his shoulder and offered his hand. "I'm Dale."

"After the solar flare, Dale made his way to my place for

refuge. I have enough ammo, food, and water to last several months."

"It's good to meet you, Danielle."

She turned and immediately recognized Tucker, her neighbor who lived three doors down. They ran into each other all the time when she went for her stroll and Tucker walked his dog, a Labrador named Millie. All she knew about him was that he had a wife and two kids.

"Thank you. Is your family safe?"

"Thank the good Lord, yes."

Danielle turned to Corvin. "What are you doing here?"

"I saw you, two kids, and a dog checking out the house earlier today. I thought you were looters breaking in to steal stuff. I gathered Dale and Tucker, and we came by to make sure things were okay."

"We're making sure no one moves in and takes what we have," added Tucker.

"I noticed on the way in that the neighborhood seemed untouched."

"We're making sure it stays that way," Corvin said firmly. "A few days ago, a bunch of assholes from Concord attempted to take over."

"What happened?"

The three men smiled. Dale said, "Let's just say it did not go well for them. You're safe here."

"Who were the kids and the dog?" asked Corvin.

"The kids are Liz and Kyle. I met them on my way here. Their parents never made it home and their babysitter abandoned them. I couldn't leave them. The dog is Chase. He adopted us."

"Where are they?"

"Hiding upstairs. I wanted to make sure they stayed safe."

"Good for you. We have several people who came here asking for help. We took in the decent ones, mostly families."

"That's nice of you."

Corvin nodded. "Swing by my place in the morning for breakfast. I cook on the grill out back. I also have a solar generator that runs the water pump and a bunch of fans in the living room. You can clean up and cool off."

Danielle was stunned. This sounded too good to be true. "Are you serious?"

Corvin nodded.

Reality struck Danielle. "What do... I mean... am I expected...."

A look of sadness washed over the men's face.

"Hon, I don't know what you went through out there," said Corvin. "But you're home now. This is your house. You're part of the neighborhood. We protect each other here. All you have to do is participate."

Danielle avoided his gaze. "I'm sorry. I didn't mean to imply—"

"You did, but there's no need to apologize. Everyone who has made it back here has nightmares to tell. The PTSD is going to last for decades."

Tucker picked the gun off the ground and handed it to Danielle. "Is this the only weapon you have?"

Danielle nodded.

"I have some extra firearms at home. You can borrow one of them. Do you prefer an AR-15 or a shotgun?"

She blushed. "What's an AR-15?"

All three men laughed, but in a good-natured manner.

"I'll bring over a shotgun and extra shells after breakfast tomorrow," said Tucker. "I'll show you how to use it if you want."

"Thank you." Danielle felt like crying.

"Don't mention it. See you at breakfast."

The men turned to leave and Corvin paused. "You're welcome to stay with me tonight if you feel uncomfortable here."

"Thank you. We'll be fine."

"Understand. If anything happens, just come across the

street and get me. Knock on the door five times so I know it's you."

"I will. Thanks again."

The men left. Danielle went back inside. As she started up the stairs, Liz, Kyle, and Chase waited for her on the landing.

"I thought I told you to stay in the closet?"

"We heard you talking with them and thought it was safe," said Kyle.

"What's going on?" asked Liz. "De we have to leave?"

Danielle climbed the stairs, stopping at the second-to-last before the landing, then leaned over and hugged the kids.

"We can stay. We've finally found a safe place to live for a while."

CHAPTER THIRTY-SEVEN

STRATMAN CAUTIOUSLY MADE his way between the trees, with Nicolai and Tyler directly behind him, each man careful to make as little noise as possible. Stratman kept his attention on the ground to ensure they did not trigger any booby traps. The raiders had left the back roads about an hour ago and approached the compound through the woods. So far, luck had been with them. However, the closer they got to the compound, the greater the chances of giving away their position.

"Boss," whispered Nicolai. "The compound is a few hundred feet ahead of us."

"Are you certain?"

"I'd stake my life on it."

"You are." Stratman glanced over at Tyler. "Is he right?"

The State Trooper nodded and pointed to the right. "I recognize that clump of fallen trees over there."

"You two stay here and keep an eye out." Stratman fell back to the others and waved over Hart and Spaz.

"What's up?" asked Hart.

"We're a few hundred feet from the compound. We'll split up here. Remember, our goal is to capture the supplies, the garden, and the horses. Once we have those, we can negotiate."

Spaz nudged Hart. "He means make those motherfuckers drop to their knees and beg for their lives."

Stratman grabbed Spaz by the shirt and pulled him close, his tone low but furious. "No fucking around. We have one shot to take this compound. If we screw this up, we won't make it through the next month. Clear?"

Spaz raised his hands. "Clear, man."

Stratman released his grip. Spaz stepped back. "Calm down."

"The first group to reach the supplies will hold their position until the rest of us can join them?"

"What happens if one of us runs into trouble before we get there?" asked Tyler.

"Fight your way through. If you can't, draw off as many of the defenders as possible. It should make things easier for the rest of us. Any questions?'

None.

"Move out."

Spaz broke to the right, taking Carlson and Sam with him. They would circle around and enter the neighborhood from the northeast.

Hart went to the left with Tyler, Mark, and Shank following behind. They would exit onto Providence Hill Road two hundred feet from the center of the compound and attempt to take it over in a quick strike.

That left Nicolai, Sarge, Big Daddy, and Pounder with Stratman. They would move straight ahead and exit the woods, across the street from the houses holding the supplies and the garden, hoping to take them by surprise.

Motioning for his team to follow, they headed out.

Success in the next two hours was crucial.

CHAPTER THIRTY-EIGHT

KIRSTIE SAT ON the front porch of Lori's house, nursing a bottle of warm water she would take on watch and thanking God the sun had set hours ago. The day had been brutally hot and humid, with the temperature in the high nineties. After sunset, the temperature dropped to the low seventies, and the humidity eased up a bit. But only a bit. Her shirt stuck to her body, covered in sweat.

Abbey came out to join her. "Have you been here long?"

"Only ten minutes. It was too hot inside the house."

"I hear you." Abbey took the rocking chair beside her friend. "What time is it?"

Kirstie glanced at her watch, maneuvering her hand to see the dial in the light from the aurora. "It's a quarter to midnight."

"Who has this watch?"

"Haellie and Lindsey."

As if on cue, the two girls exited Hawthorne Drive with Fred bouncing along between them.

Abbey stood and headed for the front door. "I'll get some water for them. I'm sure they're thirsty."

By the time Abbey came out with three bottles and a dog bowl, the others had entered the driveway and were approaching the porch. Abbey placed the bowl down and emptied one of the bottles into it. Fred pulled on the leash, so Victoria let him go. Fred ran up on the porch and slurped up the water.

"See anything?" asked Kirstie.

"Just a raccoon that was climbing a tree," said Martha Lee.

"When he saw us, he jumped down and scurried back into the woods."

"I nearly shit myself," added Victoria.

Kirstie chuckled. "You guys get some rest. We'll take it from here."

"We still have ten minutes on our shift."

"Don't worry about it." Kirstie glanced at Fred, who had already slurped down his water and lay on the porch, letting out a sigh. "We'll let him rest a few minutes, then start our watch."

"Thanks." Martha Lee twisted her neck from side to side. "I'm exhausted."

Kirstie sat for a few minutes, admiring the night sky and the fading aurora. When she rechecked her watch, it read 12:04. She stood up and took Fred's leash.

"Come on, boy. Let's start our rounds."

Roxie climbed to her feet, the nubby tail wagging, and led the way off the porch.

God, thought Kirstie. *I hope this is a quiet shift.*

DAY TEN

CHAPTER THIRTY-NINE

LINDSEY SAT IN the living room of her house on Hawthorne Road, the farthest occupied residence from the center of the compound, staring out the window. She had just gotten back from her night shift, walking the compound, and should have been trying to sleep since her turn manning the guard post near the Atkinson Country Club would begin at 0600, but fear and anxiety kept her awake. Andrew had offered to let Lindsey and her children move into an empty house closer to the others, but she rejected the offer. She felt staying in the home the kids had grown up in would help ease the pain of knowing their father had been killed while trying to screw over the compound. It helped the kids cope. The downside was that she now occupied the most isolated house in the compound. Lindsey wondered whether she had made the right decision.

If… when the raiders attacked, she would be on her own.

JORDAN GLANCED OVER at Meg. She napped against the car they were using as a defense position, which did not bother him as much as her light snoring. He reached out to wake her but thought better. Being exhausted himself, he figured if he let Meg sleep for half an hour, she could keep watch later while he napped. So long as one of them was awake—

A bark followed by the sound of running paws broke the silence. Jordan spun around in time to see Roxie rush up, sit beside him, and provide a face bath. Regan and Mikayla emerged from the shadows a few seconds later.

"Sorry," said Mikayla. "She knew you were here and wanted to be with you."

"That's fine." Jordan hugged Roxie and scratched behind her ears.

Meg woke with a start and reached for her weapon until she realized the intruders were friendly.

"Sorry, I didn't mean to fall asleep." Meg stretched. "Why didn't you wake me?"

"I figured if I let you take a nap, you could keep watch while I took one later."

"Deal." She glanced over at Regan. "I assume things are still quiet."

Regan nodded.

"Let's hope it stays that way," added Mikayla.

"We should get back to work." Jordan held Roxie's head and kissed her snout. "You're a kid girl."

Mikayla called the dog, who joined the teenagers. Mikayla took his leash, and they headed back to the compound.

"Is there any bottled water left?" asked Quinn.

"You drank yours," said Theodora.

"I'm thirsty."

"We all are." Theodora reached into her backpack and removed the last bottle. "This is mine. You can have a sip. We still have five hours until our shift ends."

Quinn screwed off the cap and took a long sip.

As she did, Theodora scanned the road and woods the two of them guarded at the checkpoint on Old Coach Road. A shiver ran down her spine, though she did not understand why. Everything was quiet.

Too quiet.

The realization dawned on her that the usual nocturnal sounds of the woods had lessened over the past few minutes, spiking her concern. Raising her flashlight, Theodora switched it on and directed the beam into the woods.

Quinn dropped the bottle of water and aimed her gun at the light. "What's wrong?"

"I don't know if anything's wrong. It seems unusually quiet."

"It could be because a bobcat is nearby. I see them in my backyard all the time."

"That puts my mind at ease." Theodora scanned the area for a few more seconds before shutting off the flashlight. "I'm probably just jittery."

"We all are." Quinn lowered her weapon and reached down for the bottle of water. Most of the content had spilled onto the asphalt.

"Thanks for wasting my water." Thedora did not attempt to hide her frustration.

"Sorry." Quinn picked up the bottle and offered it to Theodora, who waved it off. "I'll see if Kirstie can get us one the next time she's at the compound."

SPAZ HELD UP his hand for the others to stop.

Carlson crawled forward and whispered, "What's up?"

Spaz leaned closer and kept his voice low. "There's two broads manning a lookout in front of us. I can hear... Duck."

Both men lowered themselves behind the bushes as a beam of light flashed over where they had stood a moment ago. They slid their fingers around the triggers of their guns, ready to attack if the women sounded the alarm.

The taller woman with the brunette hair shut off the flashlight. "I'm probably just jittery."

"We all are."

Spaz quietly exhaled. They had avoided a confrontation that would have fucked up the assault. As the women chatted, Spaz leaned closer to Carlson. "Go back and tell Sam we'll wait until the shit hits the fan, then move in on them."

KEITH AND RYAN sat by the small stone wall running along the golf course's exterior, Keith keeping an eye on Providence Hill Road while Ryan scanned the course and the driveway leading to the country club.

"Do you play golf?" asked Ryan.

Keith was not paying attention. "Huh?"

"I asked if you played golf."

"Once, when I was in college."

"Were you any good?"

"Is one hundred and fifty-three a good score?"

Ryan snorted. "Hell, no."

Keith ended the conversation. "Keep your eyes open. I have a bad feeling."

HART BROKE THROUGH the woods into a residential backyard. He paused to check out the area and, once certain the coast was clear, motioned for the others to stay put. He slowly made his way along the side of the house to the front yard, peering around the corner and scanning Providence Hill Road for signs of movement, but saw none. The country club sat a few hundred feet to his left. Though he spotted no one, Hart assumed the compound had established a guard post there.

He rejoined the others.

"Did you see anything?" asked Shank.

"We're in sight of the country club. I don't want to take any chances of being seen, so let's continue west a bit, then move onto the road."

HAELLIE AND RENEE strolled down Geary Lane toward Justin's house, which was being used as the stable. Renee led Smokey on a leash while Haellie walked ahead of them, holding a shotgun ready to fire. When they reached Justin's house, Haellie maneuvered around the trap dug by the fence and knocked on the gate.

No one responded.

"Justin, are you there?" she whispered.

"Haellie, is that you?"

"Yes."

She heard the bolt being removed from its lock. The gate opened, and Justin peered out, holding the Mossberg ready to fire. He relaxed on seeing her and Renee alone and slung the weapon over his shoulder.

"Sorry. Can't be too careful."

"Understand. Everything okay?"

"The place smells like horseshit, but other than that, everything's fine."

"Do you want to switch out?" asked Renee.

Justin shook his head. "The horses are used to me. Having someone else take over for a while might upset them."

"Good enough. Fire three shots if you need help."

"I will. Stay safe."

"I plan on it."

As Justin closed and locked the gate, Haellie and Renee headed back to the compound, with Smokey between them.

STRATMAN'S GROUP HAD approached to within ten feet of the edge of the woods bordering Old Coach Road. He stopped, motioning for the others to do the same, then crouched and waved for Nicolai to join him.

"Is this where you were when you scouted the compound?"

"Yup." Nicolai pointed to the house across the street and slightly to the left. "That's where the garden is. The houses with the food and construction supplies are on the opposite side of the road."

"Good. When the time comes, you and Sarge take the garden. Big Daddy, Pounder, and I will... hold on."

Both men crouched lower. Two teenagers and a dog

walked along the road directly in front of them.

ANDREW SAT IN the rocking chair on the front porch of his house, watching the woods for any signs of the raiders, the MR27 resting on his lap. He assumed the raiders knew this was where they kept their supplies and, as such, it would be their main target. Andrew had urged Jeanette to take the kids to another house until this blew over, but she refused, saying she had married him for better or worse. Since arguing with Jeanette would be useless, he gave her a shotgun and Sarah a .38-caliber revolver, training them both to use them in a worst-case scenario.

Andrew knew that scenario would play out, hopefully sooner rather than later.

STROLLING THROUGH THE backyard of Lori's residence, Kathy stopped at each garden station, checking on the plants. In case a battle did occur, the garden would be the most vulnerable. If anything happened to it, they would lose their primary source of food as well as their chances of making it through the winter. She had already decided to give her life to defend the garden so the rest of the compound could survive.

When she reached the back door to the house, Kathy lifted the five-gallon gas can and swung it in a tight circle. Two gallons of fuel sloshed around inside. In the event the compound fell into the raiders' hands, she intended to make certain those assholes would not get the garden.

"SOMETHING'S NOT RIGHT," said Kirstie.

"What?" asked Abbey.

"Listen."

"I don't hear anything."

"That's my point. Why did the wildlife suddenly go quiet?"

Fred turned toward the copse of trees, his tail between his legs, and growled.

At that moment, semi-automatic gunfire erupted from the woods.

CHAPTER FORTY

LINDSEY HEARD THE weapons fire and sat upright. She grabbed the Mossberg Maverick 88 shotgun propped against the wall and ran upstairs to the children's room. Elena and Marcie, six and eight years old, respectively, sat in bed, covering themselves with their blankets, terror in their eyes.

"Mom, what was that?" asked Elena.

"The bad guys are here. Follow me. And take your water bottles with you."

She rushed into the hall, grabbed the cord to the pull-down stairs leading to the attic, and lowered it. When the girls arrived, she ushered them up, handing her oldest daughter a .38 revolver.

"I've never used one of these," said Marcie.

"Just aim it at your target and pull the trigger. Now get up there."

Once they were in the attic, Lindsey lifted the stairs.

"Aren't you staying with us?" asked Marcie.

"I have to go help the others."

Elena pushed the stairs down. "You can't leave us alone."

"You'll be fine. Don't come down unless me or one of the neighbors calls for you. And if anyone tries to get up here, shoot them. Is that understood?"

Both girls nodded.

Lindsey raised the stairs back into position, then raced to the front door.

"FUCK." JORDAN SPUN around toward the compound where the gunshots came from.

Meg moved to the front of the car and crouched by the fender, aiming her Beretta A300 12 gauge west down the road, ready for an attack.

Jordan stood and grabbed his shotgun. "Stay here and make sure no one tries to sneak up on us."

"Okay. But if I don't see anyone in five minutes, I'm joining you back at the compound."

Jordan raced off to help the others.

"DAMN IT, WE'RE missing all the fun," whispered Shank.

"What are we going to do now?" asked Tyler.

"Get our asses there as fast as we can."

Hart led his team onto Providence Hill Road and toward the combat zone.

RYAN SPUN AROUND and stared toward the compound. "What's that?"

"Gunfire." Keith grabbed his Colt M4 and stood.

"Shouldn't we stay here and cover the flank?"

"We're needed at the compound. Move!"

RENEE STOPPED WHEN she heard the gunfire. The raiders had launched their attack in the center of the compound. Smokey barked and tugged aggressively at his leash.

"Haellie, go back to Justin's house."

"I want to be where the fighting is. Those assholes murdered my family."

"Justin is by himself and might need help if they're this close."

Haellie hesitated before turning around and heading back

to Justin.

Renee and Smokey headed into battle.

"IT'S STARTED," REGAN spoke the words with resignation rather than fear. She broke into a run toward the compound.

Roxie bolted, knocking over Mikayla, who dropped the dog's leash. Roxie passed by Regan at full speed.

Mikayla picked herself up, pulled the Benelli M4 shotgun off her shoulder, and followed.

KATHY SPUN AROUND, shocked. The gunfire was across the street. Stray rounds hit the leaves in the woods beside her. She had expected the battle to start on the outer fringes of the compound, not in front of Lori's home. To make matters worse, no one was there to help her defend the garden, the plan being to have someone join her once the fighting began. No one had anticipated it would start here. The raiders would reach her before anyone else could.

Kathy moved against the wall of the house, grabbed her Beretta, and loaded a round into the chamber. Crouching, she waited.

THE BURST OF semi-automatic weapons fire straddled Abbey. Four rounds tore open her chest, splattering blood and pieces of organs onto Kirstie. Abbey turned toward her friend and dropped to her knees, shock etched on her face. She lowered her head, watching blood pour from the open wounds, before collapsing forward onto the asphalt.

Thankfully, the shooter had concentrated his fire on Abbey and not sprayed the area, otherwise Kirstie would also be dead.

Fred yelped. Kirstie thought a stray bullet might have hit him until she noticed him lying on the ground shivering from fear.

Kirstie side-stepped down the road, raised her AR-15, and fired into the woods where the initial burst came from, hoping to cover her retreat. When the breach stuck in the open position, she turned and ran for Lori's house.

Fred chased after her.

STRATMAN SLAPPED NICOLAI off the back of the head.

"Why the fuck did you do that?"

"That fucking dog spotted us."

"They might have ignored him if they thought it was a deer. Now we lost the element of sur—"

A burst of semi-automatic fire tore through the woods around them. Stratman dropped to the ground a moment before a round struck the tree he had been standing in front of. After a few seconds, the gunfire stopped.

"Was anyone hit?" asked Stratman.

The others replied in the negative.

"Let's fuck over these assholes. Nicolai and Big Daddy, you take the garden. Me, Sarge, and Pounder will head for the supply garage."

The five raiders made their way through the trees. On reaching the road, they split into two groups and headed for their targets.

ANDREW SAW ABBEY get riddled with gunfire and fall to the ground. He was relieved to see Kirstie fire back and rush over to Lori's house. At least now Kathy would not be by herself.

Common sense told him to stay put and defend his family. However, the Marine in him reminded Andrew that you leave no one behind.

Andrew was about to head into combat when the front door opened. Jeanette stepped out.

"What's going on?"

"The raid has started. Take the kids upstairs to the master bedroom and lock yourselves in. If anyone tries to enter, shoot them."

Jeanette knew better than to argue. She closed and bolted the front door.

As Andrew sprinted across the lawn, he spotted five of the raiders emerging from the woods. Two headed across the street toward the garden, and the others headed for his house. No way he would take out all of them. Raising his MR27, he took a lead on the lead raider heading for the garden and fired a single round. The round missed his head by several inches. The two raiders veered to the right and headed for cover.

The other three ducked into Dignam's driveway, one firing a three-round burst from his AR-15. Two whizzed by Andrew. The third clipped his right leg.

Andrew dropped his weapon and fell to the ground.

STRATMAN, SARGE, AND Pounder crouched behind the bushes. Stratman saw Nicolai and Big Daddy running for cover. Good. The asshole had missed.

"I think I hit him," said Sarge.

"You take care of that motherfucker. Me and Pounder will circle around and take the garage from the rear."

WHEN SPAZ HEARD the gunfire break out inside the compound, he waved for the others to attack the guard post.

Sam raised his AR-15 and fired.

Quinn and Theodora heard the rustling of trees to their right. Quinn stood, uncertain whether to fight or run. Seven rounds shattered the windows of the car and tore into her, three ripping apart her chest and abdomen. Quinn teetered for a moment, then fell against the car and slid to the ground, leaving smears of blood along the door.

At the sound of the rustling, Theodora fell prone and was raising her AR-10 when three bullets ripped into Quinn. Theodora aimed in the direction of the gunfire and fired into the woods.

The first round caught Sam in the chest. He stopped and dropped his Ar-15, at first not feeling any pain or realizing what had happened. He stared at the wound in disbelief as blood gushed from it.

"Spaz, I'm—"

The second round blew his head apart.

Spaz and Carlson ducked and turned left, maneuvering around Theodora. Several more shotgun rounds ripped through the woods, one of them striking a tree beside Spaz. A pellet ricocheted into his right hand.

"Fuck!"

Thedora homed in on the voice and pulled the trigger. The shotgun clicked.

Shit, I'm out of bullets.

The raiders would be upon her before Theodora could reload, so she tried to retreat. Two raiders emerged from the trees and lunged. Spaz punched Theodora in the jaw, knocking her off balance. He slammed his right elbow into her face, shattering her nose and two teeth. Theodora tripped over Quinn's body and fell against the car. Spaz shoved his left hand around her neck and pushed her head against the roof, raising his right hand in front of her face.

"You fucking cunt. You killed one of my men and wounded me."

"Boo fucking hoo," she gasped. "You'll live."

Fury overtook Spaz. He slapped Theodora so hard across the cheek it dazed her. Spaz let her go and picked up her shotgun, waving it in front of her.

"Is this what you shot me with?"

Theodora was too stunned to answer.

Spaz gripped the rifle so the stock pointed toward Theodora and smashed it against her face. She felt three teeth break and her left eye socket crack. He struck her two more times, the first blow breaking her jaw, the second fracturing her skull. Theodora slid to the ground, her back still propped up against the car.

Carlson grabbed Spaz's arm. "That's enough. She's out of action."

"Fuck off." Spaz pushed Carlson aside and aimed the shotgun at his face. "The bitch ain't suffered enough yet."

Carlson raised his hands and backed away.

Spaz continued smashing Theodora in the face. She lost consciousness on the fifth blow, which was fortunate. She did not feel the eighth blow that shattered her skull. Her face caved in. Spaz continued the assault until her skin tore open, allowing blood, brains, and an eyeball to ooze out.

"That's enough," warned Carlson. "She's dead."

Spaz stared at the bloody corpse, then, in a final fit of rage, kicked her in the chest so hard Carlson heard Theodora's ribs crack. Spaz dropped the shotgun, stared at the mangled corpse, then glared at Carlson.

"The others need us," urged Carlson. "Let's go."

Spaz picked up his weapon. "Come on. Let's go fuck up the others."

THE GUNFIRE BACK was becoming intense. Meg sat at the checkpoint doing nothing, which pissed her off. A prolonged burst of semi-automatic fire cut through the night.

"Fuck this shit."

Meg raced back to the compound.

HART'S TEAM REACHED the corner of Geary Lane. He raised a hand for them to stop.

"Isn't the stable down this road?"

"Yes," said Tyler. "According to Nicolai, it's three doors down on the right."

"You and I will take the stables." Hart turned to Shank and Tyler. "Help the others secure the supplies and the garden."

The team broke off into pairs and headed for their respective targets.

"THERE THEY ARE." Ryan raised his MP5 and was about to fire at Hart's team from behind when Keith placed his hand on the barrel and pushed it down.

"We can't be sure it's not our people. Besides, at this distance all you'll do is let them know we're here."

Ryan pointed toward the four men. "They're splitting up."

Shit, thought Keith. *Two of them are heading for Justin's house, who had the least defenses.*

Keith pointed to the two raiders heading down Greary Lane. "We'll follow them."

RENEE STOPPED WHEN Smokey growled and yanked on the chain, trying to break free. Two raiders were running down the street, heading toward Justin's house. She considered engaging them, but at two-to-one odds, she doubted she could take out both of them. The element of surprise was lost when Smokey barked.

Yanking on the leash, Renee headed back to Justin's to warn him and give him additional fire support, expecting at any minute to be gunned down. For some reason, the raiders did not shoot at her.

KATHY HEARD BANGING on the back fence door. She raised her Beretta 1301 shotgun, her finger curling around the trigger, ready to fire.

"It's me, Kirstie. Are you there?"

"Yes."

Kathy ran over to the fence and unlocked the bolt with her left hand while keeping the shotgun ready to fire in case it was a trap. Kirstie pushed the door open and raced inside. Once Fred passed through, she closed and locked it.

"Where's Abbey?" asked Kathy.

"She's dead. And we will be soon. Two of those assholes are heading this way."

ANDREW CRAWLED BACK to his house, his leg throbbing from the wound.

"Well, if it isn't the asshole who tried to kill Carbone."

Andrew looked up to see Sarge standing above him, his AR-15 ready to fire.

"I'm sorry I missed," Andrew huffed through the pain.

"Well, I won't."

Sarge aimed his weapon at Andrew's head. Andrew straightened his back. If this was how he would die, at least he could do so with dignity.

A growl came from the right. Both men turned their heads in time to see Roxie lunge. The dog slammed into Sarge, knocking him to the ground. He tried to use his weapon to push the animal away, but Roxie was in attack mode. She kept biting at his face. When Sarge's arms collapsed under the weight, Roxie sank her teeth into the front of Sarge's throat, yanking her head from side to side until she tore out his Adam's apple and part of his larynx. Sarge lay on the ground, thrashing around and gasping for air. He covered the wound with his hands, but to no effect. Blood from the severed artery spurted between his fingers. After a few seconds, Sarge went still, drowning in his blood.

Roxie came over and stood beside Andrew, protecting him.

"Good girl." Andrew reached up and scratched her belly. "You saved my—"

A three-round burst of semi-automatic fire tore into Roxie, killing her instantly.

Andrew turned to see Shank and Tyler approaching, smoke drifting from the barrel of Shank's Remington 870. He fired another round into Roxie's head.

"Stay."

"You're an asshole," groaned Andrew.

Shank removed a knife from the sheath attached to his belt. "If you think I'm an asshole now, wait until I start carving you up."

Tyler moved in front of Shank. "Leave him alone. He can't fight anymore."

"Fuck off." Shank shoved Tyler aside, then looked down at Andrew with a sardonic grin. "These assholes have to realize who's in charge now."

NICOLAI AND BIG Daddy reached the gate surrounding Lori's backyard. Nicolai moved his head closer to the wood and listened. The bitch he had missed when he fired on the patrol had run this way, but he heard nothing on the other side of the fence. She probably shit her pants and ran away to save herself.

He leaned toward Big Daddy and whispered. "I don't know if anyone is in there. Stay here. I'm going around back and try opening the gate. That'll distract them. When I do, climb up the fence and kill anyone inside. Got that?"

Big Daddy nodded his approval. He prepared to scale the fence as Nicolai headed for the back.

Kirstie and Kathy heard the two men whispering, followed by one of them walking along the fence's perimeter. Both women raised their weapons and tracked him. The movement stopped at the back gate. A moment later, he tried opening it, making too much noise. Both women realized it was a distraction and did nothing.

Fred barked, giving them away.

Big Daddy heard the dog and started climbing the fence, ready to spray the backyard with his Sig Sauer ROMEO4. His left arm wrapped around the top of the fence, embedding itself on the razor blades Andrew had installed along the top. Big Daddy released his grip and dropped to the ground, the blades ripping chunks out of his skin as he fell.

"Fuck!"

Kathy spotted the blood running down the inside of the fence. Rushing over, she aimed her shotgun and fired four rounds. The first shattered the fence, spraying Big Daddy with wood fragments. The second and third shots tore into their target, the buckshot embedding themselves in his lungs, kidneys, and heart. Big Daddy died instantly. The fourth round struck a bloody corpse.

Nicolai raised his weapon and kicked the gate, dislodging the lock. Since it opened outward, it did not move.

Kirstie fired three rounds into the gate.

LINDSEY APPROACHED OLD Coach Road when she saw two men coming from the other end, racing toward the compound. Since Quinn and Theodora manned the guard post, she knew these two were raiders. She stopped, raised her weapon, and fired at the lead raider. Never having used a firearm before tonight, she failed to lead the target. The rounds missed Spaz and peppered Carlson, who toppled forward onto the asphalt.

Spaz spun to the left and fired without aiming. Most of the rounds missed Lindsey. However, one grazed her right leg, cutting through the skin but not hitting bone. Lindsey screamed and fell to the ground, clutching the wound. No blood spurted, which meant the bullet missed the artery. It still hurts like Hell.

Lindsey crawled toward the nearest house to find cover

when she heard footsteps running toward her. She looked up in time to see Spaz kick her in the face. Her nose shattered. Lindsey rolled back onto the ground, dazed and in even more pain. Spaz grabbed her by the collar, lifted her, and dragged her to the nearest tree, where he slammed her back into it.

"I'm sick of you cunts taking out my team." Spaz slapped Lindsey across the face. "It's time I teach you a lesson."

HAELLIE REACHED JUSTIN'S house as the battle for the compound increased. She wanted to go back, but common sense told her Justin needed her more. She ran to the front gate of the enclosed backyard. The horses inside the garage were frantic. Haellie banged on the gate.

"Justin, open up."

"Who is it?"

"Haellie."

The gate swung open. Haellie ducked inside and stared at the garage.

"Are they okay?"

"The gunfire is freaking them out. To be honest, I can't blame them."

Justin started to close it when he spotted Renee, who yelled, "Keep it open."

Renee and Smokey raced in. Justin closed the gate and secured the latch.

"What are you doing here?" asked Haellie.

"Two raiders are coming this way."

"Shit," responded Justin. "Spread out and stay low."

"Shouldn't one of us go into the garage and protect the horses?" asked Haellie.

As if on cue, one of the horses kicked the side window, shattering the glass.

"We'd be in more danger in there." Justin crouched by the wall and trained his Mossberg on the gate.

Renee and Haellie each moved to separate corners of the gate, waiting for the raiders.

ANDREW ATTEMPTED TO punch Shank. The raider blocked the blow, grabbed Andrew's wrist, and cut a deep slice across his palm. Andrew suppressed a scream. Instead, he brought up his good leg, the knee catching Shank in the butt and throwing him over Andrew onto the grass. Andrew expected to be shot by the other raider, but Tyler stood motionless.

Rolling over, Andrew tried to get up. Shank came up from behind, yanked Andrew's head back by the hair, and placed the blade against his neck.

"I'm going to enjoy this."

"Not as much as I am," said a female voice.

Both men looked up. Jeanette stood two feet in front of them, the barrel of a revolver inches from Shank's head. Before he could respond, she pulled the trigger three times. The bullets disintegrated Shank's head, blowing off the back of his skull and sending chunks of brain and gore across the lawn. The body hovered on its knees for a moment before falling over. Blood poured from the severed arteries, staining the grass.

Jeanette spun to her right and aimed at Tyler. Instead of fighting back, he dropped his weapon, placed his hands behind his head, and dropped to his knees.

"I give up."

"Too late for that, asshole."

"Don't shoot him," gasped Andrew.

Jeanette kept the revolver trained on Tyler and stared down at her husband. "Are you serious?"

"Prisoners are a good source of intelligence. But if he tries anything, kill the motherfucker."

"Roxie!"

Jordan, Regan, and Mikayla joined the group. The teenagers took up position on either side of Tyler, each training their gun on him. Jordan dropped to his knees in front of Roxie, cradling the dog in his arms and crying.

"How did she die?" Jordan sobbed.

"She saved my life. You should be proud of her."

Jordan buried his head against Roxie and cried.

"Enough of this," said Jeanette. "We need to get Andrew back inside."

She reached down and helped Andrew to his feet, supporting him as he limped back to the house. Blood from his sliced palm ran down her blouse. Regan shoved Tyler forward, both teenagers keeping their weapons on him. Jordan scooped up Roxie in his arms and carried her into the house.

KEITH AND RYAN reached the corner of Geary Lane. In the minimal light provided by the aurora, Keith saw the battle playing out in front of Andrew's house.

"Should we help them out?" suggested Ryan.

"They have it under control. Justin needs our help."

STRATMAN AND POUNDER hid behind a row of bushes across the street from Andrew's house. Stratman watched as the dog ripped apart Sarge, the leader's wife took down Shank, and Tyler surrendered. Fucking pussy. When they got back to the VFW, his wife and daughters would be transferred to the bar, where he should have put them in the first place. If Tyler survives this, he'll tie the bastard to a chair and force him to watch.

He considered opening fire on the group, but the chances of taking down all five would be minimal and would give away their position. Shank was dead, so unless some of the other raiders were closing in on the garage, he and Pounder would have to take the house on their own.

Stratman contemplated his options. He had come too far

and lost too many people to fall back, not that he ever considered retreating an option. Tyler was a prisoner, and at least one person needed to guard him. The male was severely wounded and required medical attention. And the guy who lost his dog was too emotionally upset to fight. That left only the leader's girls guarding the house. If he could take one of them captive, the others would surrender, and he would win.

Scanning the area for other compounders and spotting none, Stratman tapped Pounder on the shoulder. "We're going to make our way around the back of the house. You go first."

Staying low, both men ran across the street, moving around the house to the backyard.

WHEN THE GATE did not open after his kick, Nicolai ducked to his right a second before shotgun bullets burst through the wood. He stopped when he reached the house, standing with his back against the wall.

"I'll give you credit. You guys are good. But you're not going to win this. Give up now, and we'll go easy on you."

"Fuck off," blurted Kirstie.

"Have it your way." Nicolai raised his arms and blindly fired his AK-47 into the backyard.

Kirstie and Kathy had crouched against the rear wall of the house, so the rounds harmlessly tore into the grass.

Kirstie fired at the raised AK-47, one of the rounds striking Nicolai's left hand and the semi-automatic. He dropped the broken weapon and clutched his wounded hand.

"God damn cunts. You'll fucking pay for that."

Kirstie leaned over and whispered to Kathy. "We have to take out this bastard before he gets to us."

"You guard out here. I'm going inside to make sure he doesn't break in and come in behind us."

MEG WAS HALFWAY to the center of the compound when she heard the gun battle break out at Lori's house. She knew Kathy guarded the garden by herself and would need backup. Breaking to the left, she went to help her friend.

SPAZ PUNCHED LINDSEY twice in the face as hard as he could. She was too stunned to fight back but still conscious. Good. The bitch would be awake enough to experience her death. He wrapped his hands around her neck, placed his thumbs on her larynx, and began to strangle her.

Lindsey gasped. Panic set in. Rather than fight back, she instinctively clasped Spaz's hands and tried to break his grip, but he was too strong. She reached up to claw his face. Spaz lifted and turned his head to one side, then pushed his thumbs harder against her larynx. Lindsey felt herself slipping away.

"Leave my mommy alone!"

Spaz turned his head to the left. A girl no more than ten years old stood five feet away, holding a .38 caliber revolver at him, her hands shaking. He smiled sadistically. Pulling Lindsey off the tree, he held the woman in front of him, one hand on her chin and the other on the back of her head.

Lindsey gasped. "Marcie, go home."

Spaz tightened his grip on Lindsey. "Is this your mother?"

"Yes. Leave her alone."

"Drop the gun or I'll snap her neck."

"No!" Marcie took a step forward. The gun shook in her hands.

"Marcie, run!"

"Don't listen to her," shouted Spaz. "Drop the gun. Now!"

Marcie hesitated. Tears flowed down her face. The girl bent over and laid the revolver on the ground.

"Good girl. Now back up."

Marcie obeyed.

"You're going to watch me kill your mother, then I'm going

to do even worse to you."

No way in Hell would Lindsey let this asshole harm her daughter. "Fuck you!"

Summoning what little strength she had left, Lindsey placed the heel of her sneaker against Spaz's right shin and slammed it down, scraping down his leg and shattering his foot. Spaz screamed in pain and loosened his grip. Lindsey shifted to the left, reached down with her left hand, and grabbed his balls, squeezing as tightly as possible. Spaz let go of Lindsey and dropped to his knees.

"Fucking cunt. You'll pay for this."

Lindsey stumbled forward, picked up the revolver, and stood in front of Marcie. "Good luck with that."

She emptied all six rounds into Spaz, tearing open his chest and shattering his ribs. Bullets and bone fragments ripped into his heart and lungs, killing him instantly. The corpse fell backward onto the ground, blood flowing from the wounds.

Lindsey dropped to her knees, every ounce of energy drained from her. Marcie raced around front and embraced her mother. Lindsey hugged Marcie, then yelled at her daughter.

"I told you to stay home."

"But… but I saved your life."

"We'll talk about this later. Let's check on your sister."

Lindsey struggled to stand, the pain from her leg wound slowing her down. When she finally got to her feet, her vision blurred, and the neighborhood began spinning. She wobbled. Only Marcie rushing over to hold her prevented Lindsey from collapsing.

"Are you okay, mommy?"

"I'm fine."

After a minute, the dizziness subsided. She took a deep breath, coughing deeply after nearly being strangled. She would be in considerable pain for the next few days. But at least she was alive.

Lindsey pointed to the revolver and shotgun on the ground. "Marcie, can you get them for me?"

The daughter picked them up and handed them to her mother. Lindsey slung the shotgun over her shoulder and slid the revolver between her pants and her back. Wrapping her hand around Marcie's shoulder and using her as a crutch, she staggered home.

STRATMAN AND POUNDER raced across Andrew's front lawn, with the latter in the lead.

Suddenly, Pounder disappeared from view. Stratman heard a loud snap followed by Pounder yelling, "Fuck! My leg!"

Noticing at the last second the pit dug in the backyard, Stratman jumped over it, then circled back to check on Pounder.

"Are you okay?"

"Of course I'm not fucking okay! My leg is broken! The fucking bone is poking through the skin!"

Stratman crouched down and studied Pounder's leg. Sure enough, he had suffered a compound fracture. That would have been him if Pounder had not been in the lead.

"Come on, boss," Pounder gasped. "Help me up."

"Sorry. We have no way to treat that."

"What do you—?" Pounder glanced up to see Stratman aiming his Remington 870 at him. He raised his hands in a futile gesture to stop the inevitable. "Wait. I can—"

Stratman fired a single round into his forehead, putting the raider out of his misery. He stood and headed toward the rear of the house.

HART SPOTTED A woman and her dog rushing to the gate of the house where the horses were stabled. He stopped and raised his weapon but did not fire.

"What are you waiting for?" asked Mark.

"For her to reach the gate. If we can take them all out, it'll make our job easier."

Hart moved in front of Mark and waited. Eventually, the gate opened. As the woman raced in, Hart emptied the Ruger AR-15 magazine onto the gate and the surrounding fence. Someone on the other side screamed.

A moment later, gunfire erupted behind them. Several rounds tore into Mark's back, splattering Hart with blood. Mark grunted and collapsed onto the asphalt.

Hart spun around and fell prone, using the raider's body as cover.

Two men ran toward him. One held a semi-automatic weapon, the other carried a shotgun. The guy with the M4 yelled, "I got them both."

Hart grabbed Mark's Remington 870 12 gauge, aimed at the approaching men, and fired when they were twenty feet away.

RYAN WATCHED THE two raiders in front of him fire on Renee as she and Smokey ducked into Justin's backyard. He raised his M4 and fired, watching as five rounds tore into the closest man's back. The body shuddered and collapsed. The other raider fell a second later.

"I got them both."

Ryan raced forward to make sure they were dead.

Keith followed but noticed that the second man aimed a shotgun at them.

"Be careful. One of them is still—"

Shotgun rounds blasted toward them. Ryan took three rounds to the chest and abdomen, killing him instantly.

Keith ducked to the left, surviving the assault. However, several pellets caught him in the right leg. He felt them tear through his skin and shatter his left fibula. Pain shot through his body, momentarily blurring his vision. Keith collapsed onto the street and remained still, hoping the gunman would think he was dead.

WHEN NEITHER MAN moved, Hart assumed he had killed them both. He replaced the empty magazine of his Ruger with a full one, then checked on Mark. No pulse. Those at the stable would pay for this.

RENEE ENTERED THE backyard as the semi-automatic weapons fire raked the gate and fence, missing her and Smokey. Justin was not as lucky. One round shattered against the gate, the fragments continuing through the wood and peppering his right shoulder, knocking him onto the grass.

Haellie screamed Justin's name and ran up to him, praying he was not dead.

Renee let go of Smokey, who ran along the fence, barking at the attackers on the other side. She spun around, closed and secured the gate, then crouched down in front of Justin, her Glock 45 aimed at the entrance.

Haellie examined the wound. Blood flowed from several holes, but fortunately, none of them had struck an artery.

"Are you okay?"

"I'll live." When Haellie touched the wound, he winced. "My arm is going to be out of commission for a while."

"Let's get you inside."

"I can still shoot with my left arm."

"Screw that. We've got to make sure you're safe. I'm bringing you into the garage."

The horses were frantic, desperate to escape. Justin shook his head.

"I'm safer out here."

Smokey began frantically barking at the fence. A moment

later, a shadow appeared on the other side of the gate. Renee fired her shotgun. The figure jumped to the side. Renee let loose two more rounds into the fence and moved to the left in case the intruder fired back.

Haellie slipped her hands under Justin's shoulder and pulled him back toward the door leading to the garage, ignoring his painful groans. Once he was out of the line of fire, she crouched in front of him, aiming at the gate.

Renee's gunfire missed Hart by a few inches. He leaned up against the garage door, considering his next move. Charging into the backyard would not work. He had no idea how many people were there. Only one person had fired at him, but he knew at least two people were in the backyard and assumed both were armed. No way could he take down both of them and the dog before one of them got him.

Hart heard the horses inside the garage. If he could break in and secure them, the others might surrender rather than lose their means of transportation. It was a long shot, but the only viable option other than scrubbing his part of the raid and having to deal later with Stratman.

Bending over, Hart tried the garage door. Fuck, it was locked. Standing back a few feet, he fired several rounds into the lock, shattering it, then grabbed the handle and raised the door.

The horses saw their chance to escape and took advantage of it. The horse closest to the opening, an American quarter horse, burst out, slamming into Hart and knocking him down. The rest followed. Two of them ran over Hart as they raced to safety. One set of hoofs shattered the bones in his left leg. Another landed on his chest, fracturing his ribcage. The broken bones punctured his heart and lungs. Hart went into cardiac arrest. He gasped for air, panicking as he felt blood filling his lungs.

The horses broke left and raced down Geary Lane. Keith rolled out of the way, the pain shooting through his leg preferable to being crushed in the stampede.

Renee swung open the gate and scanned the area with her shotgun, focusing on Hart's body. She stepped forward and trained the shotgun on him. He raised an arm toward her and gasped.

Haellie stepped up beside Renee.

"Maybe we should put him out of his misery," suggested Renee.

"Fuck him." Haellie remembered how these assholes had tormented and murdered her mother and siblings. "Let the asshole suffer."

They heard a call from further down the street. Both women spun around and aimed their weapons. Keith waved at them.

"I've been shot."

Renne and Haellie made their way to Keith, keeping an eye out for other raiders. Renee kept guard while Haellie examined the wound.

"How bad is it?" groaned Keith.

"You'll live, but you'll walk with a limp for a while. Come on." Haellie helped Keith to his feet and wrapped his right arm around her shoulders. "Let's get you back to Justin's place."

NICOLAI MOVED ALONG the rear of the house toward the closest door and stared inside. It led into the kitchen, which meant more than likely there was a door leading to the backyard. He would be able to sneak up on—

A woman stepped into the kitchen. Nicolai had to move fast.

He raised his weapon and fired three rounds into the kitchen.

Kathy had noticed Nicolai before he pulled the trigger and ducked for cover. He aimed the next six rounds at the door, shattering the lock and knob. Nicolai kicked it open and rushed inside. Kathy raised her Beretta to fire. Nicolai swung to the left and slammed into Kathy, shoving her against the refrigerator. Kathy cried out, every muscle in her back throbbing with pain. She dropped her shotgun and slid onto the floor. Kathy reached for the shotgun, but Nicolai kicked it to the other side of the kitchen, then placed the barrel of his Glock Sig Sauer P320 against her forehead. Kathy closed her eyes and waited to die. Instead, he kicked her in the groin. She curled into a fetal position from the pain.

"Don't worry, bitch. I'm not going to kill you. You and the cunt who killed Big Daddy are going back to our place to be our new whores."

"I don't think so."

Nicolai spun around to see Meg standing in the doorway, her Beretta A300 trained on him.

Racing for the door leading to the backyard, Nicolai fired in Meg's direction. Meg ducked and fired back. None of the rounds struck their targets.

Meg raced into the kitchen to protect Kathy.

"Are you hurt bad?"

Kathy grimaced and nodded. "It hurts like a son of a bitch, but I don't think he did any permanent damage."

Meg helped Kathy to her feet, who groaned and leaned against the stove for support.

"Kirstie's out back. Help her."

Meg turned and headed for the garden.

Nicolai pushed open the door to the backyard, colliding with Kirstie who was coming in to join the fight. Both tumbled down the stairs into the garden. Kirstie landed on her back, momentarily stunning her, though she had enough sense to roll to the side to make sure Nicolai did not land on her. He hit the dirt chest first and grunted. As Kirstie attempted to crabwalk away, Nicolai reached out and clutched her left leg. Kirstie slammed her right foot into his face, breaking his nose and shattering his front teeth.

Nicolai released his grip and felt his face, blood staining his fingers. "Fucking bitch."

Kirstie grabbed her AR-15, stood, and aimed it at Nicolai.

"Don't move, ass—"

Nicolai jumped and slapped the weapon out of her hands. Kirstie backed up until she bumped into the fence, ready for hand-to-hand combat, though she knew she could never win this battle, resigning herself to her fate.

Removing a switchblade from his pocket, Nicolai flipped it open. "We're still going to make you one of our new whores, but first, I'm going to carve up your face."

He took two steps toward her when something splashed over him. He paused. Both he and Kirstie smelled the odor of mercaptan. He spun around toward the house.

Meg stood five feet away holding the can of gasoline Kathy had planned on using to set the garden on fire.

"You bit—"

Meg doused him with more gasoline. It splashed in his eyes and across the wounds. Nicolai screamed. He dropped the switchblade and used the palms of his hands to wipe the gasoline out of his eyes.

Kirstie ran over to Meg as the latter doused Nicolai a third time. Meg placed the can on the ground and raised her shotgun. Kathy staggered down the stairs and joined them, removing the lighter from her pocket and flipping it open. They watched Nicolai stagger around the backyard, grunting in pain. He finally stopped and stared at the three women. Meg wrapped her finger around the trigger. Kathy flipped the lighter's flint wheel and ignited the flame.

"When the others get here, you three are going to suffer big time."

Kathy raised the lighter in front of her. "Make a move and you won't be around to see it."

"The red-headed bitch would easily shoot me, but you're not the type who would set me on fire."

Nicolai was correct. Kathy had no problem killing him but could not let him suffer like that, despite what these assholes tried to do to her and Haellie at the school. She lowered the lighter.

Nicolai chuckled. "I knew you didn't have it in you."

"I do." Kirstie took the lighter from Kathy and tossed it at Nicolai.

He jumped back several feet. The lighter missed him, falling to the ground and igniting the gasoline-soaked grass. The flames spread across the lawn, engulfing Nicolai. He released an anguished howl of agony as the clothes seared off his body in seconds. Nicolai tried to lunge at the women, but Meg shot him in the stomach. He dropped to the ground, writhing around as the flames consumed him. His skin, muscles, and tissues burned slowly as the intense heat evaporated the water inside him. Once his body had dried out, the epidermis caught fire, burning off and peeling away. The blood in his veins and arteries dried out and clotted, clogging his circulatory system. A few seconds later, those same veins and arteries began to melt. The dermis, the lower layer of skin, caught fire next, shrinking under the heat and bursting open, the fissures leaking fat onto the grass. After a minute of agony, Nicolai's flaming corpse fell forward onto the lawn.

Kathy took the Beretta from Meg. "There are some blankets on the back porch. Get them and put out the fire so the garden doesn't burn."

Kirstie and Meg ran onto the porch and emerged seconds later with five blankets. Kathy kept the weapon trained on Nicolai as they extinguished the flames, noticing neither of them attempted to stop him from burning. Once all the fires except Nicolai were out, they gathered the blankets and rejoined Kathy.

"Maybe we should put him out of his misery," suggested Kathy.

Meg offered Kathy one of the blankets. "You do it."

Kathy glanced over at Kirstie.

"Let the fucker burn."

Kirstie noticed that Kathy did nothing to help him.

The three women watched as the flames consumed Nicolai's charred remains.

STRATMAN MADE HIS way along the rear of Andrew's house. He saw several beams from flashlights illuminating the living room and quietly approached, peering through the window.

Andrew sat on the sofa, his leg resting on the coffee table. Sarah held the flashlight on the wound as Jeanette examined it. Jordan sat near the fireplace, cradling Roxie in his arms. Regan crouched by the front door, her weapon trained in case anyone tried to break in. Tyler knelt on the floor in the far corner, his ankles crossed and his hands behind his head. Mikayla stood three feet behind him, her shotgun trained on his head.

"Mom," asked Stephanie. "Will Dad be okay?"

"I'm fine, hon." Andrew gasped when Jeanette touched the wound.

Stephanie broke down in tears.

Jeanette glanced up at her youngest daughter. "There's a First Aid kit in the cabinet above the sink. Will you get it for me?"

Stephanie sniffed back her tears, took the flashlight from Sarah, and headed toward the kitchen.

Luck had finally gone Stratman's way. He ducked so no one could see him through the window and headed for the rear door.

He watched as Stephanie opened the cabinet and shone the flashlight inside. When she stood on her toes to reach the First Aid kit, Stratman acted.

He smashed the pane nearest the knob, reached in, unlocked the door, and burst into the kitchen. Stephanie turned to the noise, paralyzed with fear. Stratman raced over, wrapped his left arm tightly around her neck, and placed the barrel of his Glock against her temple.

"We're going into the living room. And don't try anything funny or I'll shoot you."

"Stephanie," Jeanette called from the living room. "Is everything okay?"

Stratman pushed the Glock's barrel against the girl's temple and led her back to the others.

Jeanette was heading for the kitchen when Stratman entered the living room. He backed against the wall so no one could sneak up on him.

"Nobody move."

Jeanette raised her hands. "Please, don't hurt my baby."

"No one will get hurt if you all do as I say." He noticed Regan stood by the front door, her weapon aimed at him. "Drop your weapons."

Mikayla placed hers on the floor. It did not go unnoticed to Stratman that Tyler did not grab it and help. Regan kept hers trained on Stratman.

He ran the gun down Stephanie's face and under her chin, pushing it up so her head lifted, aiming the barrel so the shot would kill the girl instantly. "I'm not fucking around."

"Do what he says!" yelled Andrew.

Regan hesitated, knowing if she complied, they would all be dead, but then placed it on the floor.

"Good girl."

"Boss, don't do this." Tyler remained on his knees. "These people don't mean us any harm."

"They already killed at least half my men. And I noticed you surrendered without a fight. Your wife and daughter are joining the rest of these whores at the bar when we get back."

"You son of a bitch." Tyler started to stand.

Stratman removed the Glock from Stehanie's neck and fired a single round at Tyler. It struck him in the left shoulder. A spray of blood covered Mikayla's face, stunning her. Tyler crumbled to the floor.

Andrew used the opportunity to push himself off the sofa but, because of his leg, he only made it a few inches before Stratman placed the Glock back under Stephanie's chin.

"Don't try it. There's enough bullets in this that I could take out your entire family."

Andrew settled back down on the sofa, fury in his eyes. Stratman would have to keep an eye on this one.

"You're the girls' mother, right?"

Jeanette nodded.

"You're going to go out there and tell the others to stand down. This compound belongs to me now."

"What if I get shot?"

"Then I'll send your other daughter out to finish the job."

"Asshole," mumbled Andrew.

"Don't get cocky with me. You're no good to me with that leg. Be glad I don't kill you now."

A strained silence fell over the group.

"But first, I want to see your supplies in the garage. Everyone goes first. And no funny business." Stratman pushed the Glock deeper into Stephanie's chin to emphasize his threat.

Jeanette and Sarah helped Andrew off the sofa and led the way to the garage. Regan and Mikayla followed. Jordan exited last, glaring with hatred at Stratman. When they had left, Stratman followed. He leaned over and whispered to Stephanie.

"Don't do anything foolish and you and your family will be fine," he lied.

He approached the door leading to the garage and paused. "All of you go inside the garage and stay where I can see you."

They obeyed.

Stratman stepped up to the door leading to the garage and told Stephanie, "Shine the flashlight inside."

The young girl did as he was told, the beam shaking. Stratman peered inside, his eyes widening in shock. Other than some tools and garbage bins, the garage was empty.

"What the fuck?"

Andrew grinned. "We moved all the stuff to another location this morning."

"Where is it?"

"It doesn't matter. You've lost."

Fury overcame Stratman. After all his group had gone through, every one of his team who had been killed, they came up empty handed. No fucking way was he going to let that asshole get away with it.

Removing the Glock from Stephanie's chin, Stratman aimed it at Andrew and fired two rounds, both of which struck him in the abdomen. Andrew fell back against the wall and slid to the floor, blood streaking the paint.

Stratman swung the Glock toward Jeanette but, before he could fire, something metal struck him on the back of his head, stunning him. His grip on the young girl loosened. Stephanie pushed away from him and ran to her father. Stratman swung the Glock to shoot her. Another blow struck his head, this time fracturing his skull. His vision blurred. Stratman dropped the Glock and fell down the three stairs. As he hit the cement, he saw Tyler standing in the doorway holding a poker from the fireplace. Tyler dropped the poker and leaned against the wall, resting on his good shoulder.

Regan rushed forward, picked up the Glock, and stood by Stratman, aiming at his head.

Stratman sneered. "Fuck you, bitch!"

"That ain't going to happen."

Regan shifted her aim and fired two rounds into his groin. Pain more intense than his head wound overcame Stratman. He closed his eyes and cried out. He did not see Regan shift aim back to his head and pull the trigger. Stratman's head exploded in a cloud of gore.

Regan stood motionless, staring at the body.

Mikayla moved up beside her and gently placed a hand on

her friend's shoulder. "Are you okay?"

Regan nodded. "Why do you ask?"

"Because of what you did... I mean...." Not wanting to say the words, Mikayla motioned toward Stratman.

"The asshole got what he deserved."

"Hey, listen," said Jordan.

The garage went quiet.

Mikayla shook her head. "I don't hear anything."

"That's what I mean. There's no gunfire."

Regan's shoulders slumped in relief. "That means the battle is over."

"Who won?" asked Mikayla.

"You did," answered Tyler.

Everyone turned to him.

"Stratman's goal was to take the compound or die trying. If there's no fighting, it means every one of his people is dead."

"Except you," said Jordan.

Tyler chuckled, the emotion cut short when his shoulder throbbed. "Whether I live or die depends on you."

"Let him live," groaned Andrew. "He saved us."

Sarah glanced over at Tyler and mouthed the words, "Thank you."

"Stop talking." Jeanette wiped the sweat off of Andrew's forehead. "You need to conserve your strength until we can get you help."

"There is no help coming." Andrew gasped. "We all know I'm not going to survive this."

"Don't say that!" Jeanette screamed, as if anger could cure his wounds.

"It's okay. With the raiders..." Andrew coughed. Blood spurted from his mouth onto his shirt. "With the raiders gone, the compound should be safe. Work now on preparing this place for the win...."

Andrew broke into a coughing fit, spitting up even more blood. It took several seconds for him to catch his breath.

Jordan moved over to Regan and Mikayla and escorted them out of the garage. Tyler followed. Regan removed the First Aid kit from the cabinet and joined the others in the living room. They sat silently as Regan cleaned and dressed Tyler's wound.

A few minutes later, a wail came from the garage followed by sobbing. Andrew, who had used his military experience to prepare the compound for this occasion, had passed on.

Thanks to Andrew, the rest of them had a chance of surviving.

CHAPTER FORTY-ONE

KEVIN WOKE UP early to the sound of birds chirping. It would have been a pleasant way to greet the morning if he had not been shacked up in an abandoned RV in the middle of a natural disaster.

Pushing himself off the sofa, Kevin stretched and turned his torso from side to side, the aching muscles in his neck and back snapping like popcorn in a microwave. He stepped into the center aisle and looked at Shawn fast asleep on the bed. He would let him rest a little longer before checking on him.

Kevin removed a bottle of spring water from the plastic container on the counter, twisted off the lid, and swigged down two mouthfuls. Thank God he found that water. Over the past few days, he had rehydrated himself. Not only did he feel better, or at least well enough to continue to Dunbarton, his urine had been clear since last night.

Grabbing a can of chili, he stared at it for several seconds, deciding whether he wanted to eat. He needed food and the chili provided protein, but he had been eating chili for three days and was sick of it. Putting down the can, he opted for mixed vegetables. Unfortunately, the can opener on the counter was electric. Rummaging through the drawers, he failed to find a hand-held opener. Switching out the mixed vegetables for chili, Kevin removed the pull off top, grabbed a spoon from the drawer, and consumed his boring breakfast while standing in the open doorway of the RV.

The heat and humidity were already unbearable, and it was only nine o'clock. The heat inside the RV had already reached eighty-two, turning the interior into a sauna. And it would only get worse. If there was a breeze, he could open the windows and air the place out a little, but the air had been stagnant for the past two days. At least they were not outside sweltering in the direct sunlight.

Kevin felt fortunate that the radiation poisoning had not affected his health as much as he had anticipated. He had urinated blood this morning, but nowhere near as much as Shawn had been. His stomach was upset though he had not felt the urge to vomit, which could be due to his steady diet of chili the past few days as well as the radiation poisoning. He would have to wait and see if it got worse as time passed.

Closing the door and wiping the sweat off his brow, Kevin decided to check on Shawn. He grabbed another bottle of water and made his way to the bedroom. Shawn rested peacefully on the pillows. Reaching down, Kevin placed a hand on Shawn's shoulder to wake him, then paused. Shawn's body was rigid. Kevin felt Shawn's forehead. It was cold.

Shawn had passed away during the night.

Kevin closed his eyes and said a silent prayer for his friend.

"Sorry to see you go, buddy. At least you're not suffering anymore."

Kevin unfolded the blanket on the end of the bed and laid it over Shawn's body, covering his face. It pained him not to be able to give his friend a proper burial, but such niceties had collapsed along with the rest of societal norms.

He noticed two pieces of paper sitting on the counter. Shawn had written Danielle's name and the address to their home on the outside, as well as directions on how to get there. This must be the letter Shawn had written to his sister that Kevin promised he would deliver. He folded the letter in three and slid it into his rear pocket.

"I'll get this to her."

Kevin sorted through the closet hoping to find a backpack or travel back to carry his supplies but found nothing. Then he remembered the suitcases left outside. Retrieving one with a handle and wheels, Kevin brought it inside. He filled it with the remaining bottles of water and chili, being sure to include a few spoons. Moving up to the driver's seat, he rummaged through the glove compartment and center console, eventually finding road maps. Kevin sorted through them. There were maps for every east coast state from Florida to Maine. He stumbled across one for New Hampshire that showed the entire state on one side and detailed plans for the major cities and surrounding suburbs on the back. One of them displayed Concord and, to the southwest, Dunbarton. Kevin placed it in the outer pocket of the suitcase.

Checking the RV one final time to make certain he had left nothing of use behind, Kevin paused at the door and stared down the hall to Shawn's covered body. He hated leaving his friend like this, but what choice did he have? Staying here would be of no use. At least on the road, he had a chance of survival.

Besides, he had a promise to keep.

Exiting the RV, Kevin closed and locked the door behind him, said goodbye to Shawn one final time, and started walking west along Route 101.

CHAPTER FORTY-TWO

"A RE YOU SURE we'll be safe?" asked Liz.

"Of course." Danielle meant it. However, after what she had gone through the last ten days, she kept the semi-automatic between the small of her back and her pants, hidden by her shirt, just in case.

For the first time since this all began, Danielle felt confident. She had safely made it home, though not finding Kirstie or Shawn waiting there had been a disappointment. On the other hand, knowing that Liz and Kyle were safe helped to lessen her depression over not knowing what happened to her daughter and brother. Danielle still hoped they would eventually make their way home. In the meantime, she had a new family to take care of.

A major plus was finding that the neighborhood had come together to provide a safe haven for the survivors. Now she could concentrate on getting their lives back in order, or what would be considered order in this new world. It would take years to grow accustomed to what passed for society today.

Danielle had changed her clothes that morning, shedding her dirty, sweat-soaked garb for a clean t-shirt and shorts. They had scavenged some new outfits for the kids at the church in Goffstown. The kids cheered as if it was Christmas when they shed their gross jeans and shirts this morning for the clean ones, but it wouldn't be long until they were dirty and worn down. She now stood in Kirstie's room, going through her daughter's dresser looking for more clothes for Liz and Kyle. As she rummaged through Kirstie's t-shirts, the kids sat on the bed on either side of Chase, petting him.

Danielle found an old t-shirt emblazoned with the logo of Coriky, Kirstie's favorite band. She had taken her daughter to Boston to see them for her twelfth birthday. Kirstie enjoyed that night so much she refused to throw out the t-shirt, despite it being worn and three sizes too small. Danielle held it by the shoulders.

"Liz, what about this one?"

"Who's Coriky?"

"It's a band my daughter enjoys."

"I'll wear it until she comes home, then I'll give it back to her."

Danielle fought back the tears. "Here you go."

Liz removed the t-shirt she had put on that morning and slid on the new one. She shifted her body back and forth, then lifted the collar to smell it.

"It's a little big, but it smells nice."

"What about me?" Kyle asked excitedly.

"Hang on." Danielle went back to thumbing through her daughter's shirts. She finally found one that would be a good fit for Kyle—a Minnie Mouse t-shirt that Kirstie had kept as a souvenir from when they had traveled to Disney World in Orlando four years ago. She showed it to Kyle.

"How's this?"

"Minnie Mouse? I don't want to wear that. People will think I'm a girl."

"All the other shirts are even more girlie and they're too big for you."

"That sucks."

Liz gently smacked him on the back of his head. "Language."

"Then you wear it."

"But I like this one."

Kyle crossed his arms and huffed.

"Just wear it for now," said Danielle. "Maybe someone else

has a boy's t-shirt you can wear."

Kyle sighed and rolled his eyes. "Okay."

Danielle handed him the shirt. He pulled off the one he put on that morning and slid on the new one. Moving over to the mirror, he looked at his reflection and frowned.

"I look like a girl."

Liz shook her head.

"Come on." Danielle closed the dresser drawer. "Let's head over to Corvin's house for breakfast."

The two kids jumped off the bed and cheered. Chase wagged his tail and barked.

The temperature outside was cooler than indoors. According to the thermometer by the front door, the temperature had dropped to the mid-seventies. The humidity had dissipated, and a light cloud cover prevented the sun from beating down on them. It was the most comfortable day weather wise since this all began. Danielle hoped it would be a harbinger for their future.

They crossed the street and walked up the driveway. Danielle had seen Corvin's house from a distance but had never been on his property. He was a prepper and had several firearms which he shot off in his backyard regularly. Other than that, she knew nothing about him. Others in the neighborhood also owned firearms. She often heard three or four others using their backyards for target practice. It used to bother her being surrounded by so many gun owners. Now it gave her a sense of confidence and security.

As she reached the front yard, Danielle noticed a Dodge RAM, a Subaru Forester, and two mid-size ATVs sitting on the lawn perpendicular to the house. Tire tracks surrounded the ATVs, indicating they were still functional. She wished she had stumbled across one of those in Boston.

The dwelling, a tan-colored ranch house, seemed well-maintained but was definitely owned by a guy. No ornaments adorned the front door or lawn. The only decoration was a metal sign at the top of the driveway that read TRESPASSERS WILL BE SHOT. IF YOU SURVIVE, YOU'LL BE SHOT AGAIN.

Noise came from the backyard, people laughing and amicably talking. She had not heard that since the solar flare began. It gave her more hope that things had finally got better for her and the kids.

Kyle sniffed the air. "Do you smell that?"

Liz inhaled. "It smells like bacon. Come on."

She grabbed her brother's hand and they raced around back, with Chase close on their heels. Danielle followed.

The backyard contained an inground swimming pool. Four children swam around, splashing each other and giggling. Ten adults sat or stood around a picnic table, eating and chatting. Corvin stood by a grill making breakfast.

A white American Bulldog spotted them, barked once, and ran over, its tail wagging. It stopped in front of Chase and sniffed his butt. After a few seconds, the dog's tail started wagging and it barked at Chase. Chase's tail wagged in return. The American Bulldog ran off and dived into the pool followed by Chase. The kids cheered and swam toward the two dogs.

Corvin turned from the grill and, upon noticing Danielle, waved.

"Glad you made it. Want something to eat?"

"Can we go in the pool first?" asked Kyle.

"That's up to Corvin."

The two kids spun around to face Corvin. "Is it okay if we swim first?"

"Sure. Dive in."

They dashed for the pool. Kyle dived in without removing his clothes or shoes. Liz paused long enough to kick off her shoes before joining him.

Danielle strolled over to the grill.

"I assume you want breakfast."

"Yes," said Danielle enthusiastically. "What do you have?"

"Eggs, bacon, and toast."

"I'll have all three, if you don't mind."

"Not at all." Corvin scooped them onto a plate. "We used the last of the bread since it's a special occasion."

"What's the occasion?"

"We're welcoming survivors to the neighborhood," said a voice behind Danielle. She turned around to see an attractive blonde in her mid-thirties standing a few feet away. "I've lived here for years."

"A lot of people have. But you're the only one to make it back. I'm Maleah."

"I'm Danielle." She held out her hand.

Maleah moved in and embraced Danielle. "We're so glad you made it back safely."

"I wouldn't say it was a safe journey."

"You can tell us about it later," said a young man with dark hair and a thin, well-trimmed beard. "Today is a happy day. I'm Damien, Maleah's husband."

The two shook hands.

"I don't recognize you," said Danielle. "Are you from around here?"

Maleah shook her head. "We're from Vermont. We were on vacation. We had visited Mount Washington with our son Nino and were on our way south when the flare hit. We were in Weare at the time and decided to walk to Concord. Thankfully, Corvin found us and let us stay here."

"No way was I going to let them go to Concord," said Corvin. "That place is a nightmare."

"How do you know that?"

"I have a ham radio I've been listening to. The whole world has gone to shit." Corvin handed Danielle her plate and pointed to the grill. "There's hot coffee if you want some."

"I never thought I'd have coffee again." Danielle poured herself a cup from the metal pot on the grill, nearly squealing with joy when she saw steam rising above the rim.

They joined the others at the table, who all introduced

themselves.

Danielle met Dale and Tucker last night. Alina was an extremely attractive brunette in her late twenties. She had moved to the States a year ago to be with her fiancé. They lived five doors down. He worked in Manchester and never made it home. Jake and Marie lived two doors down. Their kids, Betty and Sonya, swam in the pool. Heather and Stan, their friends from Massachusetts, had been visiting for the weekend with their kids, Little Stan and Karen, and wound up stuck here. Nate was a tall, lanky man in his mid-thirties, who had been a New Hampshire State Trooper. He was on patrol a few miles from here when his vehicle stopped working and, being single, agreed to stay and help. Sadie rounded out the group. She lived four doors down. She was a widow in her late sixties and had a friendly smile. After introducing herself, she lifted a garbage bag off the ground and placed it on the table in front of Danielle.

"What's this?" asked Danielle.

"Clothes for your kids. I have a grandson about your kids' age. He was with his father in Florida when things went south." Sadie fought back tears. "When Corvin told me about your kids, I brought them over. I thought you might be able to use them."

"They're not her kids," corrected Corvin.

"Really?"

Danielle nodded. "I picked them up while making my way home. Their parents never returned from work and their babysitter abandoned them. I couldn't leave them on their own."

Sadie took Danielle's hands in hers and squeezed. "That is so sweet of you. You'll fit in perfect here."

The group chatted for an hour while the kids and two dogs enjoyed themselves. Because the electrical grid out here was constantly going down due to fallen tree branches, most homes had a back-up generator, so they had enough electricity to use the water pumps, keep food preserved, and use fans or air conditioners to stay cool. Corvin promised to take a generator from one of the houses not lived in and install it at Danielle's home later that day. Most of them were gas powered, but Corvin assured her that was not a problem. The ATVs worked, and they used them to travel to a local gas station two miles away and gather enough gasoline to refuel them.

Around eleven, the kids finally came out of the pool, all of them having become friends and been adopted by the dogs. The kids finished off the last of the eggs and bacon. When Liz and Kyle heard that Sadie had given them fresh clothes to wear, they hugged her tightly.

Corvin told Liz and Kyle they could use his shower, getting cheers of approval from the kids. Twenty minutes later, they returned to the backyard wearing the new clothes Sadie had given them. For the first time in days, Liz and Kyle looked refreshed, their skin clean and their hair no longer matted against their heads. Both kids seemed happier than they had since she adopted them.

Then it was Danielle's turn to take a shower. The water splashing against her made Danielle feel better than she had since this nightmare began. She could feel the dirt washing off her, revitalizing her spirits. Glancing down, she was shocked to see dirty water swirling around the drain, not realizing how grimy she was. She wanted to stay under the stream of water for half an hour but did not want to take advantage of Corvin's hospitality. Shutting off the water, she dried herself odd, dressed, and rejoined the gathering.

The party broke up shortly after that. Everyone told Danielle that if she needed anything to let them know.

As Danielle walked up the driveway to her home with her new family, holding the bag of clothes, she realized how lucky she had been. Despite everything they had gone through, it could have been a lot worse. They had made it home to not only find the place intact, but she also had good neighbors that had formed a group to take care of one another. Most important, Liz and Kyle were safe. In a few days, with luck, their lives would return to a level of normalcy, or at least normalcy in this new world.

Once things had settled down, then she would look for a way to find Kirstie and Shawn.

CHAPTER FORTY-THREE

EVERYONE WHO HAD survived last night's attack gathered in Andrew's backyard at six o'clock to hold a memorial service for those members of the group who had given their lives to defend the compound. Those who had lost loved ones sat at the picnic table. Kirstie, Regan, and Mikayla faced those gathered for the event. Jeanette, Sarah, and Stephanie sat across from them, their backs to the others to conceal their crying. Ryan's wife was on a business trip when the solar flare struck, and Quinn and Theodora were single, so none of their loved ones were in attendance.

Kirstie's mind reeled from everything that had happened over the last twenty-four hours.

Andrew's plan to move the supplies from his garage to Jordan's had thwarted the raiders' attempt to take over, causing them to expend all their resources concentrating on the wrong target. Unfortunately, it had cost Andrew his life. The group spent the morning gathering the bodies. Andrew and the other compounders were placed in Andrew's garage. Jeanette wanted to cover the bodies with blankets until they could be buried, but Kathy disagreed. She wanted the rest of the compound to see what the raiders had done to them, especially the brutality enacted on Theodora, to remind everyone of the threat still out there. The bodies of the raiders were dumped onto Dignam's driveway for now.

Thankfully, the compound had not suffered as much as had been anticipated. All of the horses returned to Justin's house early in the morning, though they were nervous about going back into the garage, having to be coaxed in with hay, water, and apples. The battle for the garden had only damaged a few of the plants, which were mostly burned when they set Nicolai on fire. None of the water collection and storage units had suffered any damage.

Once the bodies were rounded up, Tyler informed Kathy about the women left behind at the bar and what they had gone through, and that Anderson was still there waiting for the raiders to return. He pleaded to be let go to be with his family. Kathy sent a rescue team for all of them. Others argued against the decision, not wanting to burden their already stressed supplies with newcomers. She overrode their protests, reminding them that Tyler's wife was a nurse who could tend to the traumatic wounds received by Keith and Lindsey. The women needed a safe place to stay and could be used to help maintain the gardens and supplies.

Kathy told Tyler to take Jordan, Kirstie, Meg, and Regan with him, hoping the presence of so many females would put the abused women at ease way. They brought along one of the trailers to transport them back to the compound. Anderson put up no resistance, which was smart considering he was outnumbered five-to-one. Jordan told him to disappear and that if he ever appeared near the compound he would be executed. Anderson grabbed some supplies and fled.

Ashley rode on the horse with her husband, the girls riding with Jordan and Meg. The four women used as sex slaves were loaded onto the trailer along with food and water from the bar and VFW Hall. Though there was limited room on the trailer, no one complained, relieved to finally be released from their nightmare. Judging by the looks on the women's faces, the bruises on their arms and faces, and their emaciated bodies, Kirstie figured it would take years for them to get over the trauma they had endured, if they ever did. The PTSD would be difficult.

When they returned to the compound, Lindsey agreed to

take in the women, feeling they would be more comfortable with her and the kids than being on their own. Ashley immediately went to work treating everyone's wounds, starting with Keith and Lindsey, then checking out the women abused by Stratman's crew. She assured everyone that, given time and proper care, they would all physically recover. Not surprisingly, none of the newcomers attended the memorial ceremony.

Kathy waited until everyone who planned on attending was present then stood by the picnic table. Kirstie noticed the nervous tension in Kathy's face and body. She empathized with her, knowing she did not have the courage to do this.

"I'm not good at this. Andrew would have done much better but, sadly, he gave his life to keep us safe. The two of us became close since this all went down. He pulled us together and made us a team. Thanks to his leadership, we were able to make it through the first few days, defeat the raiders, and now have a chance of surviving. I miss him so much. I know we all do.

"We'll miss everyone who sacrificed themselves to keep us safe. Abbey, Theodora, Quinn, Ryan, and Roxie. Keith and Lindsey were wounded defending the compound. Though the losses were painful, we were lucky. We could have lost a lot more people. We could have lost the entire compound and our freedom. We didn't because we banded together.

"If we want to honor the memory of those we lost, we have to look ahead. The next seven months are going to be tough. If we survive the winter, which is not a certainty, then we have a good chance of surviving the next few years. We can do this. We *need* to do this.

"None of us will ever fully get over the loss of our friends and loved ones, and that's normal. But we have to honor their memory, their sacrifice, by making it through this."

Jeanette wiped tears from her eyes. "I have a question. When and where will we bury our loved ones?"

Kathy took a deep breath and hesitated. "We're not going

to bury them. All the bodies will be burn… I mean, cremated."

Protests arose from the crowd, a few people yelling their disapproval. Kathy raised her hands, trying to quiet them down, but the commotion continued.

"Shut up and listen to Kathy!" shouted Kirstie.

Silence fell over the backyard. Kathy glanced over at Kirstie and mouthed the words "thank you," then resumed.

"I don't like the idea of cremation any more than you do. But we have no choice. We have sixteen bodies, nothing to seal them in, and no way to properly bury so many of them."

"Fuck the raiders," said Justin. "We'll drag them into the woods behind Dignam's house."

"And you'll attract predators and create a cesspool for diseases that will cause us even more problems."

"You wouldn't do this if you had a loved one among the dead," someone yelled.

"I would hate doing it, but it's our only option." Murmurs of descent began, but Kathy silenced them. "Listen to me. I'm not happy about making this decision, but we don't have the time and resources to dig graves. Every social norm changed when the power went out. We have to do what's best for our survival, not what makes us feel comfortable."

"She's right." Sarah stood and faced the crowd. "I hate the idea of burning my father. Dad was a Marine and would have agreed with Kathy. I know Dad did not expect us to win this battle, yet we did. He'd be pissed if we threw away our good luck for something as petty as a grave."

The protesting ended.

"How will we do this?" asked Kirstie.

"We have plenty of gasoline from the cars that no longer work, more than enough to make sure the bodies are properly cremated. There's a deserted house three doors down from me with a large cement backyard. We'll do it there. We'll set up six separate pyres so you can collect the ashes of your loved ones."

"Six?" asked Meg. "We only lost five people."

"One for Roxie."

"Thank you." Jordan held back his tears.

"What about the raiders?" asked Renee.

"We'll burn them in Dignam's driveway and spread the ashes through the woods later."

"Can we pee on them first?" suggested Justin.

Several in the crowd chuckled.

"I'm fine with that," said Kathy, forcing a smile.

Regan raised her hand. "What's next?"

Kathy took a deep breath. "The immediate danger is gone, so I suggest we concentrate on preparing for the winter. I want to set up a few more gardens and water containment systems to make certain we have enough to get us through to the spring. We also need to start prepping firewood for the winter. Those without fireplaces should consider moving into homes that have one so you'll be able to keep warm. While we're at it, we might want to move those like Lindsey who are on the outskirts closer to the center so we can consolidate our defenses."

"Why?" asked Keith. "We already killed off the raiders."

"We beat this group, but there might be others we'll run into in the future. I want to be ready for them in case that happens. Once the newcomers get back on their feet, we'll have more than enough hands to do all this. Are there any more questions?"

Thankfully for Kathy, there were none.

"If there are any questions or concerns, please bring them to me."

"Don't worry," said Justin. "We will." When Kathy looked over at Justin, he gave her a friendly wink.

The crowd split up and slowly expanded. Kirstie stood and walked over to Kathy, tapping her on the shoulder.

"Congratulations. It looks like you're in charge now."

"I know." Kathy sighed and turned to face the teenager. "I don't know if I'm up to it."

"You are. You got us this far."

"Andrew got us this far. I figured out ways for us to survive."

"Exactly. Without you, none of us would make it through the winter. Andrew would be proud of you."

Kathy flashed a genuine smile. "Thanks. That means a lot."

Both women knew the next few months would be difficult to survive, but at least they were in a much better position to do so then ten days ago.

Thank you for reading *A World Gone Dark II: Survival,* the second book in my latest series. I hope you enjoyed reading this novel as much as I did writing it.

If you like the novel, please use the QR code below to leave a review on Amazon. The more reviews a writer receives, the more exposure his/her book gets on Amazon, which means the more readers who can experience the adventure. It means a lot to us.

Acknowledgments

I've been working on *A World Gone Dark II: Survival* for over a year. I wanted to release it sooner, but my priority right now is teaching. Thank you all for bearing with me.

This series has been in the planning stages for years. I was fortunate that when I began drafting the first book, I was invited to join the *Ravaged Skies* shared world project in which thirteen of the best post-apocalypse writers drafted their novels based on a single event—a massive solar flare that disables all electronics across the globe. It is a phenomenal series. If you're a fan of apocalyptic/post-apocalyptic fiction, I highly recommend reading all the books in the saga.

The survivalist projects the Atkinson neighborhood undertakes are based on actual examples from *No Grid Survival Projects: How To Produce Everything You Need on Your Property*, the book Kathy procures from the local library. These are the only means someone can use to survive a long-term natural disaster. Hopefully, they will provide inspiration for those thinking about preparing for similar future catastrophes.

A huge debt of gratitude goes to Dan Uebel and Doc Fried, my beta readers. They tore my manuscript to shreds, finding my inconsistencies and plot flaws. My books would not be as good as they are without them.

I want to give a nod of thanks to my pets who dominate my free time. Fred, AKA Turd Burglar, my stubborn Beagle-Bassett mix, is always with me when I write, and sometimes I spend more time keeping him out of trouble than I do at my computer. My cat Archer has discovered that my plugged-in laptop makes the perfect heating pad, so getting him to move is next to impossible. At night, while editing and managing social media, my other cat, Michonne, stands in front of my desktop computer, demanding attention. They make the writing process difficult, but it doesn't matter. When I'm done writing, they are there to unconditional love and relaxation.

The biggest thanks go to my readers, especially those who have been with me from the beginning. Writing is the fun part of my job. I appreciate all of you who read my books and patiently wait for the next one. I have a lot of stories floating around inside my head, and I am looking forward to sharing them with you.

About the Author

Scott M. Baker was born and raised in Everett, Massachusetts, and spent twenty-three years in northern Virginia working for the Central Intelligence Agency. He has traveled extensively through Europe, Asia, and the Middle East, incorporating many of the locations and cultures in his stories. Scott now works as a teacher at a public charter school in Manchester, New Hampshire. He lives outside Salem, New Hampshire, with his dog Fred and two cats who treat him as their human servant.

In addition to the *A World Gone Dark* series, Scott is currently writing two zombie standalone novellas. Previous works include the *Nurse Alissa vs. the Zombies* series, his most popular zombie saga; his Tatyana paranormal series, which is also extremely popular; *Operation Majestic*, his first science fiction novel described as *Raiders of the Lost Ark* meets *Back to the Future* – with aliens; *Frozen World*, his first non-zombie post-apocalypse novel; the *Shattered World* series, his five-book young adult post-apocalypse thriller; the *Rotter World* trilogy, his first zombie series; *The Vampire Hunters* trilogy, about humans fighting the undead in Washington D.C.; as well as several zombie-themed novellas and anthologies.

Amazon Author's Page:
amazon.com/stores/Scott-M.-Baker/author/B003N4U9BK

Facebook:
facebook.com/groups/397749347486177

Twitter:
twitter.com/vampire_hunters

Instagram:
instagram.com/scottmbakerwriter

Blog:
scottmbakerauthor.blogspot.com

YouTube:
youtube.com/channel/UC5AyCVrEAncr2E0N5XoyUdg/feat
ured

Wyrd Realities Homepage:
www.wyrdrealities.net

You can also sign up for Scott's newsletter, which will be released on the 1st and 15th of every month. He promises not to share your email with anyone or spam the recipients. The newsletter contains advance notices of upcoming releases/events and short stories from the Alissa universe that will not be available to the public. You can sign up by going to the link below.

Newsletter:
mailchi.mp/0b1401f1ddb2/scott-m-baker-writer

RAVAGED SKIES

What would you do to survive the apocalypse?

What begins as a beautiful summer day ends in disaster when a massive solar flare strikes the Earth, burning out all electronic devices around the planet and plunging the world into darkness.

Kirstie and her high school friends are stranded at an amusement park in southern New Hampshire with no way to return to their homes outside of Concord. Her mother, Danielle, is trapped in Boston when the disaster strikes; rather than seeking shelter in the city, she begins the long and dangerous journey home to find her daughter. Kirstie's uncle, Shawn, the shift supervisor at the Seabrook Nuclear Power Plant, must find a way to prevent the reactor from melting down before millions die of radiation poisoning.

As society collapses, each family member must find a way to stay alive, even if it means doing things they never imagined themselves capable of.

Can they survive the first five days of the apocalypse? Will they ever see each other again?

"In typical Baker fashion, the action hits hard and fast in this very plausible apocalyptic disaster scenario. Following the actions of three people as they watch society collapse all around them, the pace never lets up. A teenager has to grow up fast. A mother in the city has to find a way out. And the supervisor at a nuclear power plant must find a way to prevent an even bigger disaster. Time is short. When there is no police or military to step in and help keep order, society breaks down quickly."—David Simpson, author of *The Solar Tsunami* and *Zombie Road* series

A RAVAGED SKIES NOVEL

A WORLD GONE DARK

RAVAGED SKIES

SCOTT M. BAKER

In a flash, the world as they knew it ended…

Madison and Zane finally called it quits.

But just as they're adjusting to life apart, a massive solar storm triggers a worldwide EMP, and in an instant, everything changes. And all they can think about is each other.

Hundreds of miles apart with society collapsing around them, they must confront the heartbreak of their past as well as the terrifying future. While Zane risks everything for a chance to see her again, Madison confronts their unraveling reality, her heart fixed on one question: Is Zane alive?

As threats multiply, survival—and forgiving past mistakes—demands brutal choices, but their love for one another, fractured but enduring, might be all they have left.

AWARD-WINNING AUTHOR
KATE L. MARY

A RAVAGED SKIES NOVEL
DESCENT
OF
DARKNESS

DARKNESS DAWNS BOOK ONE

What would you do to survive the apocalypse?

What begins as a typical summer day ends in disaster when a massive solar flare strikes the Earth, burning out all electronic devices around the planet and plunging the world into darkness.

Mike, a determined father, fights to survive and find his daughter. Living in a Los Angeles neighborhood struggling to adapt to the brutal new reality, he becomes a reluctant leader, working with neighbors to secure food, water, and safety against the threats of martial law, rampant disease, and human greed. As he navigates a collapsing world filled with devastating loss, betrayal, and violence, Mike's journey is both physical and emotional. Driven by love and guilt, he builds alliances with survivors while clashing with ruthless authorities.

A Ravaged Skies Novel

AFTER THE FLASH

Book 1 of the Michael Connors story

MARIE LANZA

RAVAGED SKIES

Burned by the sun, tested by the dark.

Alice Wilson never fooled herself into thinking her life was under control—she'd simply become an expert in pretending it was. Ever since losing her parents in a car crash, she narrowly survived, Alice has walked a tightrope of grief and self-reliance, with no one to catch her if she fell.

But during a remote camping trip, far from the safety nets of modern life, everything changes. An unprecedented solar flare unleashes chaos, wiping out power grids, severing communications, and toppling modern infrastructure.

Stranded in a world gone dark, Alice is thrust into a fight for survival she never anticipated.

Now, racing against time to find a safe haven, Alice must make unthinkable choices to protect herself and those she cares about. Can she rise above the chaos, or will the storm of a shattered world consume her?

a ravaged skies novel

FLARE STORM

a post-apocalyptic survival thriller

RAVAGED
SKIES

KELLEE L GREENE

When the sun fell, humanity followed.

Alice and the others hoped reaching the city would bring safety, but they quickly learn that certain things come at a steep price.

As the group struggles to carve out a place in the city, rumors of unrest find their way to Alice and the others. Trust becomes a dangerous game, and with threats lurking both inside and outside the city's walls, the group finds itself at a stalemate. Alice must decide whom to trust—and how far she's willing to go to protect her friends.

With safety nothing more than an illusion, they'll need to find a way to face the darkness of humanity and fight their fears head-on. Will the group rise to fight for their survival, or will the ashes of civilization bury them one by one?

FLAREFALL - BOOK TWO

a ravaged skies novel

SCORCHED FURY

a post-apocalyptic survival thriller

RAVAGED
SKIES

KELLEE L GREENE

When the world goes dark, survival becomes a whisper away from death.

Marlowe never wanted to spend her week locked in a courthouse serving jury duty. But on the second day, a catastrophic EMP strikes, shutting down power, communication, and society as she knows it. Trapped in a city unraveling into chaos, Marlowe's only ally is Cristian, a hardened sheriff's deputy with a past as fractured as the streets they now walk.

Cristian has one goal: get Marlowe to safety and find a way to survive in a world stripped bare. But as fires rage, violent gangs emerge, and desperation becomes the only currency, the pair face dangers far worse than the loss of technology. When Marlowe is injured, her already fragile trust is put to the ultimate test.

To make matters worse, Marlowe isn't just trying to survive—she's on a race against time to reach her mother, who's battling cancer hundreds of miles away. Every step forward feels like a whisper in the dark, and every wrong turn could mean no one is left to hear her scream.

Whispers in the Dark is a heart-pounding, post-apocalyptic story about survival, sacrifice, and the fragile humanity we cling to when the lights go out.

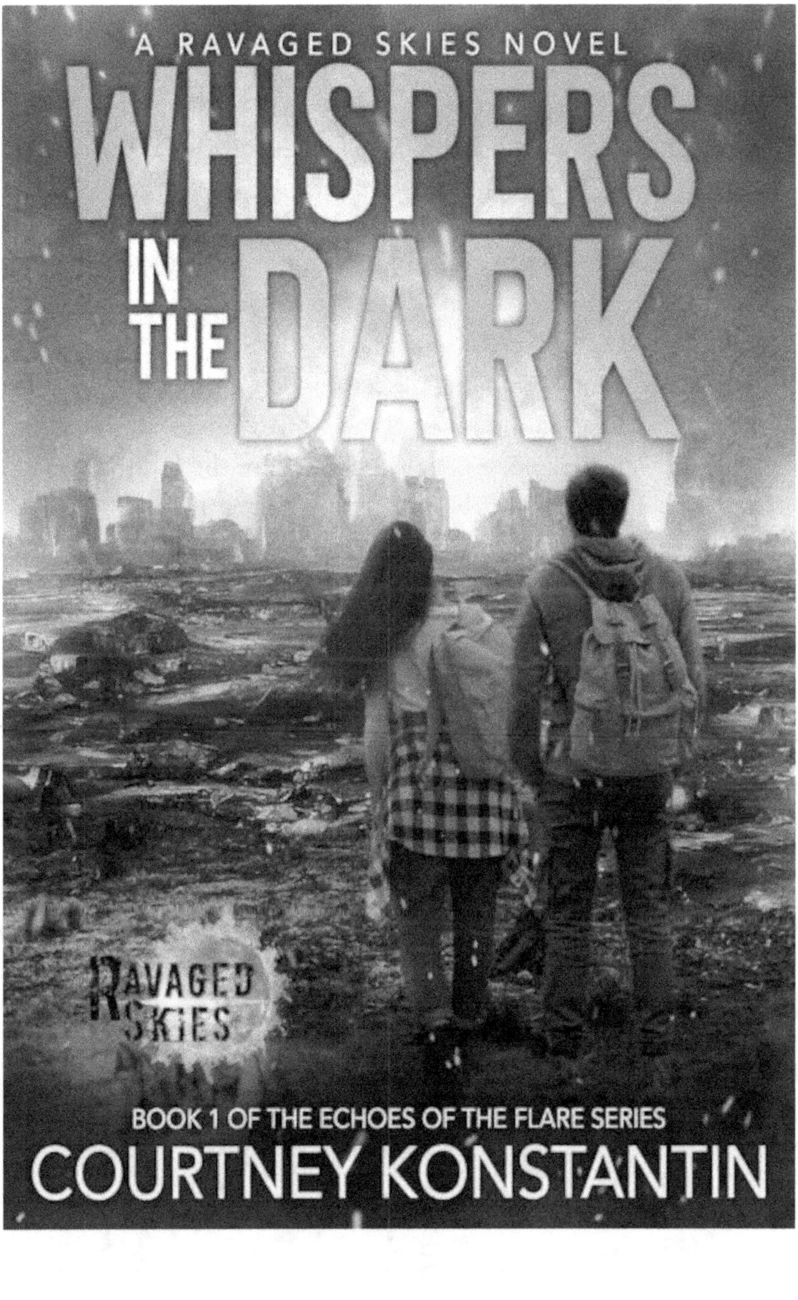
A RAVAGED SKIES NOVEL
WHISPERS IN THE DARK
RAVAGED SKIES
BOOK 1 OF THE ECHOES OF THE FLARE SERIES
COURTNEY KONSTANTIN

When a catastrophic solar flare wipes out all technology, the world is plunged into darkness. For Joshua and Lara Ryan, a simple life in their quiet New England town seemed secure—until a relentless storm floods roads, wipes out crops, and leaves their community on the brink of starvation. As desperation grows, a ruthless local family takes what they want by force, triggering the worst tragedy.

Alone and vulnerable, Lara and her children turn to their only friend—Hugh, their reclusive, movie-loving neighbor who seems a bit more prepared to weather the storms than he lets on. Soon justice and vengeance blur, Hugh's true history emerges, and soon, he isn't just watching movies on his old crank-powered projector, he's making sure the family never hurts the Ryans—or anyone—ever again.

As law and order collapse, Lara and her children must make an impossible choice: flee from the danger they know, or stand up and fight it.

The storms of light and wind may have passed, but in the rebirth of what comes next, the true reckoning has begun.

RAVAGED SKIES

THE HAT TRICK

A RAVAGED SKIES NOVEL

CHRIS PHILBROOK

128 miles to home

3 friends, stranded when the lights go out.

1 chance to escape

With high hopes, three hopeful young ladies enjoy the hot summer day with a tour at Harvard University, their sights set on changing the world and plans for the future. Little did they know, the sun had other plans.

When a solar superstorm impacts Earth, producing a Coronal Mass Ejection, with an EMP that fries the power grid. These friends must find their way back to Maine. Dangers test them to their limits and all hell breaks loose when one has reached the breaking point.

A pulse-pounding ride from beginning to end as the three friends evolve to meet the challenges of a trip through the apocalypse to meet up with friends and family. This apocalyptic adventure is part of the Ravaged Skies World of books showcasing 13 very different tales of the end.

Who will survive?

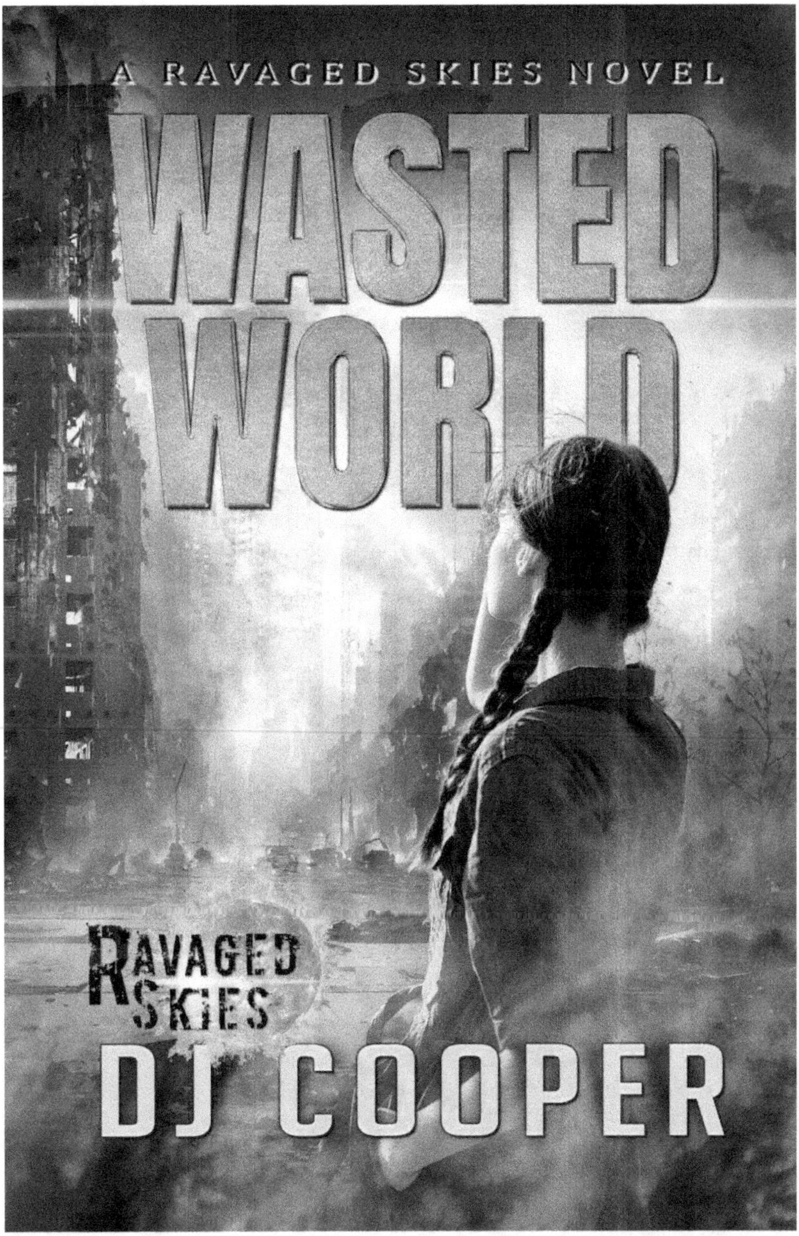
A RAVAGED SKIES NOVEL
WASTED WORLD
RAVAGED SKIES
DJ COOPER

You don't outrun the end.

You outlast it.

After narrowly escaping from the city, Alice and her group are back on their own—unarmed, starving, and fearful of being hunted. They've lost friends, supplies, and any sense of hope or possibility of safety, and the world beyond the city isn't what they remembered.

It's worse.

Desperation has turned survivors into predators, and every encounter could be their last.

With no weapons and no clear path forward, they're forced to rely on their instincts and each other more than ever before. But trust is fragile, and grief is a weight they can't outrun. As hope fades and survival grows more uncertain, one question remains… will Alice and the others find the strength to keep fighting, or will they become just another casualty of the flare?

FLAREFALL - BOOK THREE

a ravaged skies novel

BLAZING CHAOS

a post-apocalyptic survival thriller

KELLEE L GREENE

Faith, Family, and Fishing

Trapped. Attacked from all directions. Jordan Daniels felt the pressure long before the world ended. He was just trying to keep a promise to his late parents: live a good life, maintain the family cabin Up North. But peace was a luxury he couldn't afford.

The cabin was meant to be his sanctuary, the place he pursued his love of fishing after his parents passed. Yet trouble found him relentlessly, tangling him in disputes with his ex-girlfriend, her family, and even his older and crankier neighbor.

Then the CME hits, and personal problems become trivial. The good news? He's not alone. His new best friend, nine-week-old Shyla, is with him. A prepper by nature, Jordan thought he was ready for disaster.

He might not starve right away. But preparations mean nothing against the real threat. In the darkness and chaos, it's the other people you need to fear.

AURORAS & ASHES

A RAVAGED SKIES NOVEL

RAVAGED SKIES

BOYD CRAVEN III

Making it home was the easy part!

Home is not what it once was, and Maddie must overcome her grief and fears. Something is coming that no one could have expected. This second book in the Skies Afire Series brings heart wrenching struggles to the community of Cornish.

Our characters struggle to find their way in a new and changed world. They never expected the betrayal of their community from one of its own, which threatens their very survival when a new and fearsome threat emerges.

The warlord queen, whose reach is growing and her expansion out of Portland is pressing down on them with frightening speed.

Can Cornish stand?

A RAVAGED SKIES NOVEL
DECAYED
WORLD
RAVAGED
SKIES
DJ COOPER

In the end, the only law is survival.

A solar superstorm shatters civilization overnight. Now, the price of survival is written in blood.

U.S. Marshal Cody Greer is stranded deep in the Montana wilderness with a fugitive in tow, where the line between lawman and outlaw begins to blur.

Emma Greer, alone at home with her infant daughter, barely knows her new neighbors but she sees what others can't: they must organize or perish.

After a betrayal ended his military career, former Army Ranger Caleb Frost chose a different path: robbing banks. Now, his luck is about to run out.

When yesterday's enemies might be tomorrow's salvation, can they find their way through the darkness beneath the Ravaged Skies?

A RAVAGED SKIES NOVEL

DARKEST LIGHT

A.M. GEEVER

Edsel Ford has seen nearly everything over his thirty years as a long-haul trucker, delivering seafood to restaurants and grocery stores. But now an unforeseen apocalyptic event is about to cause chaos like he's never seen before.

When a massive solar flare and coronal mass ejection, unlike any ever recorded, leaves most without modern technology or transportation, Edsel is fortunate to find himself with both as his painstakingly restored, antique big rig survives the worldwide EMP.

Initially intent on looking out for number one, Edsel finds himself pulled into several episodes of looking out for others.

Now a reluctant hero, Edsel finds himself being called upon to, once again, travel the highways and byways of America. Only now, instead of delivering fresh seafood, he's delivering hope.

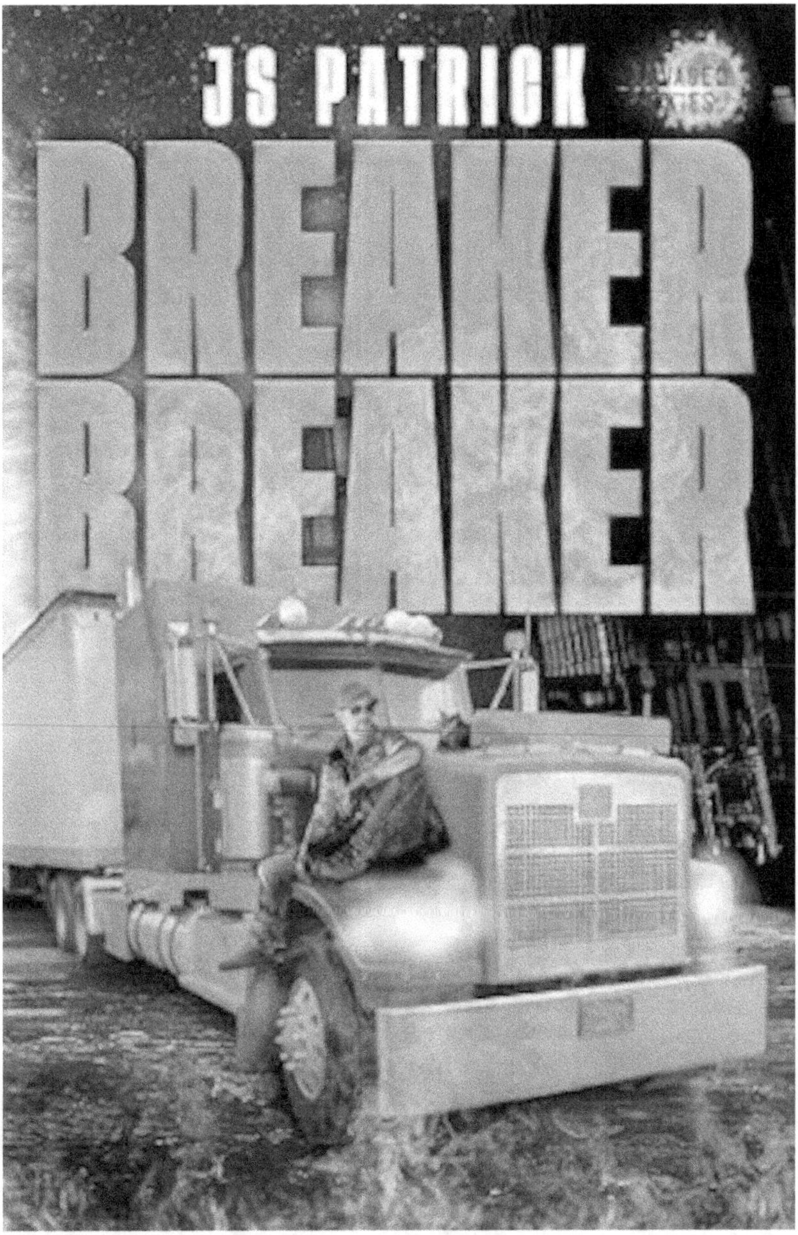
JS PATRICK
BREAKER
BREAKER

The storm made everything worse.

Cornish faces its deadliest threat when the Queen of Likes arrives with her army of broken followers. Broadcasting to a dead phone while her forces close in, turning survival into her version of twisted performance art.

Maddie is torn between emotion and reality while Matthew struggles with betrayal and loss as those closest to him shatter under pressure. And when the community's teenagers take up weapons to defend their home, childhood dies in the crossfire.

But the real enemy might already be inside the walls, and no one is prepared for the betrayal that stings worse because of their compassion.

Some crowns are built from ashes. Others burn everything down.

Can this community rise from the wreckage?

A RAVAGED SKIES NOVEL
ALTERED WORLD
RAVAGED SKIES
DJ COOPER

A solar superstorm. A deadly EMP. An escaped convict, hellbent on a twisted reunion.

Ten years after suffering a violent attack, Samantha Young rebuilds her life in a small town in Colorado. Living in witness protection, she hopes to put the past behind and forge a new life with her nine-year-old daughter, Maddie. When a solar flare knocks out the power, Samantha prepares for a minor inconvenience. And then a CME hits, dumping the entire world into darkness.

En route from Cheshire Correctional Institute to MacDougal-Walker, Stephen Silva dreams of the day he'll regain his freedom. He's obsessed with finding his first and only victim, desperate for a second chance with her. When an unprecedented storm brings the world to its knees, it's time to make his fantasy a reality.

He'll find the girl who got away. He'll finish what he started.

A RAVAGED SKIES NOVEL

FEAR THE DARK

A POST-APOCALYPTIC EMP SURVIVAL THRILLER · BOOK I

RAVAGED SKIES

T. W. PIPERBROOK

Faith, Family, and Fishing

For Jordan Daniels, the promise to his late parents was a simple one: live a good life, especially to be happy and enjoy the family cabin Up North. Disputes with his ex-girlfriend, her family, and a cranky neighbor, Jordan's personal problems seemed minor compared to the crippling CME that hit the world.

Suddenly, he is a prepper in a world of chaos, and his biggest fear is not starvation, but other people. With a new community of friends and family forming around his cabin, he must confront his own capacity for violence as they face down the harsh realities of a looming winter. He will be forced to make snap decisions to protect his friends and family, which he may regret later.

Along the way, Jordan is adopted by more strays, just not the four-legged kind. With death, anger, and old grudges boiling under the surface, Jordan has to embrace what he's becoming to keep those he cares for safe… Or will he lose himself entirely to the anger, the depression, quite possibly his friends, his new family, and his very life? Of course, Shyla won't let anything too horrible happen to them. Right?

AURORAS & ASHES

BOOK 2

A RAVAGED SKIES NOVEL

BOYD CRAVEN III

In a world ravaged by an unfathomable natural disaster…nothing is the same as it ever was.

They thought she drowned. They were wrong.

Grace Reynolds should have died in the Piscataquis River. Instead, she wakes into a broken world—and discovers that her unraveling mind is the most dangerous weapon left in it. Encouraged by her handlers Kyle, Nate, and Pete, Grace becomes **the Queen of Likes**: a skeletal warlord in glitter and pink camo who believes millions are watching her every move. Every killing is content. Every corpse is audience engagement. And the ghosts of those she's executed whisper praise only she can hear.

But while Grace chases the high of viral violence, one prisoner watches and waits. Rebecca Mitchell has played the role of shattered captive long enough. She's building a rebellion in the shadows—one meant to end Grace's reign before the Queen burns the last of humanity to the ground.

When Kyle—the man who cultivated her madness—finally tries to step away, Grace's world fractures. She discovers that even queens run out of followers, platforms, and reasons to keep performing for an audience that never existed.

This is the finale readers have been waiting for. Fast-paced, relentless, and unforgettable, Queen of Likes delivers the most terrifying villain while racing toward a climactic assault that will leave no one unchanged. The Skies Afire series reaches its heart-pounding conclusion as Grace's revenge fantasy collides with reality at the gates of Cornish—where Hannah and Maddie finally face the monster they couldn't save.

The Skies Afire **series ends here**—in a brutal, intimate collision of madness, power, and revenge. **Fast. Relentless. Devastating.**

You will not survive this finale unchanged.

A RAVAGED SKIES CHARACTER NOVEL

QUEEN OF LIKES

RAVAGED SKIES

DJ COOPER

www.ingramcontent.com/pod-product-compliance
Lightning Source LLC
Chambersburg PA
CBHW070312260626
47160CB00003B/815